⚬⚬

Ryan's lips claimed hers, reinforcing the sincerity she heard in his words. Lara melted in his arms, welcoming his affection. Every caress of his hand and stroke of his tongue erased her misgivings. She had nary a doubt. Ryan Andrews loved her.

"I love you, too, Ryan." Lara spoke the words effortlessly. They felt good, freeing. She held him closer, breathing him in. He wasn't Foster. She didn't have to be afraid of love anymore. She *had* to stop being afraid.

"I love you so."

⚬⚬

CHOICES

TAMMY WILLIAMS

Genesis Press, Inc.

INDIGO LOVE SPECTRUM

An imprint of Genesis Press, Inc.
Publishing Company

Genesis Press, Inc.
P.O. Box 101
Columbus, MS 39703

All characters in this book have no existence outside the imagination of the author and have no relation whatsoever to anyone bearing the same name or names. They are not even distantly inspired by any individual known or unknown to the author and all incidents are pure invention.

Copyright © 2008 by Tammy Williams

ISBN: 13 DIGIT : 978-1-58571-300-4
ISBN: 10 DIGIT : 1-58571-300-7
Manufactured in the United States of America

First Edition

Visit us at www.genesis-press.com
or call at 1-888-Indigo-1-4-0

DEDICATION

To my parents for their support, my three siblings for their belief, my nieces and nephew for reminding me there's always time for fun, and countless family members and friends for seeing me through. I couldn't have done this without you.

CHAPTER 1

"I changed my mind, Daddy. I don't wanna do it."

Ryan Andrews looked down as tiny hands wrapped around his leg. Those words hadn't surprised him, but his shy son actually standing inside Oakwood Primary School was a miracle, so they couldn't turn around now. Plus, it was stifling out and the air-conditioning felt great.

Ryan gazed into troubled brown eyes. "Don't be scared, Justin, it's going to be fine." He drew a deep breath. Disinfectant, a hint of fresh paint, and books hot off the presses mingled together. "You smell that? That's the smell of school. Look around." He pointed to the happy children, books, and alphabet that made up colorful borders atop the off-white walls. "Don't those kids seem to be having fun playing and learning all sorts of new things?"

Justin shrugged.

"Son, class starts on Monday. I dropped everything to bring you over to meet your teacher, because you said you were ready." Ryan shuddered at the thought of the unfinished dusting and other chores awaiting him. "I know you can do this."

"But she might be mean. She might not like me."

"She's going to love you. You're the best little boy in the world. What's not to love?"

Justin shrugged. "I dunno."

"Well, I do know. Your kindergarten teacher will be just like your grandmas—old, caring, and crazy about you." Ryan only hoped showing up out of the blue on the hot summer day wouldn't paint him in a bad light with the teacher and make things worse than Justin already thought they would be. "You ready to meet Mrs. Boyd?"

Justin said nothing. His grip tightened around Ryan's leg.

"I promise, it will be fine." Music drifted from a partially open door at the end of the hall. Maybe that was the classroom. "Come on, let's go."

The rumble in Lara Boyd's stomach made concentrating on the half-finished mobiles before her an impossible task. Marvin Gaye harmonizing about a grapevine didn't help matters. For one always spouting the merits of a complete breakfast, hers should have been more than a strawberry Pop Tart and an almost-full pot of her must-have French vanilla coffee. Rubbing her hollow tummy, she glanced at the clock on the wall. Twelve-thirty. A toaster pastry was not created to keep one going for four hours.

Tired muscles cursed her as she stood from the small square table used as her base of operations. Paint, glitter, and glue covered her hands and drizzled along the front of her T-shirt and the flaps of the colorful plaid overshirt. Lara chuckled, imagining she looked like a fudgesicle dipped in rainbow sprinkles. At least no one could accuse her of not throwing herself into her work.

Lara gazed about the classroom, finding the two things she prided herself in giving to every child who walked through her doors—education and fun. From the beginner readers and fairy tales filling the colorful wooden shelves to her left, to the toys, blocks, and veritable who's who of *Sesame Street*—she loved Ernie—lining the three-foot-high shelves to her right, to the eight computers loaded with the best and coolest "kid-approved" learning software, she had managed to create a kiddie-learning wonderland. Teaching kindergarten at one of the top school districts in South Carolina certainly had its benefits, but teaching in itself was the biggest perk of all.

She bubbled with anticipation like a good little child at Christmas. In four days, a stream of giggly, enthusiastic, and oftentimes scared five-year-old boys and girls would fill the kid-friendly space. Monday couldn't get here fast enough.

The growling in her stomach sidelined Lara's excitement about the coming school year. Though the scent of what remained of her French vanilla brew filled the air and teased her tummy, her liquid addiction couldn't compare to a ham and cheese sandwich. Quitting time had officially arrived.

Impersonating Gladys Knight and the Pips kept her mind off her empty stomach as she completed clean up. With the room in order, and her hands back to their paint-free state, Lara spun from the sink with a hearty "toot-toot" to find a tall, blond, extremely handsome stranger standing just inside the door. The curtain came crashing down on her little show. Her hand covered her pounding heart. *How long had he been standing there?*

"Oh, I'm—I'm sorry," he stammered. "I hope I didn't frighten you."

Was he kidding? Lara's suspicious eyes stayed on him. His contrite tone and the doe-like sincerity in his dazzling baby blues showed he was indeed earnest. He seemed a bit flushed, too, but that might be the heat. It was a real scorcher today.

She tabled her sarcastic retort, since he appeared to be punishing himself enough. "It's okay," Lara said, "I'm still breathing." Albeit just barely. She wasn't startled anymore, so why wouldn't her heart stop racing?

Giving the stranger a once-over, she found the answer to her question in every inch she covered. A half-buttoned, way too long denim shirt couldn't conceal straining biceps beneath a white T-shirt or the jean-covered muscles making up his upper thighs. He couldn't possibly be a member of the stuffy school board Principal Styles mentioned might make impromptu visits before the students arrived. Male board members were old, short, and on the rotund side. This man was young, early thirties, and at least six-two. Not at all the board member type. Plus, board members didn't look this good in jeans.

Near-debilitating hunger became a thing of the past as she shamelessly took in her fill of the bountiful dish before her. Specific long-dormant body parts stirred to life. The tip of her tongue bathed her dry lips. The man smiled. Her pulse quickened.

As if on cue, the Supremes' "I Hear a Symphony" played. Butterflies invaded her stomach and heat fanned her cheeks. She hadn't felt this attracted to a man in over six years, and never to a white man—except for a soap star she'd have to be dead not to notice. But impossible crushes didn't count. This man was right here and she couldn't keep her eyes off him, or help envying the T-shirt that had the great fortune of being pressed to his magnificent chest.

Careful scrutiny of his many enticing physical attributes brought Lara's attention to a pair of tiny hands wrapped securely around his Adonis-like leg. Her heart went from pounding to swelling at the cute and very appealing picture. Finding the ability to move, she stopped the Motown CD and strolled to where the stranger and his small companion stood.

The scent of lemon furniture polish flooded her senses as she approached. After smelling vanilla coffee, watercolor paint, and glue half the day, the citrus aroma was unmistakable. Lara smiled. She obviously wasn't alone in using the beautiful but hot summer day to clean. "Can I help you with something?" she asked.

Crystal clear blue eyes stayed trained on her face. "Huh?"

"Can I—"

"Oh, I'm sorry. Yes, I'm, uh . . ." His head tilted. "You have some white—" He rubbed a spot on his chiseled right cheek.

Lara wiped the spot with the collar of her shirt. That explained the staring. And she thought it was because he

5

found her attractive. She had to stop presuming. "I was just finishing up," she explained, motioning around the room.

Instinct drove her fingers along the sides and back of her dark brown hair, but good sense brought them back down. She had a new flip-wrap haircut she couldn't style without a mirror, and there was no point in making matters worse. *God, how I must look to him.* She should have worn her hair in a ponytail—and *buttoned* her overshirt.

The man's gaze stayed on her face as he reached into his back pocket and extended a piece of paper. "I'm looking for Mrs. Lara Boyd's classroom," he said.

"You've found it, but I'm not a Mrs."

Surprise registered on his face. His penetrating eyes took in every inch of her multicolored, paint-splattered frame, leaving her feeling exposed and strangely wanton.

Thick eyebrows drew together. "*You're* Lara Boyd?"

"That's what my mama told me," she answered, not quite sure what to make of his statement. "I don't think she lied, but if she did, I've been living this lie for twenty-nine years."

"I'm sorry, it's just—You don't look like a kinder-garten teacher." His gaze traveled the length of her body once again before returning to her face. "At least not any of the ones I've ever known or seen."

I don't look like a kindergarten teacher? What did he think a kindergarten teacher looked like? Sure, her appearance could be considered strange with rainbow-colored clothing and polka-dotted skin, but she found his reaction a bit disconcerting. Was he paying her a compliment or putting her down?

After two years in Denburg, had she finally met one of South Carolina's infamous hicks? The city boasted culture, big business, great shopping, and nice beaches, but it was still the South. The Confederate flags she encountered on a near daily basis remained constant reminders if she dared to forget.

Lara studied him closely. He didn't seem hostile, maybe a little wound up, but—Who was she kidding? When it came to men, she couldn't tell what was what anymore. Not since her ex-fiancé, Foster, and his *love*. Men! Why did they have to be so complicated? Was it any wonder she preferred the company of children?

"I'm not doing this well, am I?" said the stranger.

"That depends." Lara folded her arms. "If your intention is to insult or perplex me, I think you're doing a bang-up job."

His crestfallen expression said it all. He wasn't a racist hick, but his behavior still baffled her. Maybe he was a member of the school board and just taken aback by her unteacherlike appearance. Then again, he wasn't in a suit.

The owner of the tiny hands clinging to his leg peeked around the man's right side. A mini-replica of the enigma standing before her grabbed Lara's attention. The big, brown eyes shining in his handsome little face marked the only discernable difference between him and his jumbo counterpart. Her heart warmed instantly.

She waved at the boy and smiled. "Hi, cutie. What's your name?"

"Justin," he murmured before slinking behind the leg again.

The man touched Justin's shoulder. "He's a little shy at first meetings. Well, second and third meetings, too. My name is Ryan Andrews, and Justin is my son," he shared.

"He starts Monday," Lara said, remembering Justin's name from her list of students. "I guess that's what's on the sheet you gave me."

"I think you're supposed to keep it."

She tucked the sheet in her shirt pocket. "I am."

"We, uh, we were out of town until last night, so we missed Tuesday's Meet and Greet, but I still wanted to get him acquainted with his new teacher." Ryan extended his right hand. "I really feel I should apologize to you, Ms. Boyd. You just aren't at all what I expected."

"So you've said."

An electric surge swept through Lara at the touch of his hand. Her head screamed to let it go, but she didn't listen.

"My—uh, my words weren't meant to offend or said to confuse you, honest."

His caressing thumb on the back of her hand worked wonders in convincing her of his sincerity.

"I just didn't know kindergarten teachers were so . . ." Ryan wiped his sweat-glistened forehead. A shiny, gold band caught Lara's eye. "I didn't realize the way they looked from when I was five had changed so much," he finished in a rush.

A tight smile concealed her disappointment. How could she *not* know he was married? The sight of Justin's tiny hands around his leg and the smell of furniture polish screamed "settled"! One look at a gorgeous man, one tingle of long-forgotten feelings, and her ability to reason flew straight out the window. Ryan's last words had sounded like a compliment, but she was in no position to wonder, because it didn't matter.

He was married!

Her reaction to him disturbed her on many levels, but she could handle it. So what he was drop-dead gorgeous with an athletic body and a dazzling smile. He was still just a man, and a *married* one at that. She could and would rein in her raging hormones. She had no choice.

Lara rescued her hand from his dangerous touch. "No need to explain," she said with a smile she didn't feel. "I'm sure a vanilla-spotted black woman in bad plaid and old jeans wasn't what you were expecting."

Curious brown eyes peeked at her for the briefest moment and then disappeared behind denim-clad thighs. A sincere smile touched Lara's lips. That Justin was a real cutie. She'd have to work with him on that shyness.

"As I was saying," she said, "it would have thrown anybody, so think nothing of it."

Ryan nodded, his appraisal of her without shame. The seductive turn of his lips sent a titillating shiver shooting down Lara's spine and a wave of disgust crashing through her belly. Her attraction to him and struggle to keep it under wraps was one thing, but as a married man, he had no business being so overt in his attraction to her.

"So, will your *wife* be joining us?" Lara asked.

Every trace of color drained from Ryan's face. She'd definitely hit a nerve. *Good! Serves him right.*

Justin peeked from behind his father's leg. "My mommy's in heaven," he murmured.

What? Her gaze shot to Ryan's adorned finger. *Heaven?* "I'm . . . I'm sorry." Lara looked from his hand to his face and back again. "I thought—I just figured that—" She groaned. "I'm sorry."

Ryan's thumb rubbed against the top of the band. He cleared his throat. "It's okay. You didn't know."

A dark cloud of tension filled the classroom. Booming silence hovered. Lara shut her eyes and prayed for the floor to open and swallow her whole. Ryan was a widower, and she all but accused him of cheating on his wife.

Justin sniffed the air. "Ms. Boyd, do you really have vanilla spots?"

Adult laughter filled the room, evaporating the almost stifling anxiety. Ryan leaned forward. "He's at the age where he takes things literally," he whispered against her ear.

The feel of his warm breath sent more tingles racing down her spine. *Did lemon furniture polish always smell this good?* Lara nodded. "Yes, I recognize that," she said. Stooping to Justin's eye level, she reached out to him. He emerged from behind his father, accepting her proffered hand.

"I think you smell my coffee, sweetheart. My spots are just a little white paint." She glanced at her shirt. "And red paint, and blue paint, and glitter, and—you get the picture." Lara chuckled. "I do think I'm as sweet as vanilla ice cream, though. Well, on second thought, maybe chocolate ice cream."

Justin laughed. "You're funny, and you're pretty, too."

"I don't feel very pretty right now, but thanks. You're quite a handsome guy yourself, and so charming." She figured Justin's charm came from the same place he got those beaming brown eyes. Ryan could be the picture beside the word *gorgeous* in any dictionary, and he lit her fire for sure, but he wasn't the smoothest cat in the world. Justin was a different story. Lara smiled. "I'm going to enjoy having you in my class."

The boy's face lit up, as did his father's.

"Wow!" Ryan praised. "I have never seen him take to someone so quickly."

Lara brushed her forefinger against Justin's nose. The boy giggled. "I'm a teacher," she said, "we're a special kind."

"I can believe it."

Their eyes met and held as tension of another sort sparked around them like so many hanging live wires.

"Look, Daddy, there's Elmo, and Ernie!" Justin exclaimed, breaking the highly charged moment. His eyes brightened with familiarity as he pointed at the row of plush toys on the shelf.

Lara shook the small hand she held. Justin didn't seem so shy anymore. "You like Ernie?"

Justin nodded so hard his body shook. "I love him. I like Elmo, too, but Ernie's the best."

A kid after her own heart. "You want to know a secret?"

Justin nodded.

"Ernie is my favorite, too," she whispered loud enough for Ryan to hear. "Shhh, don't tell Elmo, I think he gets jealous."

"I won't," Justin said in the same loud whisper.

Lara stood to her full five feet, nine inches of height to find Ryan staring and smiling. Her knees trembled, but thankfully didn't give way. *Keep it together, Lara.* Still holding Justin's hand, she walked to her desk and picked up some sheets.

"Here's a list of all the items Justin is going to need for school: crayons, markers, a mat to take his naps on, that sort of thing," she explained.

Ryan nodded. "Okay."

"There are also some forms you'll need to fill out detailing any allergic reactions or sicknesses he might have and the name and phone numbers of individuals to call if something were to happen while he's here." She extended the sheets. "Justin can bring the forms back on Monday."

"I'll be sure to get this done," he said, folding the sheets lengthwise and tucking them in his back pocket.

"Great. Do you have any questions?"

"Questions?"

She nodded.

"Oh, questions? No, I don't—" Ryan sighed. "I don't have any questions about Justin's schooling."

He might not have questions about school, but his hesitation said something weighed on his mind and he was clearly struggling with whether or not to share. She decided his not sharing was probably for the best.

"Alrighty, then." Lara gave Justin's hand a little squeeze. "I guess I'll be seeing you soon, Mr. Justin."

"Yes, ma'am," Justin replied with his full-body nod.

"Okay, buddy, I think we should let Ms. Boyd get back to her finishing up." Ryan held his hand out to Justin as he spoke to Lara. "Thank you, for your time and everything."

"You're welcome," she said, following them to the door.

Ryan turned around. Again, he seemed to want to say something. He stared at her for a long moment before releasing a heavy sigh. "Good day, Ms. Body."

He left so quickly, Lara wondered if his Freudian slip had registered with him. She smirked. It could have been worse; at least that slip made her feel good. Ryan Andrews may have more charm than she thought. One thing was certain, he definitely had her attention.

Ryan's smile grew wider with his every thought of the breathtaking Ms. Boyd. He'd expected Justin's teacher to be a blue-haired granny, but he couldn't have been more wrong. *"I find you incredibly attractive."* Why was that so hard to say?

Justin's peals of laughter brought a momentary end to his pensive state. He shook the boy's hand as they continued to the car. "What's so funny, big guy?"

"You called Ms. Boyd 'Ms. Body.'"

Ryan stopped midstep. "No, I didn't."

"Uh-huh." Justin nodded.

Ryan slapped his forehead, sending a stinging spray of sweat into his eyes. He welcomed the discomfort as just punishment for his inexcusable behavior. Practically offending Lara with his wacky behavior was bad, but to call her Ms. Body? *Ugh.* He pinched the bridge of his nose and discovered he smelled like Lemon Pledge. His hand dropped. *This just gets better and better.* Something told him to shower first, but did he listen? No. He thought he was meeting an old lady. One that smelled too much like mothballs to notice anything else. *Damn.* He grunted.

Justin tugged on his hand. "You okay, Daddy?"

"I will be. I hope," he said, walking again.

Ms. Body. Ryan sighed. The title suited her. The over-sized plaid shirt demanded attention, but so did the traffic-stopping curves underneath. A paint-stained canary yellow T-shirt tucked inside equally discolored faded blue jeans never looked so good. And her face. Cola-colored eyes, high cheekbones hinting at Native American ancestry, and full, kissable lips perfected her beautiful countenance.

The father in him had to be restrained from smoothing away the paint staining her pretty face, but the man in him wanted any excuse to touch her creamy, milk chocolate skin, and run his fingers through her silky dark hair. Lara was absolutely stunning, even with assorted paint splatters. And her way with Justin. His son wasn't one to be so friendly and talkative when meeting people, but Lara drew Justin right out, just as she did him.

In the three years since losing his wife, he hadn't been attracted to any woman. He saw attractive women while out running errands, and a few tried to make a play for him, but he'd never been interested. All he could think about was his Shelly. But Lara . . . Ryan sighed. Lara definitely interested him, and in more than just a physical way, although the physical currently took center stage.

He looked with gratitude at his concealing shirt. If Lara had seen what she stirred in him, not only would she think him a jerk, but a pervert, too. Images of her shapely, long legs wrapped around his waist played in his head. The bulge in his jeans tightened. He hadn't felt this way in a *long* time.

"You were wrong about Ms. Boyd, Daddy," Justin said.

Ryan shook away his lascivious thoughts. "I was wrong?"

"Uh-huh, about her being old. She's young, pretty, and nice. I really like her."

"Me, too, son." Ryan turned toward the window of Lara's classroom. "I really like her, too."

CHAPTER 2

Ryan turned the corner for home to find his mother-in-law's maroon sedan parked in the circular drive. His head screamed an expletive. A man's home was supposed to be his castle, and his two-story brick Tudor was that . . . usually, but Sue Lomax's presence made his home feel like a prison.

From the beginning, they hadn't gotten along. He found Sue rigid and aloof, and she found him too simplistic for her only child. When Shelly died, they'd agreed to forge a cordial relationship for Justin's sake, but Sue had taken the bounds of polite friendship too far with her constant and unannounced visits.

Ryan always kept the house, both inside and out, clean and orderly. And thanks to his mother's insistence, he and his four siblings knew how to cook. But that didn't stop Sue, career housewife extraordinaire, from coming over three to four times a week to lend a hand. His suggestions she stop coming around so much fell on deaf ears. Sue never heard much of what he had to say, and listened to even less.

He parked behind the car. *Humph!* If she really wanted to be useful, she would have cleaned the house when he was in Wisconsin visiting his parents, and had her husband, Carl, mow the lawn. But did she do that?

No! He didn't want to see her now. He had that work to do.

Justin squealed with delight. "Grandma's here!"

"Of course she is," Ryan muttered under his breath.

Justin streaked across ankle-high grass and raced into the house. Ryan entered to find Justin on the couch with Sue jabbering a mile a minute about Lara.

"Grandma, my teacher is so great. Her name is Ms. Boyd and she's pretty, nice, funny, and sweet as chocolate ice cream. She said I was charming." Justin squinted. "What's charming?"

Ryan tossed his keys onto the table by the door, smiling at Justin's excitement. "Take a breath, son." He nodded at the petite, brown-haired woman. "Sue."

"Ryan," she returned, in her self-important way that grated his nerves. For a small woman, Sue really knew how to fill up a room. She placed her arm around Justin's shoulder. "I see this Ms. Boyd made a big impression on him."

Not just him. "She did," Ryan said.

Justin fidgeted like a cat on speed. Pure luck prevented the mauve fabric from bursting into flame from all the friction. "I'm going to have so much fun on Monday. I can't wait."

Sue rubbed Justin's shoulders. "I can't remember a time he was so enthusiastic about a stranger." Curious lines creased the corners of her eyes. "She must have magic fairy dust."

"She's a gifted teacher. Justin warmed up to her right away."

Sue brushed an invisible speck from the skirt of her lime green suit. She had never worked outside her home, but always wore business attire. Ryan never understood the reasoning behind that.

"So, you like her, too?" she asked.

"Yep, he does," Justin piped in. "Daddy said he likes her a lot." The boy laughed. "He called her Ms. Body."

Sue's head snapped up. A million questions colored her light brown eyes with suspicion.

The heat of rushing blood warmed Ryan's neck and crept to his cheeks. He drew a breath, catching a whiff of tuna fish.

"Smells like Grandma made lunch. Justin, why don't you go wash up and wait for us in the kitchen."

"All right." Justin streaked out of the room.

Sue folded her arms across her chest. "Ms. Body?"

"It was a slip," Ryan defended.

"That's an amazing slip."

Ryan placed the forms Lara had given him on the coffee table and sat at the far end of the couch. "Not so amazing, actually. Boyd/Body, they sound a lot alike."

"Right." Sue grunted. "So, you like her a lot?"

"I just met her, but from what I gather she's a very nice woman." Ryan's foot tapped an anxious beat. "Why is it I feel I'm under a microscope?"

"I'm sorry if I made you uncomfortable. I'm just curious about this teacher who seems to have bewitched you and Justin."

"You know as much as I do. She's a nice woman, and Justin likes her. Since he'll be spending quite a bit of time in her presence, I think that's a good thing. Don't you?"

"But it's not just Justin."

Ryan's jaw clenched. His foot tapping increased. "What does that mean?"

"It means my daughter has been gone for over three years and in all that time I've never once seen you take a second glance at another woman, much less get so excited when talking about one."

Ryan corralled his runaway leg. "Am I so excited?"

Sue nodded, reaching for the framed photo of Shelly from the nearby end table. "I knew this was bound to happen, but I guess I could never prepare myself."

"There's nothing to prepare for!"

Sue flinched.

"I'm sorry I snapped, but Ms. Boyd is Justin's teacher, Sue, that's all." That was all, but knowing he wouldn't mind her being something more suddenly bothered him.

Sue replaced the picture and smiled. "My Shelly is pretty hard to forget."

"Yeah, she sure is." Ryan retrieved the school forms and stood. "I'm gonna skip lunch and work in my office for a while," he said, desperately needing the escape his work provided and some time away from Sue. "I think I'll take Justin out for dinner tonight. Let me know when you're about to leave."

"I'll make sure you're not disturbed."

Too late for that. He pasted on a fake smile. "Thanks."

An hour later, Ryan sat behind his drawing board without so much as a line drawn. He began pursuing his dream of illustrating soon after Shelly died, leaving his Clio award-winning, six-figure salary to be a stay-at-home father. It didn't hurt the ad job left him financially stable until regular illustrating work came in. He now worked exclusively with three authors as the visionary behind the many characters they developed in their lines of children's books.

Ryan flipped through the pages of his current manuscript, *Sigmund the Squirrel*. How was he going to create the perfect image of this title character when all he could think of was Lara's perfect figure in those formfitting blue jeans and how perfectly guilty it made him feel?

He studied Shelly's photo on the workstation. The last picture taken before her untimely death, it captured Shelly's natural beauty. Tendrils of golden blonde curls framed her pretty face, and a shade of dusty rose painted her lips and cheeks, accentuating the brown of her eyes. Justin's eyes.

Ryan pressed the silver frame to his chest. Guilt-tinged sadness enveloped him. Shelly was hard to forget, but lately he'd been doing just that. He didn't think about her every day, not anymore. How could he let that happen? How could he allow another woman to creep into his thoughts and fill him with need and longing? He held the picture closer. "Oh, Shell."

"What?"

Ryan bristled. He turned in his swivel chair and scanned the small office. "Shell?"

"Yeah, Ryan, it's me, *finally.*"

A gauzy image of his very dead wife appeared. He closed his eyes for several seconds. When he opened them, the apparition was still there and becoming clearer. Denburg summers were warm, but he obviously had too much heat today.

"Don't close your eyes again," Shelly said, stopping him midblink. "You're not seeing things. I'm really here."

"But you can't be. You're . . ."

"Dead?" She sighed. "Yep, I am, but, Ryan, I'm not at peace. That's why I'm here. How long do you plan to mourn me?"

Ryan replaced the picture. "This isn't happening."

"Yes, it is," Shelly countered. "I'm here for a reason. It's time for you to move on. If Mom has her way, you'll be mired in my memory for the rest of your life."

"There's nothing wrong with remembering how much I loved you," he said to the picture, refusing to believe the vision behind him was real. "How much I'll always love you."

"You're wrong. There is something wrong with it. I never wanted you to stop living because I died. Ryan, you're only thirty-two years old. You're too young to retire yourself."

He turned to Shelly's image. It seemed as real as the chair beneath him. "I didn't want to retire myself, but I wasn't given a choice. You died and left me, remember?" He brushed the tears from his eyes. His voice wavered. "I didn't even get the chance to say good-bye."

"*Oh, please.* You've been saying good-bye for three years. Look, I didn't want to die and leave you and Justin, but I'm the one who didn't have a choice. You have choices."

"No. When you died, I died, too."

"You're not dead, and today proved it. Lara's fantastic! Don't be an idiot, Ryan."

"What?"

"She's beautiful, nice, smart, and best of all, she's as crazy about Justin as he is about her. I'm very happy. Somebody has finally made you take notice. I was beginning to think it would never happen, but you're going to move on, and I'll find my peace."

"What is this *peace* you're talking about?" He gave her a once-over. "And why are you in a business suit and not a flowing gown?"

Shelly looked at the gray pantsuit outfitting her slender frame. She was a little taller than Sue, and a whole lot prettier. "I was leaving from work when the accident happened. I didn't exactly have time to change before I got sent to the Pearly Gates in a burst of flames."

Ryan whimpered.

"Don't worry. It happened so fast I didn't even feel it." Shelly laughed.

"How can you joke about this? Your death was . . ."

"Unfortunate. Especially since I had only worn this suit once, and gray was never my best color. Of course, I would die and get stuck wearing it for the next three years, but I digress. All is not lost, Ryan. I can't go into too much detail, but it seems things are about to become a lot clearer."

"What things?"

"You'll have to figure that out by yourself, but I'll help you when I can."

"You'll help me when you can? Are you my guardian angel?" He looked up. "How is it up in heaven?"

"I'm not an angel, and I haven't been in heaven."

Ryan gasped. "You mean, you . . ." He looked down.

"No, I didn't go to hell! I'm an angel-in-waiting. I made it to the Pearly Gates, but I haven't been allowed entry. I need to get my wings first." She turned her back to him. "You see any wings back there?"

"No."

"That's right, you don't," she said, turning back. "My spirit has been in limbo since I died. I have to resolve things on Earth before I can get into heaven."

"You're in limbo?"

"Yes, and with Lara's help you can get me out of it. Meeting her is the difference. The door to your heart is barely cracked, and things are already better than before. You can see me and hear me talk to you now."

"Wait a minute. Before? You mean you've always been here?"

"Yep, always. And even when I'm not actually around, I always know what's going on with you. It's an omnipotent thing that happens when you die." She smiled. "I can't tell you how great it was to see you flirting again."

Ryan lowered his gaze. "I wasn't flirting."

"Yes, you were. At least you were trying. I gotta tell you, you're very rusty. Maybe I can help you polish that up a bit. Ms. Body? Tsk, tsk."

"That slipped. You know, I can't believe you're saying all this, Shell. You're actually going to give me tips on how to pick up a woman?"

"Somebody has to help you. And before you say it, I don't mean Norris."

Ryan closed his mouth. His best friend was always trying to set him up.

"You were so nervous with Lara. She likes you, too."

"She does?"

"Yeah, she does."

"How do you know? Can you tell what she's feeling?"

"I can't tell what anyone's feeling or thinking. I can only observe and draw conclusions. And from my viewpoint, she's interested. You should have seen your face when you first saw her. Whenever I say her name you glow."

"Why do you sound so calm and happy about this?" Maybe it was his male pride, but he thought she should be a little miffed. "Aren't you sad? Doesn't it bother you to know I'm—"

"Finally moving on? It's been three years, Ryan. You need a woman in your life, and so does Justin. There's something very special about Lara Boyd."

"Yeah, there is, but . . ."

"Shush, no buts. You may be able to see me, but it doesn't change the fact I'm dead. Lara has touched something in you no one else has gotten close to reaching. You can't pretend it didn't happen, and for goodness sake, don't let Mom make you feel guilty about it. You've done an amazing job taking care of Justin. Now, it's time for someone to take care of you. You need to move on."

"I don't know if I can, Shell. I've spent so much time being alone and holding on to my memories of you and the life we had. I don't know how to not do that." He twisted the wedding band around his finger. "I don't want to forget you. It's not fair I forget you. Not when you're—"

"Stuck in limbo? Ryan, not thinking about me twenty-four/seven does not equal forgetting me. Justin is our legacy, and you'll always have our memories. Besides, for a few minutes today, I'm certain I was the very last thing on your mind."

He eyed Shelly curiously. "I thought you couldn't tell what anyone was thinking?"

"I can't." Her gaze dropped to his long shirttails then up to his face. She gave him a wide grin. "I just know you, Ryan. Today wasn't the first time you didn't think about me, but it was the first time you thought about a woman, the way a man thinks about a woman, who wasn't me. That wedding band means nothing if your heart's not there. And I know it's not."

Ryan said nothing to that. He didn't know what to say about any of it. He was so confused.

Shelly paused for a long moment. "Look, only you know what you can and cannot do. But if you remember how you felt today when you met Ms. Body," she said with a chuckle, "I think you'll be able to find a way to move on." Her image started to fade. "I'll be back when you need me. In the meantime, think about what I said."

Ryan rubbed his eyes. His imagination had gone haywire. Seeing Shell? He picked up the school forms and sighed. "Ms. Lara Boyd, lady, what are you doing to me?"

—

"Lara, girl, are you ready yet?"

"I'll be out in two minutes!" Lara shouted to Celeste Monroe. She imagined her cousin and closest friend staring holes into the living room wall clock as she waited for the two minutes to pass.

"All right, but you have only two minutes. I've already been waiting for twenty. I'm starvin' like Marvin out here."

Lara laughed. Celeste was always hungry. The thirty-seven-year-old lawyer had the appetite of lumberjack, stood five-ten, and after three children, still possessed the body every woman wished she had. While Lara had to work out three times a week to keep her shapely size-ten figure fit and trim, Celeste could inhale a whole cheesecake and still look primed to take a Parisian runway.

Double first cousins, the women were members of a very close-knit family. When Lara moved to Denburg from Alexandria, Virginia, Celeste and her lawyer husband, Dan, had welcomed her into their fold and helped her find a great apartment she could afford on her teacher's salary. Besides sharing dinner after church each Sunday, every third Thursday the cousins had their ritual girls' night out to catch up and gab for hours.

Since Celeste had chosen the restaurant on their last outing, tonight Lara had the honor and decided to try a new Italian place downtown. She was dying for some pizza.

Lipstick applied, she exited the bedroom.

"Finally!" Celeste tossed the latest edition of *Ebony* to the coffee table and stood. "That's what you're wearing?"

Lara looked down at her little black dress. Celeste had impeccable fashion sense; her periwinkle pantsuit complemented her dark hair and mahogany features to perfection, but Lara thought she looked pretty good. "What's wrong with what I'm wearing?" she asked.

"Nothing. You were just in there so long I thought you were getting ready for the senior prom. What, no ball gown?"

"Ha-ha. I wasn't in there that long. Besides, I managed to get paint in my hair." Lara combed her fingers through her trendy mid-length hairstyle. "I had to shampoo and condition, plus do overtime with the curling iron. I'm still adjusting to this two-day-old hairdo you talked me into getting."

"It took me going out of town to take depositions for you to finally listen, but I'm glad you did." Celeste gently tugged the ends of Lara's trimmed tresses. "This is a nice surprise to come home to. It looks absolutely fabulous."

Lara smiled. "Thanks. I like it, too. I'll understand if you want to go home and rest. You just got back this morning."

"Are you kidding? I look forward to our nights out. You got back from Virginia the day I left for Charleston, and since Dan and the kids went along with me, my work was practically a vacation. Plus, given the fact Diana's teenage angst is giving me fits and Billy won't stop asking for a puppy, I need a break from 'Mama, I need/want' . . . fill in the blank."

Lara smiled at her cousin's halfhearted bemoaning about her thirteen- and six-year-old. Celeste had an idyllic life—a loving husband and three wonderful children. How Lara longed for that life. The unobtainable.

"Thank heavens my little Danny is too young to ask for more than his stuffed toy or a story," Celeste said of her active three-year-old. "I want us to play catch-up." She clasped her hands together. "So, Ms. Boyd, did you get the classroom all set up for the little kiddies?"

"Yes, I did, but I'm going to go back again tomorrow to finish up a few things and implement some new ideas. You know how I like things for my children."

"Yes, I do know. Just imagine if you had some of your very own." Celeste's eyes brightened. "What's going on with Mark?"

"Nothing much," she answered, surprised the question wasn't asked sooner. "We've gone out a couple of times, but I haven't talked to him in a while. He's fun and a nice guy and all, but there's just no spark."

"Spark?" Celeste planted her hands on her hips. "You think I was bowled over by Daniel Monroe from the moment I saw him?"

"Yes, as a matter of fact, I do. You were crazy about Dan from the moment you met him, and you and I both know it."

"Okay, so I was, but we're talking about you right now. What is it with you and these sparks? Sparks can come later. You had sparks with Foster Grayson, and we saw how that ended."

Lara groaned. Celeste just had to bring him up. She, more than anyone, knew Foster was a sore subject. Even after six years and no interaction, her ex hung around in her system like a stubborn cold germ. Or, more aptly, the pain of their break up lived in her heart like a twenty-four-hour armed guard. No man would get inside there again. Foster had made sure of it.

"Mark is a handsome guy with a lot going for him. Plus, he's the settling down type. You better grab that brother before somebody else does," Celeste advised. "This 'no sparks' excuse is wearing thin, Lara Rose Boyd. I didn't point him in your direction for nothing. Make that new hair work for you."

If it were only that easy. Mark was a prime catch, and a really nice guy, not unlike the other guys she had dated to keep her family off her back. But as with those guys, she didn't feel anything earth-shattering.

The same couldn't be said for the man she met in her classroom this afternoon. *Ryan.* She had felt the sparks she mentioned and so much more, and had thought of little else since. It excited and scared her to death.

"Lara? Lara?" Celeste's snapping fingers invaded her deep thoughts. "Girl, where were you?"

Lara shook off the haunting new memories. "Nowhere. I guess I'm just hungry. Let's go."

Her cousin spoke volumes with a simple look, and right now the look said *"Try again!"* Lara rolled her eyes. Celeste could read her like an open book with big, bold print.

"What?" Lara grumbled.

"You tell me." Celeste sat on the arm of the comfy, overstuffed beige couch. "What's on your mind?"

A gorgeous, white widower. "Pizza. Let's go eat." Lara opened the door and turned to her cousin. "Are you coming?"

Celeste moseyed off the couch. "I'm coming, but we aren't finished yet," she warned with a wagging finger.

Lara sighed. This was going to be a long night.

CHAPTER 3

Lara managed to keep the conversation on the family's Thanksgiving dinner and not her nonexistent love life during the fifteen-minute drive to Corlino's Kitchen. The tantalizing scent of baking bread, pizza, and pasta greeted them when they walked into the nearly packed restaurant.

Celeste took a deep breath and smiled. "I do believe you made a good choice," she said, dropping her keys into her purse.

Shown to a booth near the middle of the establishment, they placed their drink orders and decided on the house special pizza. While they sipped their iced tea and waited for the food, Celeste shared her idea for Thanksgiving.

"Our mothers will never agree on who should host this year, so if we cohost Thanksgiving dinner at my house, that would kill two birds with one stone," said Celeste. "I certainly have the room for it."

Lara couldn't argue with that. Her cousin's family of five lived in a twenty-room mansion. But their mothers agreeing to this was another thing. The sisters loved each other dearly, but had a healthy rivalry in showing off their newest home furnishings. They were always unintentionally-on-purpose trying to outdo the other. "I don't have a problem with the idea," Lara allowed, "but Mama won't get to show off her new dinette set and china at your place, and what about Aunt Bethany?"

"I know Mama will be okay with it if you tell her Aunt Evelyn is. And if you tell her you're inviting a man to Thanksgiving dinner, she'll be all for it, hmm?"

"Who is this man I'm supposed to invite to Thanksgiving dinner? When someone gets an invitation to our family's Thanksgiving, he or she eventually becomes the invitee's spouse. Minus one notable exception."

Celeste's dark eyes danced. "Yep, funny that," she said with a smile. "I'm sure Mark will be more than happy to join in our family festivities. Your birthday is a few days later, who knows, you could be getting one heck of a present this year. A wonderful new man in your life that the family loves." Celeste poked around in her purse and pulled out her cell phone. "I can call him now, give him over three months notice."

Lara's eye's widened. "Celeste!" she cried, reaching across the table.

A light tapping on her shoulder interrupted Lara.

"Ms. Boyd?"

Justin's happy face made Lara forget all about Celeste and the phone. She returned his beaming smile. "Hi, Justin."

"Hi. I told Daddy I saw you."

Daddy? Ryan was here? The fluttering returned to Lara's stomach with a vengeance. Her heart pumped wildly. It took everything she had not to jump on the seat in an attempt to locate him. Her internal conflict didn't last long as Ryan approached from Justin's rear.

"I see you were right, son." Ryan smiled. The loosened top buttons of his white dress shirt gave Lara a delicious eyeful of the sinewy blonde curls dusting his chest. Fragrant aftershave tickled her nostrils and his sparkling blue eyes continued to convince her they were the most dangerous things in the world. "How are you this evening, Ms. Boyd?"

"Fine," she squeaked, quenching her parched throat with some tea.

"Hello," Ryan greeted Celeste.

Celeste waved. "Hi."

"Where are my manners?" Lara said, knowing full well her manners, and any trace of coherent thought, disappeared the moment she heard Ryan was there. "Celeste, this is Ryan Andrews and his son, Justin. Mr. Andrews, Justin, this is my cousin, Celeste Monroe."

Ryan extended his hand to Celeste as Justin gave her a friendly wave. "It's nice to meet you," he said.

Celeste shook Ryan's hand and gave Justin an affable smile. "You, too. Both of you."

"Justin is one of my newest pupils," Lara explained.

"I see."

Ryan placed his hands on Justin's shoulders. "I hope his coming over wasn't a problem."

"Of course not, we were just grabbing a bite." Lara brushed her hand against Justin's cheek. The boy was a wonderful distraction. If she kept her focus on him, she couldn't drown in those dreamy pools his father called eyes. "This is one of my favorite little guys."

"You wanna eat dinner with Daddy and me?" Justin asked.

"Hmmm, uh . . ." Lara glanced at Ryan. His wide eyes confirmed he was as stunned by Justin's suggestion as she.

"It's okay, we don't mind. Daddy likes you." Justin looked up at his father. "Tell her, Daddy."

A bright shade of pink colored Ryan's cheeks. He cleared his throat. "Son, I think Ms. Boyd wants to have dinner with her cousin."

"She can come, too," Justin insisted.

Lara wanted to accept the invite, but Celeste's confusion made declining the best choice. "Justin, I really appreciate the kind offer, but Celeste and I need to discuss some things, and I think your father wants to spend some man-to-man time with you. What if we split a sandwich during lunch on Monday? Would you like that?"

Justin answered with his full-body nod.

Lara smiled. "Good, it's a date." She glanced up at Ryan to see the familiar "something on his mind" look she recalled from earlier. Maybe that was his normal expression. "I hope you two enjoy your meal."

Ryan nodded. "Yeah, you too." He clutched Justin's hand and led him away.

Lara turned to Celeste and her questioning eyes. Cross-examination was about to begin.

What is wrong with me? What is . . . Ryan stopped his mental kicking when he saw Shelly at his booth. He froze in his steps. *I'm losing my mind.*

"Daddy, what's wrong?" Justin asked.

Ryan continued to stare at the table. "Uh . . ."

"Only you can see and hear me." Shelly pointed in Lara's direction. "I suggest you turn around, go back to that booth, and talk to her."

Ryan opened his mouth to speak but Shelly stopped him with a shake of her head.

"If you talk to me, everyone in here will think you're crazy. You're not crazy, Ryan, just nervous." Shelly pointed at Lara. "Talk to her, and ask her out. If Justin can do it, you can, too." She shooed him away.

Ryan gazed at Lara's table. He could do this. He would do this. He squeezed Justin's hand. "We're going back."

Lara's cousin stopped speaking when he and Justin arrived. "Mr. Andrews?" she said, giving Lara a sideways glance.

"I'm sorry to interrupt again," he said to both ladies, gathering the abruptly ended conversation regarded him, "but is it possible I could have a moment with you, Ms. Boyd?"

Lara looked at Celeste.

"Hi, Justin, right?" Celeste said.

Justin nodded.

"There's this video game on my cell phone my son thinks is so cool. You want to see it?"

His eyes widened. "Yes, ma'am." He turned to Ryan. "Can I, Daddy?"

Was this his son so anxious to be alone with a virtual stranger? What powers Lara wielded. "Sure," Ryan answered.

The boy slid into the booth next to Celeste and took possession of the phone.

Ryan thanked Celeste and motioned for Lara to walk straight ahead. In step behind her, he got the full effect of her outfit. The dress accentuated her curvy hips and round backside, while showing off her beautiful, long legs. *Mmm.* He was impressed with the package, and his libido wholeheartedly agreed.

With no shirttails to hide the excitement Lara elicited in him, Ryan readily slid into the seat across from her, grateful the table was high and wide with a dangling tablecloth for added protection. Lara sat quietly, waiting for him to speak. He brushed his sweaty palms against his slacks. "Ms. Boyd, I . . ."

Lara held up her hand. "Mr. Andrews, as someone who works with young children on a daily basis, I know how they can be. They tend to share too much information in an oftentimes misunderstood way. So, if you're about to apologize for what Justin said at the table, don't. I understand what he meant."

"I was actually going to apologize, but not for what Justin said at the table. He, uh—he made me aware of something I said when I left your classroom today, and I must apologize for that. You're a very beautiful woman. Nothing like what I expected." He rolled his eyes. "I've— uh, I've said that before."

"Not the beautiful part."

"I'm sorry I called you Ms. Body." He grunted. "I can't tell you how terrible I feel about that. About the whole way I behaved. I was so . . ."

"It's all right, Mr. Andrews. Ms. Body is one of the nicer names I've been called in my lifetime," Lara offered with a laugh. "If that's all—"

"No, Ms. Boyd, that's not quite all."

"Okay."

"About what Justin said at your table."

"Like I said, I understand about that."

"I'm not sure you do. I know it sounds grade school, but what he said is true. I do like you, and as more than just his nice teacher."

Lara's eyes widened, but she said nothing.

"I haven't felt this way about anyone since my wife died, which might explain my strange behavior. I have to get used to all of this again, so if I do it wrong, please tell me."

"Do what wrong?"

Ryan drew a deep breath and let it go. "Ms. Boyd, would you have dinner with me tomorrow?"

"Dinner?"

"Yes. I mean, if you don't have any plans or—" He groaned. "You're dating someone, aren't you? I'm sorry, I shouldn't have assumed. You're gorgeous. You probably have men lined up around your block. I . . ."

"Yes, I will have dinner with you."

Ryan blinked. "You will?"

"I think it will be fun. I can give you my number so—"

"Five, five, five, zero, eight, seven, six." Her eyebrow lifted in surprise. "It was on the supply list," he explained.

Lara chuckled. "That's right. I was going to tell you to call so we could firm things up, but I guess we can do that now. Is seven a good time?"

"Seven o'clock is fine. Do you want me to pick you up or do you want us to meet somewhere? Whatever you want is okay."

"This is a date, right?"

"I hope so."

She laughed softly. "Then it's your duty to pick me up."

Ryan's nervousness disappeared. He smiled. "Okay, I'll pick you up."

"I'm at 218 Branwell Place, Apartment 3. It's a couple of miles from Fisher Park."

"I know exactly where that is. I guess I'll see you tomorrow at seven, Ms. Boyd."

"Can we dispense with the formalities? After three o'clock I'm just plain old Lara."

"Plain old Lara?" Ryan took her hand, finding himself sinking into the depths of her warm brown eyes. "Plain and old is what I was expecting when I stepped into your classroom today. But, lady, there is nothing plain or old about you. And, please, call me Ryan."

Lara maintained his gaze. Her hand tightened around his. "Okay, Ryan."

In that moment, no one else existed. If meeting Lara was a dream, Ryan didn't want to wake up.

"Ahem!"

Her cousin's clearing throat brought Lara spiraling back to reality.

"Forgive the intrusion," Celeste said, "but Justin has to go to the little boys' room."

Ryan released Lara's hand as they stood. "Okay, buddy, let's take care of that." He moved to Justin's side and gave Celeste a smile. "Thanks for watching him for me."

"No problem, he's a sweetheart."

Ryan's eyes met with Lara's. "I'll call you."

Lara nodded. "Okay. Bye, Justin," she said.

"Bye, Ms. Boyd." He waved. "Bye, Ms. Celeste."

"Good night, ladies." Ryan took Justin's hand and led him to the restroom.

Celeste wasted no time starting her grilling session once they were settled back at their table. "Well?" she said.

Lara received a momentary reprieve when their pizza arrived. The aroma of pepperoni, green peppers, onions, and sausage invaded her senses. "Mmm, that smells good." Lara handed the server her plate for a slice.

Celeste gave the young man a polite smile and took the spatula from his hand. "Thank you, but we can do this." Once he left, she placed the spatula on the pizza and slid the pan to the far side of the table.

Lara frowned. "What are you doing?"

"Eating can wait. What's going on with you and Ken?"

"Ken?"

"Your Mr. Andrews. He's like Barbie's playmate come to life. Lara, talk to me. I saw a wedding band."

"Given your description of him, I'd say you saw more."

"One thing at a time, Cuz, first things first. I also saw the way you two were looking at each other when I brought Justin to the table. Those were some serious vibes. His moment with you turned into fifteen minutes. I had to practically hack my guts out before getting your attention. What is this?"

"I don't know." Lara fell back against the soft vinyl seat. "But it feels so right, it scares the hell out of me."

"Right? Lara, the man is—"

"Widowed."

"I was going to say white, too."

"So, you did notice?"

"Kinda hard to miss. He's a widower?"

"Yeah."

"For how long?"

"I . . ." Lara shrugged. "I don't know."

"*You don't know?* His wife's body may not be cold in the grave and you're making goo-goo eyes at him? Girl, the Lord is gonna to strike you dead."

Lara laughed. Celeste sounded like the sisters at her family church in Virginia. "There's no need to worry about that. With the way Ryan is, I think she's been gone a while. At least the normal waiting period."

"*Ya think?*" Celeste mocked. "And what way is he?"

"Nervous, a little apprehensive."

"And you think that's because his wife has been dead for a while? Come on, Lara."

"I'll find out for sure soon enough. We're having dinner tomorrow."

Celeste's mouth opened like a baby bird's at feeding time. "When did you meet him?"

"This afternoon. He came over to the classroom while I was decked in my painting finery. I think he heard me singing 'Midnight Train to Georgia.'"

"And he still wants to go out with you?"

Lara rolled her eyes. *"Anyway,* he wanted to introduce Justin to his new teacher." She pressed her hand to her chest. "Celeste, when I first saw him . . . He literally took my breath away. But when we shook hands, I could have powered all of Denburg."

"The elusive sparks you mentioned earlier?"

"Yes."

"And I thought that was just an excuse."

"It was an excuse, but an honest one."

Celeste blew a long breath. "I'm going to say something you probably won't like."

"Then don't say it."

"Lara, you know I want the best for you, and I want you to be happy more than anybody, but a widowed white guy with a young son you're going to teach?" Celeste groaned. "You're setting yourself up for big problems."

"There are no problems, Celeste. We're just having dinner."

"Sure. Friday dinner tomorrow, Thanksgiving dinner in November. Girl, you are heading for some major hurt."

"Why do you think that?"

"Just a feeling."

"Well, I have a feeling, too. I have a feeling Ryan Andrews is a wonderful man, and he won't hurt me."

"Maybe not intentionally, but it could still happen. Foster left a monster dent in your heart and you didn't see that coming, either."

"Who did?" Lara shook her head. She didn't want to think about Foster. For the first time in years she felt sparks for a man. A nice man who wasn't Foster. It felt good. "Things with Ryan are different," she said.

"You're telling me. I don't have to tell you how loaded *this* situation is."

Celeste didn't mince words, but right now Lara wished she did. Her happy feeling slipped away like sands through an hourglass.

"Hey." Celeste lifted Lara's lowered chin. "If it's any consolation, I hope I'm wrong. Whatever's going on with you is definitely going on with him, too. Maybe that spark will burn out anything else that might show up. You have him completely captivated, and that little boy of his . . . That kid could charm the fur off a mink."

Lara smiled. "Justin is wonderful, isn't he?"

"I guess that's just the apple not falling far from the tree for you, huh?"

Lara's cheeks warmed. She lowered her gaze.

"Blushing?" Celeste laughed as she served herself some pizza. "Girl, you've got it bad. I guess his being fine as hell might have a little something to do with it," she said, popping a piece of pepperoni in her mouth.

Lara considered her cousin's words. All the men she dated were nice looking, and she had found them all attractive, yet she only felt the sparks with Ryan. He was white, widowed, and a father. She'd never dated a man who was any of those things, nor ever expected she would. *My, how things change.*

Ryan returned to his table with Justin. His eyes met Lara's, and like clockwork, her heart pounded. She returned his smile. Yes, this situation was different in a lot of ways.

CHAPTER 4

Ryan tossed and turned. Lara's beautiful eyes and smiling face stayed on his mind, keeping sleep elusive. At least a dozen times he had picked up the phone to call her, but hung up without dialing the first number. He wanted to hear her voice, but to phone and say that sounded really lame.

Ugh!

This was insane. He couldn't stop thinking about a woman he met less than twelve hours ago. He had to get a grip. *Go to sleep, Ryan.* He found a cool spot on the pillow. Seconds passed like hours. *Call her. Call her.* His wide-open eyes stared in the direction of the phone.

"For God's sake, call her."

Ryan shot up. "Shelly?" He twisted on the bedside lamp to find her standing at the foot of the bed. He steadied his racing heart. "You have *got* to stop doing that."

"I've been doing it for years, you just never knew about it, much to my own aggravation. FYI, you didn't need to turn on the light to see me. What are you waiting for?"

He tossed his pillow to the side. "It's ten-thirty. It's too late."

"It wasn't too late an hour ago when you first picked up that phone. Ryan, Lara only teaches kindergarten, she's not a kindergartener."

"Nah. If she's asleep, I don't want to wake her up."

"If she's asleep, I don't think she'll mind your call waking her up. Call her."

"You know, you're as pushy as ever."

"Some things never change. I'll leave you alone."

Spurred by Shelly's less than subtle prodding, Ryan grabbed the phone, tapped in the seven digits, and waited. *One ring. Two rings. Three . . .*

"Hello," Lara said, her voice sleepy.

Ryan cursed himself. He knew he shouldn't have called. "I'm sorry. I was afraid I'd wake you up."

"Ryan? I'm going to start calling you the I'm-sorry-man. Stop apologizing." She laughed. "I wasn't quite to sleep. What's going on?"

"I just wanted to say good night again and tell you how much I'm looking forward to tomorrow night."

"I'm looking forward to it, too."

"You know, Justin can't stop talking about you." *And I can't stop thinking about you.*

"I hope I don't burst his bubble when class starts. Kindergarten is a lot more than a long recess before first grade. I'd hate to turn into 'Mean old Ms. Boyd' for him."

Her cheerful laughter made his heart swell. It wasn't a pretentious, cutesy woman laugh. Hers was boisterous and honest. Pure. "You have the most wonderful laugh," he said.

"It's a side effect from my profession. The children are infectious. They are a real joy."

"Do you have any of your own?"

"Not yet. My students are my children for now. I would love to have lots of them, someday. Maybe it will happen. I just have to wait for the right guy to come along."

"He hasn't yet?"

"Let's just say the jury is still out."

Was that answer good for him? "For how long?" Ryan asked.

"For however long it takes. When it comes to the father of my children, there can be no uncertainty."

"How will you know when you find him?"

"Well, when I see him, I'll hear music, a symphony. He'll make my head spin and my heart race with a simple smile. And his touch will make my body feel like Ben Franklin's key on that fateful stormy night." She paused for a moment. "That's how I'll have my first clue. I'm still working on the rest."

Ryan smiled. "Sounds like one hell of feeling." One he'd recognized in himself earlier today.

"Oh, it is," Lara concurred, her voice whispery soft. She cleared her throat. "Metaphorically speaking, of course."

He chuckled. "Of course."

"Ryan?"

"Yes?"

"May I ask a personal question?"

"You can ask me anything."

"Tell me about your wife. How did you two come to be?"

"Well, it didn't happen overnight, that's for sure," he said, laughing. "Shell kinda grew on me. We met our freshman year at college. She was such a loudmouth. Very political, very in-your-face. It drove me nuts."

"I heard that," Shelly said.

"One moment, Lara." Ryan covered the mouthpiece. His gaze darted about the room. Shelly would choose this opportunity to be invisible. "I thought you were leaving?"

"I am. You better be nice. I'll know if you're not."

Certain Shelly was gone, Ryan removed his hand from the mouthpiece. "Sorry about that, Lara. I thought I heard something."

"That's fine," she said. "So, what changed things between you and . . . Shell?"

"Her name was Shelly, but she was so hard I called her Shell." They shared an easy laugh. "Believe it or not, graduation changed things. We clashed our whole four years of college, and the day we graduated it hit me. Shell had been the bane of my existence for four years, but sometime during the processional and the commencement address, I realized I was in love with her. I don't know when I actually fell, but by the time the speaker was done, I knew I had to find her and spill my guts."

"How did she take it?"

He rubbed his right cheek, remembering. "She slapped me."

"Ouch."

"You said it, she packed a powerful punch. But in the next moment she kissed me, and thus began our beginning."

Conversation flowed easily as Ryan shared more details of his marriage and life with Shelly, the arrival of Justin into their lives, and the purchase of their home. He even talked about Norris and their wild times together. He couldn't believe how much he'd shared, or how he didn't feel upset sharing it, which was the biggest surprise of all.

"You two sounded really happy," Lara said. "What happened to Shelly? Did she get sick?"

"A car accident," Ryan answered. "I was waiting for her to come home from work. We'd only been in the house a month, and were still decorating. We planned to spend the evening looking through more furniture books, but instead two police officers appeared at my door."

"Shelly died a month after . . ." Lara paused. "Never mind."

"No, it's alright. Say what you were gonna say."

"You said you had been in your house a month when Shelly died, right?"

"Uh-huh."

"According to you, Justin was two then."

"Yeah. His birthday was a couple of months before."

"At the restaurant you made it sound like you hadn't dated since Shelly died."

"I haven't."

"There's been no woman in your life in over three years?"

"There's been no woman. There's been no *nothing*," he answered, freely sharing his three-year sexual abstinence. "I was busy raising my son. I didn't feel like I was missing anything, except Shelly. I was missing her a lot."

"Yeah, but, three years is a very long time for a man to—"

"Measurement of time wasn't something I related to. It was all the same. I was twenty-nine years old, suddenly single, with a toddler. I had never felt so lost and scared in my life. Poor Justin had no idea what happened. He only knew when he called for Mama she wouldn't answer."

Lara sniffled. "Oh, Ryan."

Ryan sat up with a start, wishing his arms could travel through the phone lines and comfort her. "Lara, please, don't cry. I didn't tell you this to upset you; I just wanted to explain. You're such an amazing woman. The first since Shelly I've wanted to spend time with. The only one who hasn't reminded me of how much I've missed her." There was a long pause on Lara's end. He'd said too much. *Oh, God, please don't let her hang up.* "Lara?"

"I'm still here," she finally said.

"Are you okay?"

"Yeah. I'm sorry. I was just listening to you talk and it left me curious and a little confused."

"About what?"

"About how you were able to go three years without a line of crazed women beating a path to your door. After listening to you talk about your college escapades with your best buddy, Norris, two baseball jocks enjoying success on the prowl, I'm sure you're aware you're a chick magnet. Do you have some criminal record or something you haven't mentioned?"

Ryan laughed. "Thanks for the compliment, such as it is. No, there's no criminal record. Lots of women have tried to get my attention, but the one who did was the one who wasn't trying. It must have been the old jeans and colorful plaid."

Lara groaned. "You had to remind me."

"You looked great in those clothes, and you looked fabulous tonight in that black dress. You are very beautiful, Lara."

"If you don't cut it out with those compliments, you're gonna make me vain. Ms. Body wouldn't be so beautiful with a big head."

Ryan groaned. "Now who's bringing up stuff better left forgotten?" he grumbled in good nature.

"I'm sorry." Lara laughed. "I couldn't resist."

"Is it okay if I ask you something now?"

"I guess. Go ahead."

"How is it you're available?"

"I don't know, bad karma?" Lara remained quiet for several moments. "I was engaged once. His name was Foster, but it—it ended years ago."

She grew quiet again—too quiet. There was a story behind this Foster, but for whatever reason she wasn't ready to share it. Ryan decided not to push the issue. When she was ready to talk, he'd be ready to listen.

"That was my last serious romantic involvement," she went on to say. "I've dated, but my long-term love affair has been with my work. Since it makes me very happy, I can't complain."

Lara's sentence ended with a yawn. Ryan checked the alarm clock. Ten after two. They had been talking for hours. "It's so late, you must be exhausted," he said.

"No, I'm not," she replied, stifling another yawn.

"I'll give you an 'A' for effort, Ms. Boyd."

"Okay, I am a little tired. There are still a couple of things I need to finish up in the classroom, so I should call it a night. I really enjoyed talking with you, Ryan."

"Me, too."

"Good night."

"Good night, Lara." Ryan turned out the light and slid under the covers. It would certainly be a good night now.

The bright smile of Agnes Ross welcomed Ryan as he stepped off the elevator and into the reception area of Converse Accounting. The fifty-something redhead was like the favorite aunt you looked forward to seeing at all the boring family functions. A true Southern belle, she had a way of making you feel good by just being in her presence. "Good morning, Mr. Andrews," she said in her charming twang.

Ryan returned her cheerful greeting. "Hi, Agnes." He nodded to the door on his right. "He in there?"

"Sure is. You go right on in."

"Thanks." Whistling a happy tune, Ryan strolled the plush royal blue carpeting and stuck his head in the door. The scent of Italian leather permeated the air. No matter how many times he came over, that smell always seemed brand new. "You busy?"

Norris Converse stopped pounding on the keyboard and settled his glasses atop his head of dark curls. "Never too busy for my best bud." He waved him in. "Pull up some seat."

Ryan moved to the chair in front of the desk. Norris had been his best friend for as long as he could remember. There wasn't one thing he'd gone through that Norris hadn't gone through with him, and vice versa. They'd even moved to South Carolina together to attend college and ended up staying.

A good-looking guy, and well aware of it, Norris went through women like most people went through Kleenex during cold season. Born with a silver spoon in his mouth—his mother's father was a Greek shipping magnate—Norris's unlimited access to money didn't help his lady's man persona. He was also a major flirt—harmless, but major. Ryan wanted nothing more than for Norris to finally find one right woman, settle down, and lose his affinity for leather furniture.

"Was that you whistling out there?" Norris asked.

"Yes," Ryan answered. "You'll never guess what I did."

"Never? I don't think so." Norris propped the legs of his six-foot frame on the desk corner and linked his hands behind his head. "You're extremely happy, so I'll go for the big ones first. You knitted Justin a pair of socks and a sweater?"

Ryan chuckled. "No."

"You found a solution to end wax buildup on your kitchen floor?"

"Try again."

"You came up with a new way to prepare chicken?"

Ryan made a buzzing sound. "Wrong, wrong, and very wrong."

"Well, I'm stumped. What else could it be?"

"I met a woman."

Norris blinked. "Come again?"

"You heard me."

"No, I need clarification. I heard you say 'I met a woman,' but what do you mean? Did you meet a woman, or did you *meet* a woman?"

"I *met* a woman. A funny, brilliant, and very beautiful woman."

Norris made the sign of the crucifix. "Thank you, God!" Gray eyes twinkled. "Tell me all about this incredible female who has made me as happy as it appears she's made you."

"Her name is Lara, Lara Boyd, and she's Justin's kindergarten teacher."

"Justin's kindergarten teacher?" A frown erased Norris's bright smile. "The old lady you took him to meet yesterday? Damn, man, what is she, ninety-nine years old?"

"Well, actually—"

"Aw." Norris flapped his hand. "Forget it. I'll be getting you a kitten for Christmas. By the time Justin goes off to college you should have a nice cat collection."

"Norris?"

"I can see it now—the depths of summer, you sitting inside your house in a rocker, a shawl wrapped around your shoulders, a fire raging in the fireplace, and a million cats at your feet. Outside, the neighborhood kids are throwing rocks at the windows and sharing stories about the legend of the Widower Andrews." Sighing, Norris donned his glasses and turned to the copy at the left of his computer screen. His fingers glided over the ten-key pad as he resumed working with some accounting software program or another. "At least I'll have the satisfaction of knowing I tried."

"Talk about jumping to conclusions. Just because a woman is a kindergarten teacher, it doesn't mean she's old."

"You thought the same thing." Norris stopped keying and cocked a curious brow. "She's not ninety-nine?"

"No, she's twenty-nine, and *gorgeous*. Justin is crazy about her. Not that I can blame him."

"You met a beautiful, *young* woman?"

"Yep."

"I'll be damned! This is the best news."

"The news gets a little better. We have a date tonight."

"You asked her out, too? You do like her."

"Yeah, I do. I like her a lot."

"For years, *years*, I've been bending over backwards to find you a woman, and here you are waxing ecstatic about one you've found on your own. I am so happy for you."

"Since you're in a good mood, I have a favor to ask."

"What favor? Oh, I know. You want me to give you all the ins and outs of the dating game. Don't worry, pal, I got you covered. What do you need to know?"

"Can you watch Justin for me tonight?"

"The first thing is . . ." Norris shook his head. "What?"

"I don't need tips from you. I don't want to scare Lara away. I need you to watch Justin. Think you can?"

"If you were anyone else I'd say no, especially on a Friday night, but you're going out on date! This takes precedence over any and everything else. I'll have to disappoint a luscious lady, but anything for the cause. Justin and I will have a fun time, not unlike the one you'll have with your kindergarten teacher." Norris winked.

"It's not like that."

"You mean not yet, you sly dog."

"You joke, but I'm serious. Lara is special. I never thought I would feel this way again."

"Neither did I, but I'm so glad we were wrong." Norris flipped through his appointment book. "You want me to come by the house or do you want to drop Justin off to me?"

"What's good for you?" Ryan asked. His friend worked out of joy, not necessity, and he provided all of his services pro bono. New and struggling businesses and people of modest means from all over the state came to Norris for their tax and financial needs. It kept his firm quite busy.

"My last appointment is at four-fifteen, and I need to finish this fiscal report. Let's say your place at six?"

"Sounds good." Ryan made his way to the door. "I'll see you later."

"Whoa, not so fast." Norris hastened over and ushered Ryan back to the chair. "You haven't told me what this gorgeous woman looks like? Give me some details."

Ryan smiled. "Details?" He eased back into the chair. "Lara's heavenly. She's tall, about five-eight or nine. Womanly curves, no stick figure here. Legs that go on forever, deep brown eyes you just want to lose yourself in, shoulder length dark hair, and a dazzling smile. Mmm, and she smells so good." Ryan closed his eyes, visualizing Lara's gorgeous image. "She's absolutely beautiful. She's black."

"I see." Norris sat on the edge of the desk. He rubbed his chin. "Is that a problem?"

"Not for me."

"Is it for her?"

"She accepted my dinner invitation, so it can't be much of a problem. Norris, she makes me feel so good. We talked on the phone until two this morning. Lara is the best thing to happen to me since . . . since I lost Shelly. And that's another thing."

"What?"

"I saw Shelly yesterday." Ryan held up the middle fingers of his left hand. "Three times."

Norris lumbered back to his chair, groaning. "I think you've inhaled too much oven cleaner, pal."

Ryan scooted forward. "I'm serious. After I met Lara, I went home and Sue—"

Norris groaned louder. His friend didn't like Sue much either.

"Just listen," Ryan said. "Sue was there and—"

"Sue's always there."

Ryan frowned. "You want to hear this or not?"

"Continue."

"Sue got curious because Justin was going on about his new teacher and she saw I was pretty hyped about her, too. Lara's been all I can think about from the moment I saw her, but when Sue mentioned my interest, it made me feel guilty."

"Guilty? Because of Shelly?"

"Yeah."

"Ryan, Shelly's been dead for three years. She wouldn't want you to close yourself off. How long have I been saying this?"

"A long time. Shelly said the same thing. She thinks Lara's fantastic and I shouldn't be an idiot."

"Uh-hmm." Norris rubbed the back of his neck. "Well, I hope you're going to take her advice."

Ryan ignored the doubt his friend did a lousy job of concealing. "I don't think I can help myself. I feel so close to Lara, and I just met her." He wanted to be around her all the time—like right now. He moved for the door. "I have to go."

"Wait, Ryan. Can you at least tell me when I get to meet this fantastic woman?"

Ryan met Norris's inquisitive gaze. "You'll meet her in time. I want Lara to be totally crazy about me before I subject her to you. That way, she can't hold my being your friend against me."

Norris smirked. "Having a woman in your life has turned you into a comedian. Fine. I'll have to accept that, for now."

His friend's subdued response surprised Ryan. Sometimes, Norris could be like a constricting snake when he wanted to know something, squeezing and squeezing until he found out what he wanted. Ryan chose not to question the reprieve and just be grateful for it. Eventually, he would tell Norris everything, but first he had to find out what everything was.

Leaving Norris to his work, Ryan walked out of the air-conditioned office building and into the heat of the August morning. The clock on the corner lamppost put the time at just after ten, and the humidity was already so oppressive that singing birds didn't part from the shady trees. He wiped the sweat trailing down his face. Fall and its cooler temperatures couldn't get here fast enough. At least it would be cool where he was headed. Ryan smiled. He hoped Lara liked surprises.

CHAPTER 5

"Smurfette, girl, Snow White ain't got nothin' on you." Lara laughed at her unfinished picture of the tiny blue creature.

"So, you talk to yourself when Motown's greatest aren't entertaining you? I'll have to store this in my 'Things to remember about Lara' file."

Ryan! Lara turned to the familiar voice. Her heart galloped like a team of runaway horses. She couldn't imagine what brought him over, but she was glad he was there, and grateful she wore a blue T-shirt and jeans that made her look more cute than colorblind. "Hi," she greeted.

Ryan smiled. "Hi yourself."

She craned her neck to look around him. "Justin's not with you?"

"Nah, he had a date," Ryan said, laughing. He walked to her worktable and motioned at the picture. "You about done?"

Lara glanced at her unfinished picture and thought of the one still remaining. "I would like to say yes, but I'd be lying. I guess the right answer would be almost."

"Four hands are better than two. Can I help?"

"I don't know. Do you draw?"

He grinned. "I do a little something."

"Good. How are you with spring?"

"Spring?"

Lara's heart skipped a beat. He was even cuter perplexed. "I'm working on the seasons." She pointed to the pictures on the jumbo drawing paper further down the table. "I've done winter and summer. I'm working on fall, and that leaves spring. Just capture spring in a way five-year-olds can understand. That's not so hard, is it?"

Amusement crinkled the corners of his eyes. "I think I can handle the task, Ms. Boyd. Just don't try to take a peek at my picture. I'm sensitive about sharing my work before it's done."

"I'll try to contain myself."

"You do that." He glanced around the room. "Where do you keep the art supplies?"

"The top cabinet to the left of the sink. You should find everything you need there."

"Okay."

Lara watched Ryan plunder the cabinet for materials and set them aside. She smiled in appreciation of the lovely view his faded jeans provided. *Where did this man get such a nice butt?* So perfectly round and tight. She wondered if it felt as firm as it looked. Thoughts of the many ways she could find out warmed her body like hot chocolate in the dead of winter. Lara shook her head. She needed to put her brazen musings elsewhere and quickly. "So, what brought you over?"

Ryan closed the cabinet door and gathered his chosen items. "Which answer do you want?"

"Which answer?"

"Yeah, I have two. The real one, and the one I came up with on the drive over." He moved to the table across from her and dropped a box of colored pencils, a paintbrush, and a set of watercolor paints.

"Okay, I'm stumped."

"Don't be." He took a seat in one of the little chairs and opened the box of pencils. "I came over because—because I like being around you and spending time with you. I wanted to see you, so I made up an excuse about having a question about Justin's school supplies in case my unexpected visit wasn't a pleasant surprise for you." His gaze met hers. "Do I need to share specifics on the school supplies question?"

Lara smiled. Ryan had no concept of the word subtle. "No, you don't. I like being around you, too."

A while later, after conversation about Justin, her love for children, and the different activities she had planned for the coming school year, Lara added the final touch to her picture. "Well, I'm done." She made her way to where Ryan worked. He still looked incredibly comfortable in the child's chair, and he hadn't gotten up once to stretch his legs. Either he had a high tolerance for discomfort, or he was in a serious zone. "You're not finished yet?"

Ryan stood, blocking his artwork from her curious eyes. "No, Lara, I'm not." He shooed her off. "Go wash your hands or something. Play 'Midnight Train to Georgia' while you do it. That should keep you busy for a good five minutes." He snickered.

Lara's mouth dropped in mock indignation. She planted her hands on her hips. "How much of that did you see?"

"Enough. I won't need more than five minutes to finish."

"You got a peek of me at work yesterday. I think it's only fair I get a peek at your work today." She made an attempt to move around him. "One good turn and all."

He blocked her path. "Uh-uh. Have a little patience, Lara. Good things come to those who wait." His eyes engaged in a slow, deliberate journey of her body. In what became second nature, her insides melted under his blazing gaze. "I'm a testament to the truth in that statement."

Feeling a sudden need for a drink of water, Lara walked to the sink. "Okay, five more minutes."

A short time later Ryan called her. "Your wait is over." He moved aside as she approached. "I hope you like it."

"You said I would, so I . . ." Lara stopped midsentence, in awe of the finished product. "Oh, my goodness."

"Is that a good 'Oh, my goodness'?"

"Yes." Lara moved in closer. A crystal blue sky, thick green grass, blooming flowers of red, yellow, and blue, a pond, and animals, lots of animals—rabbits, a family of deer, birds, and tons of squirrels made up the nature and wildlife population in the beautiful scene. Curiously, one of the squirrels wore jeans and a baseball cap and stood on its hind legs. Children with upturned heads sat in a semicircle on the grass, while a woman, who looked an awful lot like her, sat in a wide-back wicker chair reading to them. "This is incredible."

"You can thank my subject. I think she's pretty incredible, too."

"So that is me?"

"I think it's a fair likeness, don't you?"

"More than fair. I just—I've never been captured like this before." Lara did a silent count of the varying browns, blondes, and brunettes of the faceless heads of little boys and girls. "You have sixteen students."

"I pay attention to everything you say, Lara. That's what made it take a little longer. I can see how much you love your work, so I had to account for all of your children. Nine girls and seven boys. I'm sorry I couldn't give them faces, but since Justin is the only one I know, I had them face you instead. Of course, they would be riveted to you, so it worked out."

"It's wonderful." For a picture done in a relatively short time, the attention to detail was amazing. Ryan obviously had a thing for squirrels, but he had tons of talent, too. "You're an artist?"

"An illustrator of children's books. That would explain the squirrels. The one standing off to the side is Sigmund. He's the lead in the book I'm currently working on. I was having the hardest time with him, but you inspired me."

"Glad I could be of help." She couldn't take her eyes off the picture. "This is amazing. I don't know what to say."

"You've already said it. I'm glad you like it."

"I love it." She kissed his cheek. "Thank you, Ryan."

He touched the spot on his face where her lips had lingered. His glazed eyes met hers. "Thank you," he murmured. "I mean—you're welcome." He shook his head and smiled. "You know, I should be thanking you. If I hadn't met you yesterday, I'd be home—"

"Polishing more furniture?"

"You smelled the Pledge?"

Lara nodded. "Yeah."

"Actually, I finished the furniture yesterday. Friday is the day I wax my kitchen floor." They both laughed. "I'm having a much more enjoyable time with you. Besides, no one gives me a kiss for doing a good job on the floor."

Lara's cheeks burned. She lowered her gaze, not believing her impulsiveness. "I'm sorry, I shouldn't have done that."

Ryan lifted her chin. His hypnotic eyes drew her in. "Don't apologize. I liked it. I liked it a lot." He took a step closer. "I like you a lot."

His voice dropped an octave with every word he uttered, or maybe it was the pounding of her heart that caused his speech to seem drowned. Lara didn't know, and she didn't care. She just wanted to kiss him again, and not on his cheek. Ryan's tongue darted out, moistening his full pink lips. His strong hands cupped her face, bringing her waiting mouth closer to his. Her lips tingled at the feel of his warm breath against them. Ryan lowered his head. Her eyes fluttered closed. Waiting, anticipating.

"Ahem!"

Lara's eyes flew open. *Ugh!*

Ryan grumbled an expletive and dropped his hands.

Turning in the direction of the sound, Lara found Justin and a short, older woman standing in the door. The woman didn't look at all happy, but Justin's beaming smile conveyed his utter delight.

"Hey, Ms. Boyd," Justin greeted. "Hey, Daddy."

Lara waved and returned Justin's smile. "Hi, sweetie."

"I'm surprised to see you here, Ryan," the woman said.

Ryan stuck his thumbs in the back pockets of his jeans. "I can say the same for you, Sue. I thought you were taking Justin shopping."

"I did, but I wanted to meet this Ms. Boyd he couldn't stop talking about, so I took a chance she'd be here." Her eyes narrowed. "What was it you said brought you over?"

"I didn't say," he curtly responded. "But I was helping Lara, Ms. Boyd, draw some pictures."

"Drawing?" Sue gave Lara a scathing once-over. "Yeah, that's *exactly* what it looked like to me."

Ryan frowned.

Lara sensed the anger boiling in him even without the visual of his flaming red cheeks. She touched his arm and moved to the door, extending a hand to Sue. "Hi, I'm Lara Boyd."

Sue stared at Lara's outstretched hand for a long moment before accepting it. "I'm Ryan's mother-in-law and Justin's grandmother, Sue Lomax."

Warning bells rang in Lara's ears. Sue's introduction clearly marked her daughter's territory. "It's . . . it's nice to meet you, Mrs. Lomax."

Sue ended her anemic handshake without saying a word. Goose pimples sprang on Lara's arms from the sudden drop in room temperature. Lara stooped before Justin. The warmth in his eyes was just what she needed. "So, you went shopping?"

"Yep. Grandma bought me some new clothes for school. Tomorrow, me and Daddy are gonna get the stuff from the list you gave him." He took Lara's hand. His smile brightened. "You wanna come?"

"Justin." Sue wrapped her arm around the boy's chest and pulled him away. His tiny hand slipped from Lara's grasp. "We can pick up whatever these items are today. You and your father don't need to make a special trip, and you certainly don't need to bother Ms. Boyd with any of this."

Lara stood, swallowing the pain of Sue's hurtful act.

Ryan moved to Lara's side. "Thank you, Sue, but that won't be necessary. I promised Justin we'd shop for those items together, and Ms. Boyd is more than welcome to join us." His eyes met Lara's and softened with sincerity. "If she wants to."

Lara's heart soared. Ryan's gesture meant more than she could ever say.

Sue squared her shoulders. "Fine." A family of angry dimples invaded her chin. "Were you about to leave?"

"No, as a matter of fact, I wasn't," Ryan said to the unhappy woman. "But now that you've met Ms. Boyd, you can be on your way. I'll see you later."

"Yes, you will."

The warning in Sue's voice didn't escape Lara. Ryan would have his hands full later.

"Good-bye, Ms. Boyd," Sue said.

Lara shuddered. If Sue's words were a witch's spell she would definitely be a distant memory. Needing more warmth, she turned to Justin's happy face and caressed his smile-puffed cheek. "I'll be seeing you, okay?"

"Yes, ma'am." He nodded. "See ya, Daddy."

Ryan tussled Justin's hair. "See ya, champ."

Sue gave them one last glare, grabbed Justin's hand, and stormed out.

Ryan groaned. "I'm so sorry about that, Lara."

"You mean the cheery Mrs. Lomax?" She shook her head. "You don't have to apologize for her."

"Yes, I do. That was uncalled for."

"C'mon, our first meeting didn't exactly go like gang-busters." Ryan's curious expression called for an explanation. "Maybe I made her nervous like I made you, and it caused her to be a little strained with me."

"Oh, Sue was strained, but not because she was nervous."

"She did find us in a compromising position."

"There was nothing compromising about our position. I was about to kiss you, and I still want to, but right now . . ."

"The mood is a little broken?"

"Yeah, just a little." He made a tiny space between his thumb and forefinger. "I need to talk to Sue. She needs to understand she can't dictate what I do with my life. I've mourned Shelly for a long time, but now I'm ready to move on."

"She doesn't seem too thrilled with that idea."

"Sue doesn't have to be thrilled, because I'm thrilled enough for the both of us. I'll see you at seven."

"Ryan, wait. How should I dress?"

"So as not to cause mass hysteria, I'd say in clothes." He laughed. "Seriously, whatever you choose will be fine. We'll go where your wardrobe takes us."

Lara watched Ryan leave, trying to remember what her life was like the minute before he walked into it. The conversation she had with Celeste echoed in Lara's head. She didn't think Ryan would hurt her, but she still had her own issues, and after meeting his mother-in-law . . . *Oh, boy.* What had she gotten herself into?

～

Ryan made it home to find Sue had yet to arrive. He paced the floor like a caged lion, clenching and unclenching his balled fist, trying desperately to calm down before the woman showed. He grabbed a throw pillow from the couch and jammed his closed fist into it.

Shelly appeared at his side. "Pretty mad at Mom, huh?"

He usually jumped out of his skin when Shelly popped up, but he was so incensed her appearance barely rated a blip on his radar. Ryan stopped pacing and dropped to the couch. "Tell me you can talk to her," he said, nearly squeezing the stuffing out of the wrung out pillow.

"I wish I could. Mom is—she's . . ."

"She's being a pain in the butt!"

One calming breath followed another and soon Ryan's blind rage became a blurred agitation. He loosened his stranglehold on the pillow. "Shelly, when I lost you, I was so lost. Sue was a big help to Justin and to me, and I'll forever be grateful, but enough is enough. Her constant drop-bys are bad enough, but I won't have her give me grief for wanting to spend time with Lara, and I sure as hell won't apologize for it."

"You don't have to. I'm sure Mom will come around in time." Shelly smiled. "You really like Lara, don't you?"

Ryan fiddled nervously with a corner of the pillow. "I don't feel particularly comfortable talking with you about her."

"Why not? I'm one of your biggest supporters."

"You're my wife."

"Your *dead* wife, and I want you to be happy. You were going to kiss her before Mom showed up."

"And you're mentioning this because?"

"Because you're so at ease with her. You're becoming the old you again. I should be getting my wings in no time."

"What's this about your wings, and what does my being with Lara have to do with it?"

"You'll have to figure it out. But for my money, I think she's the one."

"The one?" Ryan resumed his pacing. He'd be lying if he didn't admit to wanting more than a couple of fun dates. But what exactly did that mean?

"You only pace for two reasons: when you're angry or when you're in deep thought. The angry pacing stopped."

"What do you mean by 'the one'?"

"What do you think I mean?"

Ryan shrugged. He had no idea how to answer that. His pacing increased.

"Look, you want to be with her all the time, and you want to share everything with her. That means something, Ryan. Lara could become very important to you, if you let her."

He stopped pacing. "And my being with Lara will help give your soul its peace?"

"In more ways than one, yes. But it's more involved."

"More involved?" Ryan felt as if he'd been zapped to an alternate world. "I don't understand this. Yesterday my life was so different and today . . ."

"What a difference a day makes." Shelly laughed. "Don't drive yourself crazy trying to analyze everything to death, just let things happen. Even at the warped speed you think this is happening, it's a natural progression. When you take Lara out tonight, wear the navy blue suit your mother gave you for Christmas. You look great in that suit. And with the collarless white shirt," she made the okay sign, "very sexy."

"Shell . . ."

"And be firm with Mom. I want this for you, and I need it for me. It won't be easy, Ryan, but I have faith in you. Hold on to this happiness and don't let it go, no matter what."

"No matter what? What does—" Justin and Sue's arrival brought a premature end to his sentence.

"Daddy, who were you talkin' to?" Justin asked.

Ryan looked around. No Shelly. She said he was the only one who could see her anyway. He laughed nervously. "Looks like myself, huh?" Sue's indistinct mumbling made it all the more clear they needed to talk.

"Hey, listen, buddy, you've had a busy afternoon, so it's nap time for you."

"Aw, Daddy," Justin grumbled. "Do I have to?"

"Yes, you have to. Uncle Norris is coming over tonight, so I want you to be well rested."

Justin's face lit up. "Uncle Norris?"

"Yeah, he's going to stay with you while I take care of some things." Justin loved spending time with Norris. Ryan only hoped his son wasn't being groomed to be the next Don Juan.

"Yea! Okay, I'll go take my nap." Justin raced upstairs.

Sue joined Ryan in the middle of the floor. "Why is Norris coming over?" she asked, the answer obvious in her unhappy eyes.

"You heard what I said. I have some things to take care of."

"Some *things*, or *someone?*"

"Does it matter?"

"Yes, it matters! What are you thinking? And why didn't you ask me to watch Justin?"

"I didn't ask you because I don't want to explain myself to you. And I think you have some nerve showing up at Lara's classroom and treating us both like we were little children caught doing something wrong."

Sue tossed her purse to the couch. "I never said you did anything wrong, but if you're bothered, you must think so."

Ryan closed his eyes and drew a breath. He didn't want to argue with her, and he was determined to try not to, but if she pushed one wrong button . . . "Listen, Sue, I can't thank you enough for all you've done, but . . ."

"But you have this kindergarten teacher you met *yesterday* you'd rather have take care of you and my grandson now!" Her eyes blazed. "Is that what you were going to say?"

"I'm not going to defend my actions to you."

"Because you can't!" Her balled fists thrust toward the floor. Her body shook with rage. "This is indefensible! How can you mar my daughter's memory like this?"

"Mar Shelly's memory? She's been dead for over three years. Years I've spent wishing she was with Justin and me, missing her like crazy, and knowing the feeling would never end. But yesterday changed everything." He snapped his fingers. "Just like that, I met a woman who made me remember I didn't die with Shelly."

"You're ready to start dating again, that's understandable, but you don't need to rush this."

"Rush? After three years of mourning, wanting to spend time with a kind, intelligent, beautiful woman is rushing things?"

"You forgot something." Sue walked to the couch and sat. "This kind, intelligent, beautiful woman is Justin's teacher and she's also—"

"What?" Ryan resumed his pacing. "Finish up, Sue!"

"I think dating her is going to confuse Justin, and it's best you don't."

"I disagree."

"Of course you do, because you're thinking with the wrong part of your body!" Sue barked. "You were all over that woman, and you just met her. You're a man with urges, that's normal, but you need to take a step back and look at what you're getting yourself into." She sucked in a breath. "This Ms. Boyd is just . . . she's not suitable. She's all wrong."

Ryan put an end to the groove he was working into the carpet and stared at Sue. "What's your idea of suitable? White?"

"She's Justin's teacher, and I don't think you should be getting involved with her. It's inappropriate."

"Inappropriate? Okay. I don't think Lara being Justin's teacher will be a problem with us seeing each other, but I'll be sure to ask her tonight when we're having dinner. As for her being unsuitable . . ."

"Ry—"

"You'll know when I'm finished!" Sue scoffed. Her gaze dropped. "You don't have to like that I'm interested in her, but you have to accept it, because I'm going to date her. I would never keep Justin from you, but I'm making this clear: you won't spew your venom to him, and you will refrain from involving yourself in my life. What I do and whom I do it with is my business."

"Ryan, I think—"

"I think you should go, and leave your key."

Sue's eyes stretched. "What—what are you saying?"

Her stunned expression and attempt at playing dumb didn't faze him. "I've had enough of your constant visits," Ryan clarified. "Starting now, things will be different."

"Is this because I have a problem with the woman? That . . . that kindergarten teacher?"

"She has a name, and no, it's not. I'm just tired of your presence in my house. Justin and I can manage just fine without you." Ryan extended his hand. "The key, Sue."

"Let me take Justin home with me. He loves spending time with his grandpa, and Carl—"

"I've already made plans for Justin. I don't want to be rude, but I have a few things to take care of, so . . ." His hand remained extended in wait for the key.

Stomping to the couch, Sue pulled the key from her purse and tossed it toward the coffee table, where it skidded off the finished surface and landed on the floor. "I'm sure my Shelly is rolling over in her grave right now." She bounded out the door, leaving it wide open.

Ryan shook off the woman's anger and closed the door. "So, Shell, are you rolling in your grave?"

"Talkin' to yourself again, Daddy?"

Ryan looked up to find Justin descending the stairs. "I think that had to be the shortest nap in history."

"I wasn't real sleepy." Justin plopped on the couch. "Grandma left?"

"Yeah." As Ryan pocketed Sue's key, he remembered she had another. He'd have to change the locks.

"Daddy, is Ms. Boyd your girlfriend?"

Ryan sat with Justin on the couch. "Is she my girl-friend?"

Justin nodded. His eyes shiny with hope.

"No, she's not my girlfriend."

Justin' happy light vanished. "You haven't kissed her yet?"

"No. Why do you ask?"

"After you kiss Ms. Boyd she'll be your girlfriend."
Justin gasped. "You didn't know?"

"Uh-uh. Who told you?"

"Grandma Sue. She was watching her show and this
man kissed a lady, and Grandma said she was his girlfriend. Are you gonna kiss Ms. Boyd soon?"

"Justin, I think you misunderstood your grandma. If
I kiss Ms. Boyd it won't mean she's my girlfriend."

"It won't?"

"No."

"Don't you want Ms. Boyd to be your girlfriend?"

"Well, I . . . I . . ."

Justin smiled. "You do, dontcha?"

"I wouldn't mind," Ryan admitted.

"Yea!" Justin clapped.

"Yea?"

"Uh-huh." Justin nodded eagerly. "I like Ms. Boyd,
you like Ms. Boyd, and I think she likes us."

"Me, too. But it doesn't mean she'll want me to be her
boyfriend."

"But she might want you to be her boyfriend?"

If things went well at dinner, she could be his girlfriend very soon. "Yes, she might," Ryan said.

Justin smiled. "Good."

"Since you're not tired, let's go get our hair cut."

"Aw, Daddy, I don't wanna get my hair cut."

"I know," Ryan whined in lighthearted response.
"But your hair is getting so long." The one thing Justin
hated more than getting his hair cut was eating lima

beans. Ryan brushed his fingers through the slightly curling locks around his son's ear. "You don't want to look like a big grizzly bear and scare Ms. Boyd on Monday, do you?"

"Uh-uh, I don't want to do that," Justin answered with a vigorous shake of his head.

"Okay, then, let's go get handsome. And if you're good, we'll get ice cream on the way home."

Justin's eyes brightened. "Chocolate ice cream?"

Ryan chuckled. "Yeah, chocolate."

"I'll be good."

"That's my big boy." Ryan took Justin's hand. "Let's go."

CHAPTER 6

Hangers scraped against the steel rod of the closet as Lara continued her maddening search for the right outfit.

She couldn't believe it—perfect hair, flawless makeup, but not a thing to wear. "You know, you really didn't have to come over," she said to Celeste, who had shown up to be nosy in her own caring way.

"Of course I did." Celeste placed her hands on Lara's shoulders and led her to the bed. "If I hadn't, I wouldn't be able to get you to sit down and catch your breath."

Lara shot off the bed and back over to the closet. "I can't sit down. Ryan will be here in less than thirty minutes, and there's nothing right in there."

"Oh, girl, you have a closet full of beautiful clothes. Besides, Ryan is taking *you* to dinner, not your wardrobe." Celeste walked to the closet and pulled out a wine-colored halter dress. "Wear this. He won't be able to remember his own name when he sees you in that."

"This might work," Lara said, stepping into the dress.

"It will work. Not that it . . . nothing."

Hearing the tone, Lara smoothed down the dress, and against her better judgment, asked, "What were you about to say?"

"I guess I was just thinking about the scene you told me about. Ryan's mother-in-law sounds like a lot of fun."

Lara pulled out a pair of gold open-toe slides from her closet shoe rack. "Technically, Sue's not his mother-in-law anymore." She stepped into the shoes, grateful she'd splurged for a pedicure when she got the new hairstyle.

"Technically or not, the woman is going to be a part of his life for the rest of her life because of Justin. If she has a problem with you, it's going to be a problem for all of you."

"Ryan said he was going to talk to her."

"He's going to *talk* to her? Think he can sit down with the Grand Wizard when he's done?"

"Come on, Celeste. I wouldn't label her a racist. I just think she was a little surprised at what she walked in on."

"Surprised?" Celeste gasped, holding her hand to her chest. "*Is that . . . No, it can't be. Yes, it's a colored woman. My daughter's husband is sniffing around a . . . a . . . ohhh.*" She fell to the bed in a dramatic swoon.

Lara tossed a pillow at her giggling cousin. "You are a barrel of laughs tonight, aren't you?"

"Sometimes you gotta laugh to keep from crying." Celeste sat up, holding the pillow to her chest. "This has a lot of potential for ugly."

"It also has a lot of potential for beauty. It could be very beautiful. I don't rush into things, Celeste, but I can't explain this amazing attraction I have for Ryan."

"Apparently not. It also seems you can't control it. Today you almost kissed a man you met yesterday. That's not like you."

"No, it's not, but at the same time it is." She joined Celeste on the bed. "There's something about Ryan."

"There's a lot about him. I believe I mentioned a few of the things last night at dinner. You can add his mother-in-law to the ever-growing list."

Lara groaned. She didn't want a rain shower on her parade, yet Celeste seemed determined to put a dark cloud in the path of her sunshine. "I thought you were going to support me in this."

"I am, Lara. I'm just seeing it from all sides. I do want you to be happy, but I also don't want you to be hurt. I'm your biggest cheerleader, and I always will be, but I'm going to keep your vision clear when the stars blinding your eyes make things too cloudy. Understand?"

"My cousin, my protector. Yes, I understand."

"Good." Celeste gave her a hug and pulled back, smiling. "You look great. Ryan's not going to know what hit him. Make sure you have a good time."

"I don't know how I can't." Lara walked to the full-length mirror on the back of her closet door. The dress was perfect. The hem stopped a few inches above her knees to display the legs she worked religiously on her stair stepper to keep toned, and the V-neck cut was deep enough to be sexy, but not scandalous as it showed off her cleavage. When it came to breasts, she was grateful her cups were full, but they didn't runneth over. Lara smiled at her reflection. "As anxious as I was about what to wear, I'm not at all nervous about going out with Ryan. It feels like I've known him forever."

"Forever? What's going on with you?"

Lara rolled her eyes. Celeste was thinking her thoughts again. "I don't know what you're getting at," she said, rifling her jewelry box and choosing a pair of diamond stud earrings.

"I think you do. Talk to me."

Lara sat on the bed and put on the earrings. Celeste would read into things if she didn't get an answer, but Lara didn't know how to answer. She felt comfortable around Ryan, she liked being around him and watching him interact with Justin, and she was extremely attracted to him. And that meant what? She had no idea. "I like him," she said. "I haven't had this much interest in a man since . . ."

"Foster?" Celeste offered. A familiar ache stabbed Lara's chest, a constant with the mention of her ex. "Whenever you go to Alexandria, you get all melancholy for Foster."

"I don't have to go to Alexandria to do that."

"Maybe not, but you've never met a man this soon after your return trips either. Maybe this amazing attraction you have for Ryan is just a little touch of jungle fever. Ryan's a good choice to get it for."

"I hate that jungle fever thing, Celeste. It's not that, and it's more than just attraction. I don't know what more, but I think I'd like to find out." The nervous feeling returned to her stomach, her heart pounded. Lara took her cousin's hand and placed it on her chest. "You feel that?" Celeste nodded. "That's what thinking about Ryan does to me."

"You're saying your heart beats for him?" Celeste smirked.

Lara dropped her cousin's hand. "I'm baring my innermost feelings to you and you're being funny."

"I'm sorry, I couldn't help it." Celeste laughed. "He makes you happy?"

"He does."

"That's enough for me. As long as he keeps making you happy, he's okay in my book."

"Thank you. That means a lot."

Celeste stood from the bed. Worry lines creased her forehead and apprehension colored her dark eyes. Lara prepared herself for another speech.

"I can't lie and say I'm not concerned," Celeste said. "You know how cruel people can be, Lara. Are you prepared to deal with the repercussions of dating him?"

"I don't know what I'm prepared for, all I know is I like him. Ryan may look like Ken, but I wasn't dressed incognito as Barbie when we met. He knows what he's getting."

"Yes, but does he know what he's *getting into*? That, my dear cousin, is the question."

The chime of the doorbell brought an end to the discussion. Lara looked to the living room and stood. "That's Ryan now."

"I'll let him in on my way out." Celeste started to the bedroom door and turned around. "I don't care how late it is, call me when you get home," she instructed with a wag of her finger. "I want details."

Lara waited out of sight by the couch as Celeste opened the door. "I guess that's not for me, huh?" said her cousin.

Fingers snapped. "Darn, I knew I was forgetting something," Ryan said, evoking a laugh from Celeste. "It's good to see you again."

"You, too." Celeste slipped Lara a thumbs-up. "Don't mind me, I was just leaving. You kids have fun," she said, closing the door behind her.

Carrying a single rose, Ryan made his way over to Lara. His eyes shone with appreciation as his gaze swept over her.

Lara smiled as she engaged in a body sweep of her own. Who needed to go out? She could stay at her apartment staring at him all night and it would be time well spent. How she managed not to drool she'll never know. Celeste gave Ryan a thumbs-up, but the touchdown signal would have been more appropriate. She'd never seen a blue suit look so good.

"Wow! Lara, you look—you look . . ." He continued his shameless ogling. "Wow!"

"Thanks. You look pretty wow yourself. You cut your hair."

His gaze stayed on her. "Yeah, Justin and I both—we, uh, we both needed a trim."

"Nice flower."

"Flow . . ." He blinked. "Oh, it's for you." He extended the bloom. "I hope you like roses."

"They're my favorite flower, and my middle name." She inhaled the soft scent. "Thank you, it's lovely."

"Not nearly as lovely as you." Ryan's gaze swept over her yet again. His radar fixed on the V-neck of her dress. He swallowed audibly. "You really look incredible."

The butterflies fluttering in her stomach grew more active. She definitely got the desired reaction from Ryan, but the reaction he stirred in her . . . She needed a moment alone. "I need to get my purse, and then we can go."

"Okay."

"You can have a seat if you like," she said, walking into her bedroom.

"I'm fine." Several seconds of quiet followed. "You have a terrific apartment."

"Thanks, it's functional, and the neighbors are nice and not nosy, so it suits me." She grabbed her purse and keys from the dresser. After sucking in a few steadying breaths and swiping another look in the mirror, she returned to the living room where she found Ryan tapping the African drum next to her fireplace. "Do you play?"

"Oh, no, I was just admiring it and got a little carried away." He chuckled. "You have wonderful pieces."

"You like African art?"

"I do, but not as much as Norris. He went to Kenya on a safari a couple of years ago, and he fell in love with the country and the art."

"Is he an artist, too?"

"Norris? No, he's an accountant and full-time lady's man. I guess that sorta makes him an artist in his eyes." Ryan laughed. "But he's playing babysitter tonight."

"Sounds like an interesting guy."

"Interesting is the very least he is. Maybe you'll get to meet him sometime soon."

Lara smiled. Meeting the best friend. This was a good thing. "I think I'd like that."

"So, are the people in the pictures here your family?"

"Yes. This one was taken earlier this year at my parents' fortieth wedding anniversary party," she explained, handing him the centermost picture from the mantle.

"I see I'm not the only person to get a haircut."

"Oh, yeah, my Sade look. Celeste badgered me forever to get rid of it, insisting long, straight hair went out with Cher and the seventies." Lara laughed as she combed her fingers through her hair. "It's only been a few days, but I like it."

"Me, too. It's beautiful." Their eyes met and held for several electric moments. Ryan cleared his throat. "So, uh, who are these smiling people?" he asked, glancing from the picture to Lara. "I'm betting the lady next to you is your mom. You look like her."

"You're right." She pointed at the different faces. "My parents, Evelyn and Robert. My sister, Gillian, and my brothers Marshall and Travis."

"Marshall and Travis? They look identical."

"They are identical, but my parents wanted them to be individuals so they didn't go down the normal twin route. No similar names and no dressing alike. They were just brothers born on the same day."

Humor brightened Ryan's eyes. "Interesting," he said. "How so?"

"I'll tell you on the way to the restaurant. I take it you're the youngest of this brood."

"Right again. Gilly is older by eight years and the twins by seven, and my brothers teased me mercilessly. Mama didn't dress them alike, but she bought them the same clothes, and my brothers were cagey." She laughed. "Suffice it to say, I think I was four before I was convinced they were two people and six before I was able to tell them apart."

"Sounds like you had a wonderful childhood."

"I did, although I didn't think it was so wonderful at the time."

Ryan pointed at the remaining pictures. "Nephews and nieces?"

"Some of them. Niece, nephew, and cousins," she explained of the five children in the remaining three frames. "The cousins belong to Celeste."

"Oh, yes, Celeste." Ryan returned the picture to the mantle. "I see you two are very close."

"We are. Our moms are sisters and dads are brothers, and she's also my best friend. There's not a lot that goes on in my life that she's not aware or a part of."

"Something else to add to my Lara file."

"This file is starting to get thick."

"Slowly but surely. Are we ready to go?"

"Yes, we are." They walked to the parking lot. "So, where are we going?"

"I don't think there's a restaurant in the state worthy of your divine presence, but I hope Martin's will make a halfway decent attempt. I made reservations."

"Martin's?"

"Yeah, it's over on . . ."

"Lakeshore," she said. "You made reservations?"

"Yeah."

"What if I had worn jeans and a pullover?"

"Well, then I would be sitting in The Burger Barn or Taco Heaven in a nice suit." He smiled. "Luckily things worked out."

"I don't know, Ryan. Martin's is pretty—heck, it's *very* expensive," she said, feeling a little uneasy with him spending so much money for a first date. She already liked him; he didn't have to go the extra mile to woo her.

"Don't worry, Lara. After we've eaten, I promise you won't have to wait while I wash dishes." Placing his hand on the small of her back, Ryan ushered her to a forest green Jeep Cherokee. "I'm a gentleman. I'll call a taxi for you first." He laughed heartily as he unlocked the door and helped her inside.

Lara liked that Ryan was quick on his feet, even if it was at her expense. "I didn't know you moonlighted as comedian," she said when he slid behind the wheel.

"I don't, it's just one of my hobbies. I do a magic trick, too." He reached behind her ear and produced a shiny quarter. "Ta-da."

She took a quick glance at the coin. "That's your trick?"

"Justin loves it."

"Wait till he turns six." She laughed. "I think you better stick to your day job."

He tried to look serious but his reluctant smile gave the lightheartedness away. "Keep this up, Ms. Boyd, and you'll find yourself washing dishes with me."

Lara laughed as Ryan started down the highway. Even if he were serious, she could think of worse ways to spend her evening than washing dishes with him.

Lively conversation about Ryan's upbringing on a small Wisconsin dairy farm with two sets of male/female fraternal twins with similar sounding names passed the time on the drive to Martin's Lakeside Restaurant. Lara couldn't decide which she liked more—Ryan's wonderful childhood memories or being in his company to listen as he shared them. The way his eyes twinkled whenever she laughed at the funny parts made her realize being in his company was definitely the best part.

"Sounds like you had a pretty wonderful childhood, too," she said.

"It was certainly interesting." Ryan glanced at her for a moment before focusing back on the road. "Being slap dab in the middle of two sets of twins, not too young for my older brother and sister and not too old for my younger brother and sister, left me honorary tiebreaker for everyone. Being the blend child, I was also the sibling everybody came to when they needed Mom and Dad to agree to something."

"The blend child?"

"Yeah. I was the perfect mixture of Mom and Dad. I have Mom's blue eyes and Dad's blonde hair, Dad's nose and Mom's smile, Dad's humor and Mom's good nature. And given the fact I was the lone single child, the novelty of the family, my brothers and sisters took it to mean that I was the child my parents couldn't tell no."

"Was it true?"

"Not hardly. Matthew and Justine Andrews had absolutely no problem telling their lone child no. Fact is, since I was making the argument alone, it took them even less time to say."

A few minutes later, they arrived at the restaurant. Lara ignored the curious eyes of the other patrons as the hostess showed them to an elegantly set round table in a quiet corner. After helping Lara with her chair, Ryan took the empty seat across from her. The hostess handed them each a menu, informed them their server would arrive shortly and left with a smile.

Lara scanned the menu. "So, what looks good to you?"

"Tell me that's a rhetorical question."

Lara peered over her menu to find a mischievous glint in Ryan's eyes. She couldn't believe this was the same man who sweated bullets in her classroom the day before. "I meant the menu, funny man," she said.

He chuckled. "Oh."

"I think I make it too easy for you to tease me. I'll have to watch that."

"Tell you what, you say whatever you want, and I'll watch you. My God, you are just so beautiful."

The butterflies in Lara's stomach took flight at the way he looked at her. Ryan's hand inched toward hers.

"Lara, I thought I'd—"

A slender young man wearing a bright red jacket and black slacks interrupted Ryan's words and creeping hand.

He placed a basket of rolls in the center of the table and filled their empty crystal glasses with ice water.

"Hello, my name is Felipe and I'll be your server for the evening. Might I interest you in an appetizer or cocktail?" he said, smiling in Ryan's direction.

Lara did a double take. She didn't doubt Felipe's capability as a waiter, but along with his rotten sense of timing, he had the nerve to be hitting on Ryan. Crazy stuff like this only happened in movies. She snatched a roll from the basket and popped a small piece into her mouth.

She gave the waiter a once-over. Felipe appeared to be in his midtwenties, but his slight stature and abbreviated height could easily shave a few years off the actual number. His spiked dark brown hair resembled the quills of a porcupine, and a minimal but obvious amount of makeup dusted his alabaster complexion.

As he rambled about some potato and bacon soup, Lara looked toward Ryan, whose face was completely obstructed by the open menu. She couldn't help wondering what he was about to say before the interruption. After reciting the evening specials and giving short but mouthwatering descriptions of their chosen entrees, Felipe left to place their orders and get their iced tea.

Ryan cleared his throat. "Felipe seems like an okay waiter, but a strange guy." He leaned forward in his chair. "Was he wearing makeup and hitting on me?"

"I thought I was the only one who noticed."

"Why do you think I was hiding behind the menu?" Lara covered her mouth to keep from laughing out loud.

"Talk about unnerving." Ryan shuddered. "Women have always hit on me, but a man? The dating scene *has* changed a lot." He draped his napkin over his lap. "But no matter, if dinner is half as good as he made it sound, I'm liable to pull one of Justin's bad habits and lick my plate clean."

Ryan laughed, but Lara found the image of his tongue mopping over his dinner plate strangely exciting, and it stoked the embers of curiosity she had for that same tongue mopping languidly over hers. Her spine tingled. Feeling flushed, she grabbed her water glass and took several small gulps.

"Somebody's thirsty."

Lara dabbed her lips with the red linen napkin. "It's the bread." She pulled off another small piece of the roll. "So, uh, you were saying something before Felipe came over."

He took a swallow of water and smiled. "I was?"

"Ryan?" She frowned.

He laughed. "Okay, I was. You're an amazing woman, Lara Boyd. The fact I'm sitting here with you, having more fun than I ever thought I could again, is a testament to that. You know what Justin asked me today?"

Mid-chew with another piece of bread, she shook her head.

"He asked if you were my girlfriend."

The bread slipped down her throat. She took a sip of water, avoiding a major coughing fit. "What did you tell him?"

"The truth." He sighed. "You aren't my girlfriend." Ryan took a roll from the basket and set it on his plate. "Poor guy was pretty bummed about it."

Lara smiled. Was there any wonder she was so crazy about that little boy?

"He had a lot of questions, and quite a bit of insight, too." Ryan scooped some of Martin's famous whipped honey butter on a piece of bread and popped it in his mouth.

"What insight?"

Downing about a third of his water, Ryan wiped his hands with the napkin and said, "He could tell I wanted you to be my girlfriend." Lara barely had time to process his words when he took her hand. "When I lost Shelly, I lost a piece of me I thought was gone forever. Imagine my shock when yesterday it showed up right out of the blue." His hand tightened around hers. "Lara, there is something good happening here. It's very exciting, but I gotta tell you, it's scary as hell."

Lara nodded. "I know what you mean."

"Are you too scared to walk this path with me?"

"No, but . . ."

"But?"

"As scary as what we're feeling for each other seems to us, imagine how scary it would be for others."

"The race issue?"

"It is an issue. The stares we're getting now notwithstanding, does this afternoon with your mother-in-law ring a bell?"

"Sue is misguided, but what she thinks doesn't matter, and I told her so. She's Justin's grandmother, but she's not my mother, and she has no say in my personal life. Our racial difference is not a problem for me." His fingers moved gingerly along the back of her hand before linking with hers. "Does this bother you?"

Lara didn't know if he meant his touch or their differing skin colors. Either way, the answer was the same. "No, it thrills me." She stared at their twined fingers. She was middle of the road when it came to coloring, a perfect mixture of her mother's fair and her father's dark brown complexions, but the contrast in her skin tone to Ryan's was striking. "But there is a difference here, Ryan."

"You're right. You're a gorgeous woman, and I'm a man."

Lara sighed. He was going to make her spell this out. "Ryan, I—"

"I enjoy being with you, Lara, and I want to be with you as much and as often as I can. Do you feel the same way?"

"Yes, I do."

"Great. Is seeing me a conflict of interest because you're Justin's teacher?"

"There's no rule against fraternization between parents and teachers."

"Even better. I only have one last question. Is my being white a problem for you, yes or no?"

"It's not that simple."

"Yes, it is. Is my being white a problem for *you*? Not for the world, not for the people who might orbit your world, but for you?"

"You know the answer to that."

"I do, but I want to hear you say it."

"Fine. Your being white is not a problem for me."

Ryan smiled. "Now, did that hurt?"

He sounded like a pediatrician after giving a shot. "No, *that* didn't hurt," she said. "But this, you and me together—dating, could hurt a lot."

Ryan's expression soured. Lara rolled her eyes. She sounded like Celeste. And like she with her cousin earlier, Ryan didn't want to hear the negative aspects of their being together. Still, she knew ignoring it wouldn't be sensible.

"Have you ever dated a black woman?"

"Unless you count tonight, no."

"Ryan, take a look around this restaurant." The place was crowded, but they were the lone interracial couple. As such, more than a passing glance, some curious and some downright hostile, came their way, and she couldn't help noticing. "Tell me what you see."

"You," Ryan answered, his eyes never leaving hers. "You're all I see. Lara, you don't have to paint a picture for me. I know what year it is, and that interracial couples are still seen by many as taboo. I also know there are people in this country, in this state, even in this restaurant, who would rather see us dead than together. But if I let the fear of these ignorant people determine my life's direction, it's like I'm conforming to their narrow-minded views of right and wrong, and I can't do that."

A smile touched Ryan's lips. Lara's heart fluttered. His gorgeous smile got her every time.

"When I woke up yesterday morning, I never imagined my dreams for that night would be of my son's kindergarten teacher, but they were. Just like I never imagined I'd marry Shelly, but I did. I've learned people can't plan for things. I never planned to be a widower at twenty-nine, but I was. And I never thought I'd meet someone who would so readily captivate me, but I did. You make me feel more alive than I've felt in years. Some people might frown when they see us together, but I believe even more will smile. A little guy named Justin in particular." Ryan expelled a breath. "So, Lara, would you like to date me?"

Would she like to date Ryan? Lara liked the idea of it, and she certainly liked him. She looked at their twined fingers. This ride could be bumpy, but she was fastening her seat belt. *Please, Lord, don't let these sparks burn me.* She nodded. "Yes, I think would."

Like in her classroom earlier today, an intense urge to kiss Ryan overwhelmed her. The fact they were in a crowded restaurant didn't matter, only feeling his lips against hers. Seeing the same need reflected in Ryan's eyes, she eased forward to meet him as he leaned over the table.

His warm, honey-scented breath caressed her lips. He cupped her cheek. Brilliant blue eyes disappeared behind lowered lids. "Lara," he whispered.

"Two iced teas!"

Felipe's falsetto voice was like a firecracker going off in a library. Lara dropped to her chair, struggling to catch her breath.

Balancing a tray with two full glasses of the brewed beverage, Felipe took a final step to the table. Lara wanted to take that tray and douse him. Every fiber of her being screamed he planned this ill-timed return, and the self-satisfied grin on his face confirmed it.

Anger burned in Ryan's eyes as he shot poison daggers at the waiter. Felipe's pleased smirk disappeared, and not even his pale makeup could hide the fear on his face as Ryan addressed him. "You better hope this is the best damn tea in the world."

CHAPTER 7

Lara's laughter grew louder as they approached her apartment door. Ryan marveled at the joy he derived from listening to that simple act, but everything she did charmed him.

"I can't remember the last time I laughed so hard." Lara fanned her face. "You are very funny."

"What's very funny is Felipe," Ryan quipped. "He was hitting on every guy in the place. I thought the man seated in front of us was going to hit him with two uppercuts."

"I think he would have been one of a dozen of others. Between the men and the women they were dining with, Felipe was a marked man." Lara touched Ryan's hand. His heart skipped a beat. "Do you want to come in for a nightcap?"

Do I! "Sure, that would be nice," he calmly accepted.

"I don't keep anything stronger than wine on tap. I hope red is okay."

"Anything is fine." He would drink toilet water if it meant he could be with her a while longer. They spent hours together after leaving Martin's, walking around the park and talking about anything and everything under the sun. He didn't want the night to end.

Lara dropped her purse on a nearby table and kicked her shoes underneath. "Make yourself comfortable and I'll be right back."

Ryan unloosened the top two buttons of his shirt and dropped his suit coat along the back of the couch. He was admiring her art when Lara returned with two full glasses. He took a sip of the chilled beverage. "Very good. It's vibrant and sweet, just like you."

"Enough with the flattery. Let's talk." She settled on the sofa with her legs tucked under.

Ryan always wondered how tall women could sit like that without their legs going crazy, but Lara did look comfortable, and so sexy with a couple of inches of her bare milk chocolate thighs exposed to his hungry eyes.

"You can come over." She patted the cushion in the middle of the sofa. "I won't bite."

Yeah, but I might. He made it to the couch, trying mightily to avert his attention from her gorgeous lower limbs but having very little success.

Lara tapped his shoulder, prompting their eyes to meet. "I think you should be looking up here. One of the first things I teach my children is to look at people when talking to them."

"Well, in my own defense, I wasn't talking yet." Lust clouded his vision as he took one last look at her shapely legs. Meeting her gaze, he found the playful spark he'd grown familiar with over the past few hours. "You're doing this on purpose."

Lara shrugged. "I'm just sitting here. I don't know what you're talking about." She took a sip of wine. Her twinkling eyes peered at him from the top of her glass.

"Sure you do, you flirt." He brushed his shoulder against hers. "Let's dance."

"Dance?"

"Yeah." Ryan placed his glass on the coffee table and walked to the stereo in the corner. Lara had eclectic taste in music, and he found they had many of the same CDs. Finding the perfect song, he made his way back to the couch and extended his hand as the opening melody began.

Lara smiled. "Luther Vandross." She lowered her glass to the table and took his hand. "This is one my favorite songs."

"Mine, too."

The soft curves of her body nestled against him. His arms curled around her waist, holding her close as their bodies swayed to the music.

Her fingers threaded the back of his hair. "This is nice," she murmured.

"Yes, it is." His hand trailed gingerly along Lara's arm. She had the softest skin and most intoxicating scent. It had been so long since he held a woman in his arms. And this woman, with her dangerous curves and slow-moving hips, made him all too aware of how long it had been.

In a desperate scan of the room, he searched for a distraction. Something, anything, that would help smother his growing fire down below. Though very attracted to Lara, he didn't want her to think his interest was purely physical. He liked everything about her—her engaging mind, wonderful wit, and caring spirit. The fact he found her so physically appealing was the icing on the cake.

Ryan continued his hunt for a distraction. Lara had a really nice apartment and seemed partial to browns, as its varying hues made up the primary color scheme for her furniture and art pieces. He could ask more about her art, but they'd already talked about that. Pedestals housed beautiful, flowing green plants, but his thumb was anything but green.

Completing his second once-over of the room, Ryan spotted a toy Smurfette on the end table. Now seemed the perfect time to find out Lara's interest in the tiny blue creature. "What's this about Smurfette?"

She lifted her head from his chest. Confusion colored her brown eyes. "Where did that come from?"

"My curious nature, and—" He motioned to the tiny blue toy. "What's your fascination with Smurfette? Why is it Snow White has nothing on her?"

Lara laughed. "You really do hear everything I say, don't you?" she said, as they began dancing to the next song.

"Absolutely."

"I like Smurfette because she was the coolest little thing when I was growing up, and she didn't hide away her feminine wiles. She was hot stuff and she knew it. Snow White had seven dwarfs, but Smurfette had almost one hundred little blue creatures entranced by her. None of them was immune to her charms, not even Papa Smurf."

"You make a great point for Smurfette being the hottest blue chick in animation, but your argument has one tiny flaw."

Lara paused the dancing. "A flaw?"

"Yep." Ryan continued their movements. He could stand here dancing with Lara and discussing this frivolous Smurf matter all night long. "There is a flaw," he said.

"Please explain."

"My pleasure." Having watched more than his share of the classic Saturday morning cartoon, he was quite capable of doing just that. "You stated Smurfette had all the Smurfs in the land gaga over her, right?"

"Yeah. All the Smurfs loved her."

"All of them?" He paused for a moment to look in Lara eyes. Confusion swirled. She honestly didn't know where he was going. "Vanity, Lara, the Smurf like old Felipe from Martin's."

She laughed. "I forgot all about Vanity."

"You forgot? How can you forget Vanity? He was the Smurf that made you wonder."

"Come on. Vanity was in love with himself, that's why he carried the mirror, and the flower made him feel good. He was just very pleased with himself. Thus, the name Vanity."

"Lara, there's being happy with yourself, and just being *happy*. Vanity was happy all right, happy and *gay*." Lara's soft laughter grew as he continued. "I could get past him carrying the mirror wherever he went, but the pink flower in his hat? That's taking happiness to a whole new extreme. You've got to admit, if Vanity left Smurf Village, he would have no trouble fitting into Greenwich Village."

"I guess you have a point. A very little point." She gave his shoulder a playful swat and resumed their dance. "You're terrible."

"Hey, don't get me wrong, I have no problem with gay Smurfs, or even gay people. Felipe's interest in me was a bit disconcerting, especially since nothing like that had ever happened to me before, but I'm secure enough in my masculinity not to let it bother me."

"So, you're a man who knows who he is?"

Ryan stopped dancing and peered deeply into Lara's eyes. "Who he is and what he wants."

"And what does he want?"

"To kiss you."

His mouth gently covered hers, moving against her lips in a slow, deliberate manner. Lara had the sweetest lips. She told Justin she was as sweet as chocolate ice cream, and Ryan now knew for a fact she spoke the truth. He could easily make a glutton of himself, feasting on her mouth until he had his fill. Lara's arms curled around his neck. Their bodies grew closer, their kiss deeper.

Blood roared in Ryan's head and loins while moans of pleasure echoed in his ears. His heart pounded in time with the throbbing throughout his body. Losing control could be so easy, too easy, but he cared about Lara and didn't want to ruin what could be something special by rushing into things. Besides, he wanted Lara to think of him as her Prince Charming, not some horny toad.

Their kiss came to a mutual end.

"Wow." Lara breathed heavily. "It's been how long since you kissed a woman?"

"About five seconds." Ryan licked his tingling lips, savoring the sensation her kisses left behind. "Prior to that, over three long years."

"You haven't lost a step." She smiled. "You're a great kisser."

He remembered being great at something else, too, but now was not the time to think such things. "I'm glad you liked it."

"I did. I like kissing you, being around you, talking to you. This thing we have it feels so . . . so . . ."

"Good? Right? Incredibly wonderful?"

She nodded. "Yes."

"And this is just the beginning, Lara." He pecked her lips. "How about breakfast tomorrow, say about nine? I'll be bringing someone along."

Her eyes lit up. "Justin?"

"He'll enjoy seeing you."

"Good, because I always enjoy seeing him, too."

"Then it's a date?"

"It's a date."

Ryan checked his watch. "One-ten." The night had practically flown away. "As much as I hate to say this, it's time for me to go," he said, retrieving his jacket from the couch.

"I didn't realize it was so late."

"The old adage is true: time flies when you're having fun." He pulled her into a warm embrace. "Thank you, Lara."

"For what?"

"Everything." He kissed her tenderly. "I'll call you when I get home." Ryan walked to the car with a lilt in his step. *Lara Boyd.* He smiled. Yes, indeed, she might be "the one."

CHAPTER 8

Ryan barely had his foot in the door when Norris started his verbal onslaught.

"Six hours! Over six hours you were gone? All right, buddy, let me—" Norris stopped speaking and inched closer, sniffing.

"Man, what are you—" Ryan moved away.

"Perfume?" Norris followed, staring at Ryan's face. "Lipstick? Oooh, somebody got some sugar," he teased.

"Cut that out." Norris fell on the couch in a fit of laughter. "How's my son?" Ryan asked, wiping away the evidence of Lara's sweet kisses.

"Justin's fine. He went down hours ago. The little guy talked himself to sleep. I heard all about Ms. Boyd, her nice cousin Ms. Celeste, Ernie, Elmo, the toys, blocks, and the computers in the classroom."

"Okay, I get it."

"I'm not done yet. You didn't tell me you called her Ms. Body or you almost kissed her in the classroom today. She must be something, because Justin couldn't say enough about her."

Ryan closed his eyes, remembering the feel of Lara's sensual kisses and lithe body against his. "She is, Norris. She really is." His eyes flew open. "Gimme one second."

Making a mad dash to the phone, he turned his back to Norris and punched in Lara's number. The sound of her voice brought a smile to his face. "Hi."

"Hi." Lara said. "I gather you made it home safely?"

"Yeah, I did."

"Thanks for calling. I wish I could talk with you, but Celeste is on the other line anxious to finish grilling me about our date," she grumbled in good humor.

He laughed. "Okay. Tell her I said hello."

"Will do. Good night."

"Good night."

Ryan turned around to find Norris looking very much like a curious father, sitting back on the couch, his arms folded across his chest, and his legs extended and crossed at the ankles on the coffee table. Ryan frowned. He hated feet on his coffee table, and Norris knew that.

Overlooking the pet peeve for now, he addressed the question in his friend's eyes, knowing, too, his grilling session was about to begin. "Yes?"

"What was all that?" Norris asked.

"What was all what? The phone call?" Ryan placed the phone on the charger. "I just called Lara to tell her I was home."

"And you had to turn your back and speak in low tones to say 'I'm home'? This is me. What happened tonight?"

Ryan knew it wouldn't last. The constrictor was back, with a grip that showed no signs of loosening. "We had a good time."

"What kind of good time?"

"Not your kind of good time." Ryan shoved Norris's feet off the table and joined him on the couch. "We enjoyed each other's company. We talked, laughed, danced—"

"Kissed," Norris said.

Ryan smiled. "And kissed. She's such a wonderful woman. I felt this pull toward her from the moment I saw her, and I knew there was an obvious attraction, but now . . . There's something going on between Lara and me. Something good and real."

"Real? Does Lara feel this 'realness'?"

Ryan smiled. "Yeah, she does."

"Did she say so?"

"We both did."

"So you guys talked?"

"I told you, we talked a lot."

"You know what . . ."

"Yes, Norris, I know what you mean. We discussed the race issue. We discussed the hell out of the race issue."

"And?"

"And it's not an issue."

"Ryan?"

"Okay, it's not an issue for us. I can't control what the world thinks or how people react to us, just like I can't deny this connection I feel to her. All I can do is accept it's there and live with it."

"Can you live with it?" Norris asked. "*All* of it?"

"I think the better question is can I live with the suffocating sadness I would feel if I didn't have Lara in my life." Ryan looked squarely at his friend. "The answer to that question is no. She wanted me to be fully aware of what our being together would mean, and I know and understand, and I'm ready to tackle it all head-on."

"It's going to be tough, Ryan. I'd like to believe we live in a progressive society, but there are a lot of narrow minds out there."

"You would know. You've dated women of every ethnicity."

"Wrong. I don't *date* anyone. Not in the traditional sense, anyway. I go out and show women a good time, so they can come back to my place and show me one. No relationship, no ties. It's a little different for you."

"We got some stares and whispers tonight, but I can endure anything to be with Lara."

"You sound determined."

"I am."

"In all our years, I've never seen you like this."

"That's a good thing, right?"

"No, it's a wonderful thing." Norris gave Ryan a spirited pat to the back. "If anybody deserves happiness, it's you. I'm behind you 110 percent, pal." Norris shook his head, grinning. "Just look at you. All lipstick and perfumed down, a big smile on your face. You really are the picture of happiness, but . . ."

"But?"

"As happy as you seem, there's something I can't quite put my finger on. What is it?"

"You know me too well."

"Twenty-five years will do that. You gonna tell me what?"

"I already did, earlier today."

Norris groaned. "Not that Shelly thing?"

"It's not a thing. I saw her."

"Of course you did." Norris looked around the room, motioning at every picture he encountered of Shelly. "She's everywhere. Come on."

Pictures of Shelly covered the room from corner to corner. Ryan had never realized there were so many. Lately, he realized a lot of things he hadn't before.

Norris checked beneath the sofa and under the cushions.

"What are you doing?" Ryan asked.

"All evening it's just been Justin and me, minus Shelly's pictures. Now unless she's playing hide and seek . . ."

Ryan frowned and the mock search ended.

Norris sat. "If this was anyone but me, the men in white coats would be coming for you."

"You think I'm crazy?"

"No, I think you're feeling guilty. For three years you've been mourning Shelly, when all of a sudden you meet this incredible woman, and then you start seeing your dead wife everywhere. It's a textbook case."

"A textbook case? What are you talking about?"

"Survivor guilt. You're moving on without Shelly and your subconscious is holding you back. You want this happiness with Lara, but think you shouldn't have it because it's not with Shelly. Seeing Shelly is a reminder that she's the one your happiness was supposed to be with. It's your mind playing tricks on you."

"Freud would be proud, Norris, but I think you should stick with accounting and leave the psychology to the experts."

"Fine, don't listen."

"Trust me, I won't. I did feel guilty for a while, but I don't anymore. And I didn't imagine I saw Shelly, I know I did."

"So you're not feeling survivor guilt?"

"No."

"Then why are you're preoccupied with Shelly?"

"I'm not. I just have to deal with her in being with Lara."

"*Deal with her?* Shelly's been dead for years."

"But I have to help her to find peace." Ryan frowned when Norris shook his head. "Don't look at me like you just saw my last marble roll away. I'm totally sane. Shelly is happy for me and she wants me to be with Lara, but she's in limbo. Somehow, my being with Lara is supposed to help her get peace."

"Why are you telling me this?"

"I'm running it past you before I tell Lara. I want to be sure it doesn't sound as strange as I think it does."

"You gotta be kidding me. I assure you, there is no easy or sane way to break this to Lara. I think I'd wait before springing this on her. You don't want her running for the hills before you get her in the valley," he said with a wink.

"Is sex all you think about?"

"Mostly, but I'm serious. Give it some time, and when it's the right time to tell her, the words will come."

Norris stood and stretched. "I'm beat. I'll catch you tomorrow, pal."

"Maybe not. I've got breakfast plans with Lara and, with any luck they'll extend to dinner, so I'll call you, okay?"

"Yes, sir, lover boy. You guys have fun." Norris grabbed the doorknob and turned around. "When am I going to meet Ms. Wonderful? You scared I'm going to sweep her off her feet?"

"The answer to the last question is not even a little bit, and the first is soon. How's that?"

"How soon?"

"Soon enough. Good night, Norris."

"It's good morning, pal." Norris tapped the face of his overpriced designer watch. "In case you forgot, this date lasted over six hours. I'm happy you're getting your love life back, but I want to be able to keep mine, too, okay? We can't do the double date thing if I'm Justin's babysitter and I don't have a babe sitting with me."

"Go home, Norris." Ryan pushed his friend out the door and did a quick sweep of the room. Shelly's pictures had to go. Minutes later, almost a dozen photos gathered from his office and the living room lay in a box on the floor. Only one picture of Shelly, holding a newborn Justin, remained on the fireplace mantle. Ryan covered the box and set it on the top shelf of the hall closet, surprised the undertaking wasn't nearly as painful as he expected.

Ryan gazed at the gold band on his left ring finger. Shelly was right, his heart wasn't there anymore. The ring was just a fixture, a symbol of what was. In the midst of removing it, he stopped and looked up. "I'm finding my peace with Lara, Shell, but I think I'll keep this ring where you put it until I've helped you to find yours. When I know you're as happy up there as I am down here with Lara."

━━

"You sure you don't need any help with anything, Ryan?" Lara asked, watching him disappear behind the swinging door of his kitchen. After purchasing Justin's school supplies, Ryan suggested a picnic at the lake, and with the fun they all had at breakfast, she couldn't say no. "I'm an old hand with sandwiches."

Justin looked up from the school items he had laid out on the floor. "Old hand?"

Lara laughed. "I'm good at making them," she explained.

"Thanks but no thanks, Lara," Ryan shouted from the kitchen. "I can have the picnic basket packed and ready in fifteen minutes. You and Justin just sit tight and I'll be right back. Do you want anything to drink? Water, juice?"

"I'm good, thanks."

Lara took a moment to examine her surroundings. The comfort of Ryan's home grabbed her. She loved the lighting the windows provided and the contrast of his mahogany wood furniture to his light-colored walls, though he could use a few plants. With nary a speck of dust or item out of place, and Ryan's warm hospitality and desire to prepare lunch, he was a true Mr. Mom.

As she continued to look around, Lara spotted pictures on the fireplace mantle. She made her way over. Three of the photos were of Ryan and Justin, and one other of a woman holding a small baby. She looked closer.

"That's me and my mommy," Justin said, confirming Lara's thoughts. "Daddy says I have eyes like her."

Lara nodded. "You do." She waited for discomfort at the situation to besiege her, but it didn't happen. This woman with kind brown eyes and a nice smile was Justin's mother and the wife Ryan mourned for over three years, and Lara didn't feel at all threatened. Shelly would always have a place in their lives, why not a picture on the mantle? "Your mommy was a very pretty lady," she said.

Justin smiled. "Just like you." He took her hand. "I'm glad you're having a picnic with me and Daddy, Ms. Boyd."

"Me, too, Justin." She smiled. "Me, too."

Hours later, Lara and Ryan sat curled together on her couch watching prime-time reruns while cartoons kept Justin occupied in the bedroom. Ryan kissed her hair. Their fingers twined. Lara nestled against his chest, enjoying the simple sweetness of the moment and Ryan's tenderness.

"Let's have brunch tomorrow," he whispered against her ear.

"Oh, I'm sorry, Ryan. I can't do brunch."

Ryan arms fell away from her. "What?" He looked like a little boy who was just told there was no Santa. "Didn't you enjoy our day?"

"I loved it." Justin's laughter rang out. After the picnic, they had returned to her place, where Ryan had prepared a delicious dinner and they'd played hands of Go-Fish with Justin. It was the perfect day. "I enjoyed being with you both," Lara answered.

"But you can't be with us tomorrow?"

"I can't do brunch. I'll be at church until early afternoon. Afterward I'm having dinner with Celeste and her family. It's what we do."

"Oh," he grumbled.

"Don't sound so disappointed, Ryan. You *can* come with me."

His eyes brightened. "Dinner with Celeste and her family?"

"And church services, too."

The light in Ryan's eyes dimmed. He sucked in a breath.

"What?" Lara asked. "Do you want to go to your own services?"

"It's not that, it's just . . . I haven't been to church in a while."

"What's a while?"

"Shelly's funeral."

The gasp escaped before Lara could stop it. She wasn't a perfect Christian, but her religion was extremely important to her. And though it had only been a couple of days, spending so much time with Ryan was making him important to her. "Why haven't you gone back to church?"

"Why?" he repeated, as though it needed no explanation. "Lara, God had taken my wife from me. I didn't feel like telling him thanks for making me a widower. I figured if I stayed out of his life, he'd stay out of mine." He sighed. "Justin's gone to church a couple of times with Sue, but he didn't much like it, and I didn't force it."

Feeling he had more to say, Lara prompted him. "And now?"

"Now, I guess I feel a little uneasy, because . . ."

"Because you're past your anger at losing Shelly and you see how blessed you are to have a home, your health, and a wonderful little boy? You're thankful?"

"I guess, yeah."

Lara took Ryan's hand between hers. "You're not alone in feeling this way, Ryan. When things go wrong, people get angry and want to blame God. The good thing is he understands our shortcomings and forgives us anyway." She jiggled his hand. "Come to church with me. I have a feeling both you and Justin will enjoy it. I know you'll enjoy dinner at Celeste's. Her son Billy is a year older than Justin, and her husband, Dan, is the most wonderful guy. It'll be great."

"Alright, we'll come." Ryan caressed her cheek. Her skin tingled and body warmed all over. For a man with such big, strong hands, he had the gentlest touch, so caring and sensitive. The same qualities that made him such a good father. "You know, you mentioned the things I have to be thankful for, but you left out one of the most important things."

"What?"

He kissed her tenderly. "Meeting you."

CHAPTER 9

Ryan pulled into the empty space beside Norris's car and turned to Lara. "You sure you want to do this? If we hurry, we can catch up with Justin and the Monroes at the movies." As Lara had predicted, church services and dinner with Celeste and her family went great. Justin and Billy had become fast friends, as did he and Dan, so spending the evening together wouldn't be a hardship. "It's okay to change your mind."

"I'm not changing my mind, Ryan. Justin is hanging out with his friend, and I'm joining you in hanging out with yours. It's going to be fun."

"Fun? Possibly. But our idea of fun and Norris's is a little different. He is my best friend and I love him like a brother, but he's a bit . . . He can be a bit much."

"You told me he's a flirt, but if he's your best friend, he can't be too bad. You trust him with your life and your son. That means something. I'm sure I'll like him." She smiled. "He has this friend I think is a pretty amazing guy."

Ryan leaned toward her. "Does he?"

"Uh-huh."

He brushed a sweet kiss to Lara's lips. In the two weeks he'd known her, his life had changed so much for the better. Besides Justin becoming more outgoing, Ryan now looked forward to Sunday as more than a day to sleep in late. Lara brought him sunshine he didn't know was missing from his world, and warmed the cold spaces in his heart that froze over when Shelly died. She brought him joy.

Following another kiss, Ryan escorted Lara to the door. Norris greeted them with a smile that became wider when he turned to Lara. Ryan shook his head. Lara would get the full Norris treatment tonight.

"Ah, so this is the lovely Lara Boyd. My, my, my." Norris pressed a kiss to Lara's hand. "Ryan's said plenty, but not nearly enough." He kissed her hand again. "It's my extreme . . ."

Ryan pushed Norris away, stopping the man from getting in a third kiss. "Enough with the slobbering already." He guided Lara to the love seat. Norris's condo was much like his office just on a grander scale. Art and leather abounded. "You'll have to excuse him," he said. "Flirting comes as easily as breathing to this one."

"C'mon, Ryan, you kept her to yourself for two weeks. I'm just happy to finally meet her. And be able to give her a very important warning."

Lara's eyes widened. "A warning?"

"Yeah." Norris nodded toward Ryan. "He didn't tell you?"

"Tell her what?" Ryan asked.

Norris sat on the couch across from them, his face deadly serious. Weird ripples filled Ryan's stomach. He scooted closer to Lara, taking her hand. What was Norris about to say? He couldn't shock her with stories from college; Ryan had already told her about the wild old days.

"Lara, I don't know how to tell you this," said Norris.

Ryan could only shrug when Lara looked his way.

"What is it?" she asked, foreboding evident in her voice.

"Ryan told me you have a drum from Ghana."

"I do," she said. "I love African art. Ryan told me you did, too. I can tell you have quite the eye."

"You're right. That's why I have to warn you. You're a kindergarten teacher, and Ghanaian folklore has it that a U.S. kindergarten teacher owning a drum from Ghana equals seventy-six . . . No. Eighty. Eighty years of bad luck."

Ryan joined in Lara's laughter. Norris was so stupid.

"Listen, Lara, the only way you can spare yourself is to give that drum to an accountant. We're immune to the evil forces."

Lara pressed her hand to her chest. "Norris, I don't know how to thank you for this wonderful warning, but I think I'll take my chances with the drum."

"You sure?" He glanced at Ryan with humor in his eyes. "Look at that guy beside you. I don't know. You might want to reconsider."

Ryan pointed. "Hey." He curled his arm around Lara's and kissed her cheek. "I told you about him."

"Told her what?" Norris cocked a brow. "What did he say?"

"That you're an original," Lara said, extending her hand. "It's nice to finally meet you, Norris."

Norris accepted her hand and smiled. "You, too."

Lara gaze settled on Norris's wall of fame—his collection of prized African masks. She snapped her fingers.

"You know, that mask second to the left reminds me of a story I heard about accountants and leprosy. I might be able to spare *you* a horrible fate." She left to take a closer look.

"Don't get too excited, Lara, I don't scare easily." Norris leaned over and slapped Ryan's shoulder. "You did good, pal, she's a keeper," he said before joining Lara to continue their banter.

A keeper. Ryan smiled. He thought so, too.

"M-A-R-O-C-A-I-N?" Ryan frowned. This is what he got for playing Scrabble with a teacher with a master's degree. "Lara, what's a marocain?"

"It's not a what, it's a thing. Ribbed crepe fabric used in women's clothing." She scribbled her points on the notepad. "Double letter score on the 'C' makes the total . . ."

"Enough for you to win, I get it," he said, his tone playful as he gathered the tiles. "The next time I'll come out on top."

Lara leaned over her kitchen table and kissed him. "I'll look forward to the challenge." She helped him collect the tiles. "You might have gotten more points if you hadn't chosen to spell such uninspired words."

Ryan laughed. "Sorry, Lara, we can't all come up with words like marocain and xenia."

He dropped the last of the letters in the bag. For the last hour he had tried to find a way to broach the delicate subject of Foster by choosing words like "past," "him," and "hurt," but in the mix of the others, Lara didn't seem to pick up on them. Or maybe she did and just pretended she didn't.

They'd been dating over six weeks, and he still knew nothing about Foster, but he did know he was falling in love with Lara. Whenever he mentioned the man's name, a cloud of sadness would fill her usually bright eyes and she'd find a way to change the subject. He wanted to know what happened, but he wouldn't press her, not yet.

"So what do you want to do now, Lara?" He handed over the game and followed her out the kitchen. "It's still early."

"Let's go out. This apartment is too quiet without Justin's laughter. I know he enjoys his sleepovers with Sue and Carl, but I miss him when he's not around." She placed the game with the others on her bookshelf and took his hand. "How about the movies? I'm even willing to sit through that action flick you've been dying to see."

Ryan's eyes widened. "You hate action movies."

"But I like you. And since you were nice enough to play Scrabble with me, I guess I can sit through explosions, car chases, and gun fights with you."

"Wow. You must *really* like me," he said with a laugh.

Lara nodded. Her hand tightened around his. "Yeah, I *really* do."

Ryan's heart knocked against his chest. The way Lara said those words, the breathy quality of them, and that look in her eyes. Were they on the same page? Did she feel for him the way he felt for her? "Lara, I . . ."

The chime of the doorbell ended his sentence.

Lara closed her eyes for a long moment. "I'll get it." She checked the peephole and then pulled open the door. "Celeste, Dan, hi." Lara greeted them each with a kiss and ushered them inside. "Ryan, look who's here."

"Hello." Ryan bussed Celeste's cheek and shook Dan's hand. He wasn't happy about the interruption, but was always glad to see them. "What's going on, guys?"

Dan smiled brightly. With the height of a basketball player and body of a pro wrestler, Dan Monroe was a gentle giant with a love for his wife and family as big and strong as the man himself. "Long story short, our house-keeper is staying with us a few days while her place is being painted. In her gratitude, she offered to sit with the boys and keep an eye on Diana while Celeste and I go out on the town." He pulled Celeste close. "We're inviting you to join us," he said.

"Nothing fancy," Celeste added, "just some adult company and conversation. It'll be fun. You guys game? Millie wouldn't have a problem with watching Justin."

"Justin's with his grandmother, so it's just us," Lara shared. She turned to Ryan. "It does sound like fun. What do you think?"

"I think it looks like we'll be having a great time on the town tonight," Ryan answered.

Celeste clapped. "Great, let's go."

Ryan's gaze met with Lara's. The electric spark between them sizzled all the more. The confession in his heart would have to stay there a while longer, but that was okay. The words unspoken were being lived between them every day, and tonight their already wonderful relationship had taken an even bigger turn for the better. He realized they had fallen in love.

~~~

Lara smiled to herself, Ryan's surprise visit to her classroom still fresh on her mind. In the past few weeks they had grown even closer. She spent every day with him and Justin, and every minute revived her suppressed desire for happily ever after. Helping Justin at bath time, convincing him to eat his vegetables, and helping Ryan with mundane tasks like folding laundry were now her favorite things to do.

Stares and hushed whispers occurred more often than she cared to admit, but that was the only overt hostility she and Ryan encountered, with the exception of Sue. Since their initial meeting in her classroom, Lara had been spared Sue's wrath, but it was no question her developing relationships with Ryan and Justin did not make the woman happy. Sue refused to speak when Lara answered Ryan's phone and never came inside the house when Lara was there. Amazingly, Justin remained oblivious to his grandmother's attitude. How long that would last was anyone's guess.

Lara gazed at the cupcake on her desk. Her smile widened. Ryan became a familiar fixture in her classroom as involved parent extraordinaire, always available for Parents' Day and a willing chaperone on field trips. Not surprisingly, he had won over all the students with his quarter from the ear trick. A last-minute business trip to Atlanta had kept him from the Halloween party, but on his way to the airport this morning he had dropped off two-dozen cupcakes for the children to enjoy. He also left with a promise to give Lara a special treat later tonight. She couldn't wait.

With the countdown to the weekend rapidly approaching, Lara worked on completing her remaining biweekly progress reports while the children made final preparations to go home.

"Ms. Boyd!"

Lara looked up to see Tommy Jones approaching.

"Ms. Boyd, I am trying to put the blocks away, but Justin will not stop playing with them. My mother is waiting outside for me." He pushed his slipping glasses back in place. "It is my duty this week to put away the blocks, and I want to do my duty so I can go home and begin trick-or-treating."

Lara searched the room for her able assistant, Penny Thompson, and found the pretty twenty-five-year-old brunette helping the other students into their sweaters and jackets in preparation to lead them to their waiting parents. Knowing Tommy as she did, Lara knew he wouldn't have gone to Penny anyway. Tommy wanted her attention, and wouldn't have stopped until he got it, especially when it came to Justin.

The little boy grabbed her hand and dragged her to where Justin sat with the blocks. "See," he said, pointing an accusatory finger.

Justin stopped playing with the interlocking plastic blocks and looked at Lara. "I tried to tell him I'm leaving with you today and I'll put the blocks up when I'm done." Justin frowned at Tommy. "He won't listen."

"He is supposed to stop playing when playtime is over. Playtime is over, Ms. Boyd. Justin has to stop playing now so I can put the blocks away. I want to do *my* duty before I leave."

Lara rolled her eyes. Tommy was a sweet boy, but a real stickler for details, and the only person she knew who never used contractions. All the students knew "Justin's daddy" was her boyfriend, and the look on Tommy's face as he waited for her to handle the situation demanded she not deviate from the normal procedure because of that fact.

Tommy brushed his platinum blonde locks from the rim of his glasses and smoothed his hands along the front of his perfectly pressed white dress shirt. "Well, Ms. Boyd?" he said.

Why did Tommy have to make a big deal out of this? Justin playing with the blocks a little longer wasn't a problem. Any other child would have happily relinquished the duty to him, but Tommy would push this to the end.

Lara touched Justin's shoulder. "You know the rules, sweetie. It's time to let Tommy—"

"Ahem!" Tommy stuffed his hands in the pockets of his light brown trousers.

"It's time to let *Thomas*," she corrected, "put up the blocks."

"But I—" Justin began, his eyes doing the twinkle she couldn't resist.

Why did he have to do the eye thing? "Justin, please," she said, her voice soft but stern. "Playtime has been over for a while. Let Thomas put up the blocks so he can go home."

Justin got up from the floor. "Okay," he grumbled.

"Why don't you go look at one of the picture books while I finish my work." She brushed her hand against his hair. "It won't be much longer, okay?"

Justin nodded and flashed an understanding smile. "Yes, ma'am."

Mrs. Thompson and all the children had been gone about five minutes when Lara heard another voice call her name. She looked up from the progress reports to find Sue Lomax frowning down at her. Lara sighed. And just when her day was going so well. She placed her ink pen atop the papers.

Justin scurried to the woman's side. "Hey, Grandma. I didn't know you were coming here."

Sue leaned forward and gave him a squeeze. "I know. I wanted to surprise you."

"You did. Me and Ms. Boyd are leaving soon, but I can show you some of the pictures I did while she does her work."

"I would love to see them, but first I need to speak with Ms. Boyd." She cupped his cheek. "You go back to your book while I step outside with your teacher for a bit, okay?"

"All right."

The women stepped outside. "Justin's not the only one who's surprised," Lara confessed.

"I imagine not."

The abrasive edge in Sue's reply confirmed she wasn't there to apologize for her rude behavior over the past couple of months. Lara folded her arms. "Are you here to talk to Justin's teacher or Ryan's girlfriend?"

"I don't have a problem with Justin's teacher, so long as she stays in her place."

"Her place?"

Sue's eyes narrowed and her thin lips became an even thinner line. "How dare you raise your voice to my grandson!"

"Excuse me? I have never raised my voice to Justin."

"Oh, no? What was that a few minutes ago?"

"What was what?"

"You were short with him about something as insignificant as blocks. I don't care what you think you are to his father, but you are not Justin's mother. I will not have you chastise him in front of anybody, especially other children."

Tension attacked Lara's neck and shoulders. Sue didn't like her, but these accusations were groundless, not to mention hurtful. She closed her stinging eyes. She wouldn't cry. She couldn't show Sue any signs of weakness. Gathering her composure, Lara met the woman's gaze.

"Mrs. Lomax, I'm aware I'm not one of your favorite people, but you don't know me, and you most certainly have no idea what you're talking about right now. I have never raised my voice to Justin or any other child, and I could never, nor would I ever try to take his mother's place."

"As if you could." Sue took a step closer, eyeing Lara from head to toe. "You're not even half the woman my Shelly was." The woman's eyes narrowed to tiny slits. "You will never be anything more than a bed warmer for Ryan and a babysitter for Justin. The ring on Ryan's finger tells me all I need to know. His heart will only belong to one woman, and it's not you."

Sue's verbal jabs sent Lara reeling; effective one-two punches that were both powerful and unexpected. Lara spent a lot of time with Justin, time Sue used to spend with him, so the babysitter comment didn't really surprise her, but the bed warmer thing really jumped out at her. She had fallen in love with Ryan, and she felt certain he loved her, but neither had actually said the words to the other, nor had they been intimate, at least not in the way Sue meant.

Doubt seeped into Lara's head like a slow-moving poison. Attacking her faith in Ryan. She had a key to his place and he to hers. An exchange that happened for practical reasons with Justin, and because sketching at her place stroked Ryan's creative juices, but a key exchange all the same. That meant something, didn't it?

What about that ring?

From the moment she learned Ryan was widowed, the ring hadn't bothered her, but maybe it should have. Had the stars Celeste thought would blind her vision done just that?

Angry and confused, Lara ached to forget she'd been taught to always respect her elders, and unleash a slew of curses that would make a drunken sailor blush. Her hand itched to slap the taste out of Sue's mouth. A big believer in time-outs, Lara closed her eyes and engaged in a silent count to five.

With five reached, she pasted on a sweet smile and met the woman's gaze. Scorn twisted Sue's mouth, and contempt flared in her eyes. Enjoying the woman's reaction, Lara smiled more.

"You're spoiling for a fight, Mrs. Lomax, but you're not going to get one from me. I'm going to go back into my classroom, finish my work, and take Justin home."

Sue blocked Lara's path as she headed for the door. "That won't be necessary—the taking Justin home part. He'll be leaving with me."

"No, he won't," Lara countered. "Justin was left in my care. I'm the adult with permission to take him home, and I'm the one who's going to do it."

"I'm his grandmother."

And a wretch of a human being, but that's neither here nor there. Lara maintained her phony smile. "Ryan asked me to take Justin home, and that's what I'm going to do. If you have a problem with that, take it up with him. He should be back from Atlanta around four-thirty."

Sue grabbed Lara's arm as she made another attempt for the door. "You wait one minute!"

Lara stared at Sue's tightening hand around her arm. Willing herself not to shout, she snatched her arm away. Her fake smile vanished. "Don't you *ever* touch me again," she said, her voice deathly calm. "That is the first and last warning I'm giving you." Lara took a menacing step forward. If she couldn't hit Sue, at least she'd give her pause. "Now you say good-bye to Justin and then get on your broomstick and fly back to wherever you came from. I'll give you five minutes with him. If you're not out of my classroom by then, I will make a call and have you physically removed. Do you understand me?"

Lara's words went unacknowledged as Sue walked around her and into the classroom. Smoothing her hands over her black slacks and adjusting the sleeves of her orange blouse, Lara entered the classroom and took a seat behind her desk. Justin's smiling face confirmed he hadn't heard any of the exchange. Relief flooded her tense body. One less thing to worry about.

She picked up her pen to finish the reports, but shaky hands made it impossible. Nagging questions plagued her. What did this relationship mean to Ryan? What did she mean to him? No matter how she tried, she couldn't dismiss what she perceived as truth in Sue's words. One visit from that miserable hag had her doubting Ryan and what she knew in her heart they felt for each other.

Memories of Foster and how they ended resurfaced to torment her. Lara had thought he loved her, too, but she couldn't have been more wrong. Foster was her deepest pain. She had wanted to share it with Ryan on the many occasions he'd asked, and even times when he didn't, but she didn't know how to explain something she couldn't understand herself.

Come to think of it, Ryan never pushed when she side-stepped him on Foster. Was Sue right? Was their relationship nothing more than a passing dalliance and readily available childcare while Shelly still lived in his heart?

Lara groaned. *What's wrong with me?* Ryan's touch on her body and his dizzying kisses made her heart pound. She could see his love for her every time she looked in his eyes. Couldn't she?

Conflicting thoughts pulled her in different directions. She never felt threatened by Shelly's memory, or the place Shelly would always have in Ryan's heart as the mother of his child. How now could she let Sue, of all people, make her second-guess herself?

Sue approached the desk with Justin. "I have something in my car for him."

"Fine. I'm done here." Lara gathered her things. She wouldn't get any more work done today. "We'll follow you out."

She settled Justin in the backseat of her silver VW Beetle while they waited for Sue to bring over her "something." His tiny hand covered hers as she fumbled with the safety belt.

"Ms. Boyd, are you all right?" he asked. "You look sad."

She clicked the belt and gave him a smile. Justin was always so concerned about her well-being. "I'm okay. I guess I just have some things on my mind. Grown-up stuff. Nothing for you to worry about."

"Your eyes look sad." Justin reached into his jacket pocket. "I like you with happy eyes. Daddy said these make his eyes, mouth, and stomach happy. Mine, too," he added with a laugh, dropping something into her hand.

Lara looked to find a foil-covered chocolate. "A Kiss." She ignored the frown on the approaching Sue's face and pressed her lips to Justin's wind-chilled cheek. His eyes brightened, as did Lara's disposition. "Thank you, Justin. I feel happier already."

━━

Lara made her way down the stairs after tucking Justin in. Considering his successful night of trick-or-treating—he was the cutest little Ernie—she was amazed he went down so fast. Only a few pages of his favorite story had him out like a light.

Halfway to the kitchen, she spotted Ryan on the couch in the living room. "Hey, I thought you'd still be busting suds," she said, joining him as he rifled through the giant orange treat sack Sue had given Justin.

"I decided to let the dishwasher wash the dishes tonight." Ryan removed mini racing cars, coloring books, crayons, homemade cookies, candy, and an ungodly amount of sugarless gum from the bag and set them on the table. "Justin asleep?"

"He went down just like that," she said, snapping her fingers.

"I didn't know Sue was planning to visit him today."

"Of course not, it was a surprise." Lara rolled her eyes. She didn't mean to sound so sarcastic.

Ryan dumped the items in the bag and set it aside, curious eyes fixed on her. "Tell me what happened," he said.

Lara shrugged. The last thing she wanted was to get into that scene with Sue and all the doubts it brought up.

"It's nothing." She kissed his hand. "Let's talk about your day. With Justin's excitement with trick-or-treating, I didn't get to ask about your trip. Was the flight good? Meeting productive?"

"Yes and yes. My interpretation of Sigmund the fun-loving squirrel was a big hit. Now, it's your turn to talk."

Lara stiffened. He wasn't going to let this go.

"You livened up as the night progressed, but I knew something was wrong from the moment I got home. What happened with Sue? Justin obviously doesn't know, because he would have told me already."

"It's nothing."

"Stop saying it's nothing, Lara. You're being evasive, so I know it's something. What is it?"

"Mrs. Lomax accused me of raising my voice to Justin."

"You would never do that, but I know there's more to this."

She sighed. "You know the boy in my class—Tommy?"

"Thomas, the anal kid?"

Lara frowned. "Andrews, that's mean."

"But true. What about him?"

"He wanted to put away the blocks."

"Huh?"

"Playtime was over, and it was his turn to put up the blocks. Since Justin was leaving with me, and still playing with them, he told Tommy he would do it." Lara groaned. "Tommy wanted to put up the blocks, and wouldn't take no for an answer. I personally didn't mind

Justin playing, but with our relationship, I couldn't bend the rules for him, even though his eyes were doing the little thing they do that makes it impossible for me to tell him no."

"I know the look."

"You ought to." Justin had his mother's eyes, but the look was all Ryan's, and they'd shared many a close call on the couch because of that very look. "I had to be firm," Lara explained, "but I wasn't loud or angry when I told him Tommy was right, and to let him put up the blocks. Apparently, Sue heard this and made it what she wanted."

"What then?"

"We stepped outside the classroom to talk, and that's when she made her accusations and . . ."

Ryan sat upright. "And what?"

Dread tightened in Lara's stomach as his inquisitive gaze bore down on her.

"Lara?"

"She said some things."

"What things?" Silence hung in the air. "Lara, please, just tell me what she said to upset you."

"She said I'm not half the woman Shelly was, and because of the wedding band you still wear, I'll never be more than a bed warmer for you and a babysitter for Justin. That Shelly would always have your heart." Lara walked to the window and then turned to face him. "There."

He watched her intently, never once batting an eye. "Tell me you don't believe that."

"I don't. I mean—I didn't." Lara closed her eyes, trying to dam the tears threatening to spill but having no luck. "I don't know."

"Oh, Lara." Ryan rushed over, lifting her downcast chin. "Are you standing here telling me you don't know how important you are to me? How much you mean to me?"

Sniffling, she half nodded and half shrugged. "I do know, but I don't *know* know. You know?"

He chuckled. "Amazingly, I do."

"I don't know why Sue's words bothered me so much. I never felt like I was in Shelly's shadow, but—"

"Shhh." He pressed his forefinger to her lips. "You don't have to say another word." He brushed away her tears. "It's time I did the talking."

She nodded.

"For a very long time, this ring on my finger meant exactly what Sue said. Shell was all I knew and wanted to know, but everything changed when I took Justin to meet his kindergarten teacher. From the moment I saw you, and heard that off-key voice, I knew you would forever be special to me. I could recite a poem or come up with a lyrical ditty to express how I feel about you, but it's as simple as saying three little words that aren't at all simple in meaning. I love you. I love you so, so very much, Lara Boyd, and I have for a long time."

Ryan's lips claimed hers, reinforcing the sincerity she heard in his words. Lara melted in his arms, welcoming his affection. Every caress of his hand and stroke of his tongue erased her misgivings. She had nary a doubt. Ryan Andrews loved her.

"I love you, too, Ryan." Lara spoke the words effortlessly. It felt good, freeing. She held him closer, breathing him in. He wasn't Foster. She didn't have to be afraid of love anymore. She had to stop being afraid. "I love you so."

CHAPTER 10

Ryan walked out of the kitchen with two steaming mugs of coffee. He smiled, admiring Lara's beautiful backside as she talked to a couple goblins at the door.

"You have a good night," Lara said.

"Think that's the last of the trick-or-treaters?" he asked after she closed the door behind the giggling children.

"I hope so, because if not, you might find your gorgeous shrubbery toilet-papered in the morning." Lara approached with the candy bowl held upside down. "You're all out of treats."

After setting the full cups and empty dish on the table, Ryan wrapped his arms around her. "If push comes to shove we can always give them some sugarless gum. With all Justin has, I'm sure he won't miss it. Lucky for me, I have my favorite treat right here." His lips brushed hers and trailed to her graceful neck. "So tasty." After another kiss, he escorted her to the couch. "Come, your French vanilla awaits."

Lara joined him and motioned to the remaining cup. "Have I finally converted you, or is that your man coffee?"

"Babe, the stuff you drink is dressed up cocoa." He took a big swallow of his Colombian blend. "This is real java, the way nature intended it to be."

"If you say so." She took a sip, peering at him from the top of her cup. "You're staring, Ryan."

"I was thinking about what happened today with Sue." He placed his cup on the table. "I'm really sorry about that."

"I'm not."

"Are you serious?"

"Yes." She set her cup on the coaster next to his. "I'm not *happy* it happened, but it made us open up about our feelings for each other, so I can't be upset."

"In that case, me neither." Ryan kissed her softly and brought her to recline against his chest. His chin rested on her shoulder. He had been waiting for the right time to tell Lara about Shelly's ghost and the ring, and now seemed to be it. "But we still have other things to discuss." He felt Lara's body tense against him. She thought he meant Foster. Her continued disinterest in discussing her ex worried him, but Ryan felt once he'd explained everything about Shelly and why he wore the ring, she'd be ready to talk freely about her past. "There's something I need to tell you."

"Sounds ominous."

"I'm sorry."

"The 'I'm-sorry-man' returns." She laced her fingers with his. "Is it that bad?"

"I don't think—Well, no, not really." How could he answer that? If she didn't think this some crazy Halloween story, she would probably believe he was off his rocker. Telling the woman he loved about visits from his dead wife's ghost . . . Her reaction could be almost anything.

Ryan buried his face in Lara's hair. Strawberries and cream. He loved the scent of her hair. He loved everything about her. If all went well, she would still love him and not think him ready for the loony bin when he'd told his story. "Do you believe in ghosts?"

"Is this a story to commemorate the holiday?"

"It might sound like it, but it's not."

She snuggled into his arms. "I'm listening."

"It started the day I met you . . ."

At the conclusion of his revelation, Lara faced him on the couch, sitting in that woman way with her feet tucked under her bottom. "Aren't you going to say something?" he asked.

"I'm trying to think of what to say. Shelly has been paying you visits?"

"Not lately, but, yes. And like I said, she thinks you're great. She's one of our biggest champions."

"You've been seeing your wife's ghost?"

That wasn't the response he was going for. "Yeah," he answered with a hesitant nod. "Lara, what's going on in that beautiful head of yours?"

"All sorts of things." She moved to the unlit fireplace.

Ryan followed. He remembered he needed to call the chimney sweep people. With the cold weather coming and Lara in his life, he had plans for that fireplace that went far beyond keeping the house warm. It was a principal part of more than one of the romantic fantasies he had about her. He hoped he would still need it after Lara had shared her thoughts. "Feel free to unburden yourself," he said.

"I don't know what you want me to say."

"That you don't think I'm crazy and you still love me sound good."

"I do still love you."

"Uh-oh."

"Do you know how this sounds?"

"I do know, but I told you because I need you to help me."

"Yes, to help Shelly find her peace." She sighed. "You said the last time you saw her was when?"

"The day we had our first date."

"It's been over two and half months since our first date, and you haven't seen Shelly since. Maybe what you told me Norris said was right, and it was your subconscious giving you the okay to move on guilt free. Didn't you say she was very positive about us?"

"Yes, but I didn't imagine it. Lara, she was as real as you are right now."

"Did you touch her?"

"No, but—"

"Did she touch you?"

"She's a ghost. I don't think you can touch a ghost. Sweetheart, I didn't dream her up. She was right in here, and she talked to me. She told me how much she likes you, and she was glad I finally found a woman that made me feel alive again. Then she told me our being together would help her get her wings so she could finally get into heaven. This all happened."

Lara grew quiet. Ryan gnawed his bottom lip. He was usually very good at reading her, but this time he drew a blank.

"Where do you want to start?" she finally said.

His eyes widened. "You believe me?"

"I believe you think you saw Shelly's ghost, and that's enough for me. I'll do whatever I can to help you. I am curious, though. How will you know you helped?"

"I think Shelly will tell me. It sounds strange, I know."

"No more than what I've already heard." She picked up the picture of Justin and Shelly.

"When I first saw Shelly's ghost, I thought I was going crazy. I had just met you and I couldn't stop thinking about you. I felt confused and hurt, because you were in my thoughts and on my mind and Shelly wasn't." Ryan gazed at the photo in Lara's hand and smiled at the happy memory. "Shell helped me see that caring about you was a wonderful thing and I shouldn't feel guilty. I got that lesson quick," he said.

"And you're going to wear the ring until you think Shelly's peace is achieved?"

He nodded. "I know Sue mentioning it bothered you. Does it still?"

"Should it?" She replaced the picture and walked back to the couch.

"I asked my question first." He sat beside her. "Is this ring a problem for you? I want you to tell me the truth."

"Honestly, no. I think it should bother me. I think it's crazy it doesn't, especially after my run-in with Sue today and hearing you say you've been seeing Shelly's ghost, but it doesn't. It did in those moments before I learned you were a widower, but since then, it's just been there. I see it, but I'm not threatened by it. I'm amazed I can say that and mean it after what I—"

"After what?" he asked, seeing the flicker of a Foster memory in her eyes.

She shrugged. "Nothing."

Nothing again. Ryan wanted her to spill the story, but he wouldn't push. Not yet. She was still processing a lot of information, and he didn't want her overwhelmed all at once.

"Tell me about the rest of your last visit with Shelly. Exactly what happened?" Lara asked.

"It was right after you met Sue. She knew how bad that scene was in your classroom and told me to deal with her mother, and not to give up on you and what we had, no matter what."

"No matter what? Does she know something we don't?"

"From what she said, I think she just observes and draws conclusions. I assumed Shelly saying not to give up no matter what was in regard to Sue's issues with us. And after what happened today, I definitely have to talk to Sue again."

"You may have to talk to her, but it shouldn't be for my benefit. I don't need you fighting my battles."

"Hey." He kissed her softly. "Your battles are mine."

"I can handle Sue, Ryan. She upset me, and she angered me when she grabbed my arm, but . . ."

"Whoa! When she what?" he erupted.

"Ryan, shhh. You'll wake Justin."

"Why didn't you tell me about this? Did she hurt you?"

"Not at all. That's why I didn't want to mention it. She wanted to take Justin home with her, and when I told her it wasn't happening she didn't receive it well. I stood my ground with her, so I'm sure she won't be grabbing me anymore."

"I'm really sorry that happened, Lara."

"Me, too. Physically, Sue didn't hurt me, but she pounded me pretty good emotionally. She has a real problem with me, and she hates I'm so close to Justin."

"I know."

Lara hugged a throw pillow close to her chest. "It killed me to tell him he couldn't play with those lousy blocks. I love Justin, Ryan. I would do anything for him."

"And that, my lady, is what Sue dislikes. She knows this, so do I, and so does Justin. He is absolutely crazy about you. The fact I'm in love with you is just more reason for her to be upset."

"It may be more of a reason, but I don't think it's the main reason. Sue does have a problem with my closeness with you and Justin, no doubt about it, but my being black seems to be her biggest problem. You do know that, right?"

"That you're black?" The hint of a smile twitched her lips, but the humor didn't quite reach her eyes. Ryan sighed. There was no lightening this moment. "Yeah, babe, I know." He took the pillow and placed it on his lap. "Come here."

Lara rested her head. "I'm disappointed," he admitted, combing his fingers through her hair. "I was never a big fan of Sue's, but her reaction—I didn't expect that."

"I have a feeling Sue is not going to be the last surprise you'll encounter. The stares and the whispers are nothing." She repositioned her head so their eyes met. "We've been fortunate."

"We are fortunate. But we shouldn't have to deal with blatant hostility because we love each other."

"No, we shouldn't, but it's the way of the world."

"It's still wrong. What we have together isn't." He stared at her full lips, struck with an overwhelming need to kiss them. "I don't want to talk about the ignorant people of the world anymore. In fact, I don't want to talk at all."

Sliding his hand from her hair, Ryan cupped her cheek and covered her mouth with his. Lara's arms curled around his neck, holding him close, but not nearly close enough. With little effort, he coaxed her lips apart, deepening the kiss. His tongue invaded her mouth, taking hers as a willing hostage. Lara's sighs of pleasures increased his need for her. His hand traveled a slow path along the curves of her body, stopping only when he reached the swell of her breasts. Her heart pounded against his hand, beating in time to the throbbing in his slacks. Never breaking their inflamed kiss, he worked feverishly to unbutton her shirt. "I want you, Lara," he whispered against her lips. "I want you so much."

"I want some water, Daddy."

Startled by Justin's drowsy voice, Ryan dropped his exploring hand. Lara scooted to the other end of the sofa, straightening her shirt. "You, uh, you say you want water, son?"

Justin nodded, rubbing the sleep from his eyes.

Ryan stared at the pillow on his lap. There was no way he could get up right now.

Lara stood. Amusement shone in her eyes as her fingertips grazed his pillow. "Why don't I get the water for you, sweetie," she said to Justin. "I'm feeling a bit thirsty, too."

Justin nodded and took her hand. "Okay."

When Lara returned, Ryan praised her quick thinking with a kiss. "Thank you," he said. "You just saved me from trying to explain how I got a baseball stuck in my pants."

"You're very welcome." She licked her lips. "But I'd watch that if I were you. Justin was only too tickled to share he saw us kissing just now."

"I guess it's a good thing he walked in when he did and not a few minutes later, huh? Poor kid might have been traumatized for life." They laughed. "But you're right. R-rated fun is over for tonight. Let's talk."

"About what?"

"Thanksgiving. It's right around the corner."

Lara paused for a moment before nodding. "Yeah, it is."

He waited to see if she would say something more, specifically, *"Hey, Ryan, why don't you and Justin join my family and me for Thanksgiving?"* She didn't say that, or anything else. "I heard you and Celeste talking when we stopped by her place tonight. Sounds like you guys have big plans."

"I guess, sure." She reached for the coffee cups. "I'm gonna take these into the kitchen."

He covered her hands. "Why are you so fidgety?"

"I'm not."

"Why haven't you invited me over for Thanksgiving?"

"You're going to Wisconsin, right?"

"I didn't say that."

"You haven't visited with your family in a while, though, and your sister Kristyn is pregnant."

"Kristyn is always pregnant, this is child number five. Besides, my folks are going to be in London, and I saw everybody during the summer. I want to spend Thanksgiving with your family, Lara. I'm ready to meet your parents."

"No, you're not," she countered, swooping up the coffee cups and literally sprinting into the kitchen.

CHAPTER 11

Lara sat at the kitchen table, struggling to settle her overactive brain. All the normally quiet sounds seemed magnified ten times over—the soft hum of the refrigerator was as loud as a lion's roar, the quiet swirl of the dishwasher a fierce windstorm. Even the glistening white of the appliances seemed brighter.

Everything seemed bigger, bolder, more out of control. Like her feelings for Ryan. She loved him with all her heart, and she wanted him to come to Thanksgiving dinner, but . . . *But?* What was that "but" about? She groaned. Who was she kidding? She knew what.

She plucked an apple from the fruit bowl and washed it at the sink. Still smarting from her run-in with Sue, she hadn't given the burgers and fries Ryan prepared for dinner the attention they deserved. Hopefully, a little sustenance would soothe her anxious thoughts.

Making her way back to the table, Lara spotted a white tissue waving from the partially cracked door. "Ryan, what are you doing?" she asked, biting into the apple and filling her mouth with sweet, tangy juice. Either she was extremely hungry or this was the best apple in the world. She took another bite as she waited for Ryan's reply.

He stuck his head in the door. "I'm waving a surrender flag. You're so opposed to my joining your family for Thanksgiving, I figured I did something wrong."

Lara chewed and swallowed the bit of apple in her mouth. "You didn't do anything wrong." She took another bite. He was doing everything right. That was the problem.

Ryan entered and straddled the chair next to her. "Then why don't you want me to have Thanksgiving with you?"

"I want you to come, but inviting someone to my family's Thanksgiving dinner is a big deal. It's a *huge* deal, and everybody, and I do mean *everybody*, is going to be there. Besides my parents and Celeste's, there's going to be our siblings and their spouses and children. I'm talking seventeen people you haven't met, twelve of them adults."

"That's exactly why I want to come. Lara, I want to meet your family. I want to talk to the people who created this wonderful woman I love so much. I want to meet the twin brothers who teased you, and the older sister who wouldn't share her nail polish. It feels like I already know them, you've talked about them so much. I want formal introductions now, not just pictures and stories."

Suddenly, the apple wasn't so tasty. She twirled the half-eaten fruit like a spinning top.

Ryan's eyebrows furrowed. "What's wrong? Don't they know about me?"

"They know I'm dating someone."

"Exactly what does that mean?" he asked, grabbing the apple and taking a big bite.

"It means . . ."

He held up his finger, swallowing the bit of apple in his mouth with a loud gulp. "You didn't tell them I'm white, did you?"

Lara shrugged. "They didn't ask."

"You think it will be a problem for them?"

"I don't know." She left the table and headed for the living room.

The apple core hit the bottom of the trash can with a thud as Ryan followed. "Is that why you just don't want me to share Thanksgiving dinner with you and your family? Because of how they might react to me?"

"That's part of it." Lara dropped to the couch. "We're different, Ryan. The looks we get when we go out are just the tip of the iceberg. Things are not going to get any easier for us. If anything, they might get worse."

"Worse?" He stood, pacing. "What do you mean it could get worse?"

"I think you know," she said, trying to discern if this was his angry or thinking pacing.

"We don't always get looks. Come on, you don't think we can handle a few snide comments or a couple of lingering stares? Lara, I don't give a damn what strangers think."

"We're not talking about strangers. This particular conversation started after you asked about Thanksgiving. I don't know about you, but I'm afraid of how my family will react to us." She threw up her hands. "There, I've said it."

He sat beside her. "You think they'll be upset? Disappointed?"

"I think more surprised and shocked than disappointed. Falling in love with you shocked me, and it happened to me. Being in love again, and with you . . ." She shook her head. "I can only imagine how my family will react to it. Have you told your folks about me?"

"Of course. You've talked to my parents on the phone."

"Yes, but I've been told I sound white."

He raised an eyebrow. "You sound what?"

"White."

"Sweetheart, it's impossible to sound like a color."

"I don't mean literally. That's what black people get when they speak in complete, succinct sentences. They're assimilating. Trying to sound like the man."

Ryan shook his head, frowning. The more she spoke the more perplexed he looked.

"Never mind, I'll try to explain again later," she said. "I'm asking if your family knows I'm black. Did you tell them?"

Ryan shrugged. "They didn't ask." He grinned.

After her bout with laughter, she fixed him with an admonishing gaze. "Don't distract me with humor, Ryan. We need to talk about this."

"Lara, we can talk about this until the end of time, but it will only be speculation until we face it."

"Meaning?"

"Meaning, we won't know what will happen until it happens. All I know is I love you." He smacked his lips.

"My folks have only spoken to you briefly on the phone, but I gathered they like you. If that changes because they find out you're black, I'll certainly be hurt and disappointed, but I'll get over it. What I won't get over is you, Lara. You're my heart." He finished his words with a tender kiss.

"Ryan, this dinner means serious commitment."

"Isn't that what we have?"

Lara's heart fluttered. *It sure felt like it.* And that's what scared her even more. "Ryan . . ."

"I want to come, Lara. I'll be honored."

"You'll be grilled. Did you forget my father is six-five, and my brothers are just a hair shorter than that? They are big." She made a wide space between her arms.

"You can't scare me. Your family and I will get along great. If you decide to invite me, I won't be your first honored guest, will I?"

"No."

"Foster?" Ryan asked.

"Yeah, he was the first and only guest for me." He was the first and only in a lot of things for her. He fit in perfectly with her family at the first Thanksgiving and the one that followed, but the way their relationship ended was hardly perfect.

"You rarely talk about him."

"Why should I?"

"Because he was important to you. I talk about Shelly."

"That's different."

"How's it different?"

"Shelly was your wife, and she's the mother of your child, plus your friendly visiting ghost. Foster was just—"

"A man you loved and were going to spend your life with. That's a big deal, Lara. I'm secure in my feelings for you, and yours for me. I don't mind hearing about him. I want to know how he hurt you so I'll never do the same foolish thing. Are you going to tell me more about him?"

Lara considered Ryan's question. He'd opened up completely about Shelly and she felt obliged to do the same with Foster, but she didn't know how, or if she would even if she did. She did know she wasn't ready tonight. "Maybe some other time."

"Thanksgiving?"

She groaned. "You're not going to let this go, are you?"

"No. I want to be invited. I'll even help you and Celeste cook. My string bean casserole is to die for. And my German chocolate cake." He kissed his fingers like a French chef. "So?"

The puppy dog look he and Justin mastered had the same effect on her as kryptonite had on Superman. Lara sighed. She never had a chance.

His blue eyes filled with hope. "What?" he asked.

"Ryan, it would be my pleasure if you and Justin would join my family and me for our Thanksgiving dinner. Will you come?"

"Absolutely." Ryan pulled her into an embrace.

Lara closed her eyes. *Thanksgiving.* If this didn't go well . . . She held Ryan tighter. It had to go well.

~~

The sound of the doorbell interrupted Ryan's trek to the laundry room. He lowered the basket of dirty clothes to the arm of the couch and checked his watch. Who could be at his door at eight on a Saturday morning? Lara had a key and an eight-thirty hair appointment the hounds of Hades couldn't keep her from. The doorbell rang again. *Jehovah's Witnesses?* He shuddered. Not today. He had too much work to do.

"I'll get it, Daddy."

Justin left the couch and his cartoons and raced to the door before Ryan could stop him. He'd taught his son to check the window before answering the door, but at five, Justin had yet to grasp being inconspicuous, so if Jehovah's Witnesses were at the door, they couldn't pretend no one was home.

"Daddy, it's Grandma and Grandpa," he happily shared.

Ryan groaned. Carl he didn't mind seeing, but what did Sue want? Not to apologize for her treatment of Lara on Halloween, that was for sure. He'd only seen her once since then, and the woman had looked through him as if he were glass. Justin loved his grandmother, but Ryan was in no mood to play nice. "Go on and open the door," he said with as much enthusiasm as a candidate for a root canal. "I'm going to finish the wash." He picked up the basket and trudged toward the laundry room.

As the washer hummed to life, Ryan retrieved the still warm laundry from the dryer and began to fold. With any luck, Sue would be gone when he got finished.

"Ryan Christopher Andrews, is doing laundry more important than saying hello to me?"

"Mom?" Ryan turned to find his grinning parents and a smiling Justin perched high on his father's broad shoulders. "When Justin said Grandma and Grandpa, I thought he meant Sue and Carl." He dropped the bath towel he was folding to the basket and greeted them with a hug. "What are you two doing here? I thought you'd be halfway to England by now."

"We took this flight because it had a layover here before connecting to O'Hare," Matthew explained, lowering Justin.

"Yes, a four and a half hour layover," Justine reiterated. "We decided to surprise you."

"Well, you certainly have. It's so good to see you."

"It's so good to see you both." Justine gazed down at her namesake. "I can't believe how big you've gotten since the summer."

"I've been eating my vextables," Justin shared with pride. "Ms. Boyd said they'll make me big and strong like Daddy."

Justine's face lit up. "Yes, Ms. Boyd. She's the main reason we're here."

"Lara?" Ryan repeated.

"Yes. Your mother and I couldn't wait another second to meet this woman who's making you and Justin so happy," Matthew explained. "Since we'll be out of the country for several weeks, we wanted to meet her before we left."

"Is it at all possible we can?" Justine asked.

Ryan checked his watch again. Eight-twenty. He sucked in a breath. Lara's appointment started in ten minutes, and she had been complaining about her roots all week. But with his parents here, last week's speculation of how they would react to her could finally be put to rest.

"So, Ryan, can we meet her?"

"I can't make any promises, but I'll see what I can do."

Excusing himself to the kitchen, Ryan picked up the cordless phone and dialed Lara's cell.

She answered on the second ring, something he knew she wouldn't have done if not for his special ring tone. "Ryan, sweetheart, I really can't talk. I'm about to see Dahlia, and she has a million people on her book today."

"Yeah, I know. Lara, I wouldn't ask if wasn't important, but I need you to come over right now."

"Come over? To your place?"

"Yeah."

"Now?" She groaned. "Ryan, I just pulled up to the salon. My roots are giving me fits. You know that."

"Babe, it's important."

"My roots are important." She paused. "What? Is it Justin?" Her voice trembled. "Oh, God, is he sick?"

"Oh, no, no," he assured her.

She breathed a loud sigh of relief. "Then whatever it is can wait."

"No, it can't."

"What is this about?"

Ryan stuck his head in the laundry room to see his parents in lively conversation with Justin. "It's a surprise.

I promise, I wouldn't ask you to come over if it wasn't necessary. Can Dahlia maybe squeeze you in a little later?"

"How long will this surprise take?"

"In theory, not too long, but it could change."

"Oh," she groaned.

Ryan smiled. He could tell from her grumbling she was coming over.

"I'm one of Dahlia's best customers, so maybe she can back my appointment to nine. Taking time for the drive, I can give you fifteen minutes, twenty tops."

"Whatever you can do. I know what your appointments mean to you."

"It's a good thing I love you so much is all I'm gonna say on that. I'll see you in a few."

"Well?" Matthew asked when Ryan returned.

"Lara should arrive shortly. She can't stay long, but she'll be here."

Justine clapped. "Wonderful. I can't wait to meet her. She sounds so lovely on the phone."

Ryan tensed. He still hadn't told them Lara was black, and he wouldn't. A genuine response to the woman he loved was what he wanted. Lara wanting his head for not telling her she was about to meet his parents was another thing. She would ream him for sure. He drew a deep breath. "I can't wait for you to meet her, either, Mom."

Lara pulled into Ryan's driveway and dashed inside the house. *This better be one heck of a surprise.* "All right,

Andrews, I'm here. What's so important I had to—" She stopped speaking when she spotted a pretty brunette with Ryan's eyes and a handsome, older man with Ryan's blond hair sitting with him on the couch. Ryan *was* the blend child.

The enormity of this moment took root. Lara's hands flew to the baseball cap covering her head. Jeans, a red sweatshirt, and sneakers did not equal the meet-the-parents look. Why hadn't he given her some warning? She could have at least changed. "Hi," she squeaked.

"Hey, Ms. Boyd!" Justin raced over, wrapping his tiny arms around her legs.

Lara smiled down at Justin, returning his hug. "How's my favorite boy?"

He tilted his head to meet her gaze. "I'm good. My grandma and grandpa are here," he whispered in his loud way.

"I see," she whispered back, glaring at Ryan. She would get him for this.

Ryan stood. A tight smile touched his lips. "Lara, babe, there are a couple of people I want you to meet."

"Oh, you, hush up." Justine flapped her hand at Ryan as she and Matthew made their way over, smiling brightly. "There's no point in making unnecessary introductions when your father and I are quite capable of speaking for ourselves."

Lara thought to look over her shoulder. Were they really grinning so broadly at *her*?

Justine took Lara's hand in hers. "It's wonderful to finally put a face to the name Lara Boyd," she said.

"An extremely beautiful face at that," Matthew added, kissing Lara's cheek. "It's a pleasure to finally meet you."

"The pleasure is mine." She studied their faces, finding not the slightest hint of discomfort or shock, but ever-growing smiles. "I wish I'd known you were going to be here," she said, shifting her gaze to Ryan. "*Somebody* neglected to mention this to me."

Ryan squirmed. "Yeah, about that—" he began.

"Don't be too hard on him, Lara," Justine interjected. "He didn't know we were coming. We had a layover and decided to take advantage of the situation. I think I can speak for Matt when I say you are everything we could have hoped for and more."

Lara raised a curious eyebrow. She looked from one to the other. Did they really not care that their son was involved with a black woman? "I am?"

"Yes," she answered as Matthew nodded. Justine smiled down at her grandson, who was still fastened to Lara's legs. "The way Ryan and Justin's faces lit up when you walked in . . . Their happiness is all that matters to us, and you, young lady, make them happy. We've waited a very long time for this." Justine squeezed Lara's hand and pressed a kiss to her cheek. "Thank you for loving them."

Lara's heart swelled. The look on Ryan's face mirrored the happiness she felt. *Could Thanksgiving go this well?*

"I understand my son dragged you from your hair appointment."

Lara adjusted the visor on the cap. "Can you tell?"

"You look like I do when I go to mine—very comfortable." Justine smiled. "You can get back now. We'll have lots of time to get to know each other better. I'm just glad we finally met."

"Me, too, Mrs. Andrews."

"Justine, dear."

"And Matt," Matthew added, linking his arm with his wife's and pressing a kiss to her gray-streaked hair. "I'm sure we'll be seeing you again real soon. Ryan, you walk Lara out to her car. We'll stay with Justin."

"You comin' back for dinner, Ms. Boyd?" Justin asked.

"Would I miss your daddy's spaghetti bake?"

His head shook vigorously. "Uh-uh."

She brushed her finger against his nose. "Okay, then, I'll see you later." Lara turned to the elder Andrews. The smiles of delight on their faces were almost childlike. She really liked them. "It was a pleasure meeting you both."

"It was all ours," Matthew said.

Justine shooed them off. "Go on, Ryan, walk Lara out."

Lara stifled a giggle as Ryan led her out the door. Now she knew where he got his lack of subtlety.

Ryan stopped in front of Lara at the driver's side of her car. "Are they still watching us?" he asked.

Lara laughed. "Yep, they're still watching," she answered, looking over his shoulder in the direction of the living room window.

"No surprise there." His hands swept up and down her arms. "What's the verdict on my folks?"

She gave him a big squeeze. "I think they're wonderful."

"They love you, Lara. I wanted to know their true reaction when they first met you, and that's what we got. You're not upset I didn't tell you they were here?"

"I was a little peeved at first, but things went great. All we need to do now is get through Thanksgiving."

"It's going to be fine." He leaned in closer. His thumb caressed her cheek. "Why don't we give my folks something to really talk about on their flight to London." The sweet taste of French vanilla flavored his tongue when it brushed against her lips. "You and your coffee," he murmured.

Lara's soft chuckles made way for sensual moans as his tongue plowed deep in her mouth. The curves of her body molded to him, fueling his endless need for her. Encircling his waist, her hands moved lower, squeezing his bottom. Driven by pure instinct, he thrust against her, pinning her to the door, grinding against her.

"Whoa." Lara broke the kiss. "Ryan, sweetheart, your parents *are* watching us."

"Lara," he murmured, attempting to reclaim her lips.

She slid from his amorous clutches. "I think we've given them more than an eyeful. And if I stay another minute out here with you . . ." She glanced at the bulge forming in his jeans. "Bye."

Ryan's gaze turned to the window after Lara made her quick exit. His mother stood alone. Regaining composure, he headed inside. "Where are Dad and Justin?"

"The kitchen," Justine answered, approaching. "That was some fireworks display out there."

He smirked. "Lara can't keep her hands off me."

Justine's eyes brightened. "Poor girl's contagious," she said, mussing his hair. "Really, she's incredible, son."

"Thanks, Mom." He kissed her cheek. "Hearing you say that means a lot to me."

"Society has a ways to go, but your father and I don't. Lara is a gem. It's obvious you love her very much."

"With all my heart."

She raised his left hand. "Then, what's with this?"

"It's a long story." Ryan walked to the couch and sat.

"It must be, but you need to close the book and take off this ring. Think of Lara's feelings."

"Mom, this ring doesn't bother Lara. We've talked about it and she knows why I wear it. Shelly is my past. Lara is my future. She knows how much I love her."

"Even with this invisible third party in the mix?"

"There might be an invisible third party in our life, but it's not Shelly."

"What?"

"Things with Lara and me are great . . . mostly, but she's not been able to be completely open with me."

Justine joined him on the couch. "Open? You mean you haven't—you know?" she said, jutting her head.

Ryan shuddered. "Mom?"

"Isn't that what you men mean when you say 'open'?"

"I guess it sorta means that, but when I used it I meant it in the confiding sense," he said, not believing his mother was asking about his sex life. "There's a guy from her past, her ex-fiancé, Foster, who hurt her terribly, and she won't talk much about him. When I think she's about to open up, she shuts down on me."

"You think she still has feelings for this Foster?"

"No, I don't. I know how she feels about me, but she's not been able to trust me with this Foster thing, and I need her to trust me. We can't progress fully with this between us. I want Lara to tell me what the hell this guy did to her." He sighed. "I need to know what's got her so wary of sharing this part of her past with me."

CHAPTER 12

"C'mon, Daddy, this is the good part!"

Ryan couldn't remember how many times he'd heard that phrase over the course of the lazy Saturday. But he was having so much fun. All the parts were good for him. "All right, I'm coming." Carrying a fresh bowl of popcorn, Ryan took his place next to Justin, who was snuggled against Lara's side, and placed the bowl on the boy's lap. "What am I missing?"

"Wile E. Coyote is about to get a serious headache at the hands of Roadrunner—again," Lara answered, grabbing a handful of popcorn. She chuckled. "When will he learn?"

Beep! Beep!

Justin erupted in laughter at the foiled coyote as Roadrunner sped away. "That's so funny. He has a big knot on his head."

"That's the last cartoon on this disk," Ryan announced, using the remote to stop the DVD.

"Let's watch another one, Daddy," said Justin.

"Another one?"

Justin nodded.

Ryan couldn't have planned this better. Justin wanted more cartoons, and he didn't want Lara to leave. Her hair appointment last week had robbed them of precious hours together, and today he was determined to make up for lost time. He'd used all of Justin's bathroom breaks to steal kisses, whisper sweet nothings, and try to persuade her to stay the night. She hadn't given him an answer, but with Justin's help, he'd get the right one now. "I think you should ask Ms. Boyd, son," Ryan said. "We might have to stop to take her home."

Lara stopped munching on the popcorn. She met his gaze, dressing him down like a mother who'd caught her child's hand in the cookie jar. Ryan smiled broadly and shrugged. Maybe he should be ashamed of his tactic, but he wasn't. He wanted her to stay, and wasn't above using Justin's influence to make it happen.

"Aren't you having fun, Ms. Boyd?" Justin asked, his little voice as morose as Ryan hoped.

"Of course, sweetie. I'm having a great time," she said.

"Then stay."

"Yeah, stay," Ryan chirped.

Justin stroked Lara's hand and pressed his head against her chest. Ryan sighed. If only he could trade places with his son.

"Please, Ms. Boyd." Justin's brown eyes peered up at her.

Seeing Lara's resolve cracking, Ryan decided to chisel the rest away. His arm stretched along the back of the couch, and his fingertips trailed gingerly against the side of her neck. Up and down. She sighed softly. Ryan smiled. Blocks of resolve were crumbling to the floor.

"It's already dark, and it's so cold and nasty out there," Ryan said, pointing to the rain-splattered windowpanes. "Justin and I will drive you home in the morning, prepare a nice little breakfast while you get ready for church, and once we've eaten, we'll go to services together. After dinner with the Monroes, we could go to the movies and get some dessert. Doesn't that sound like fun?"

"Yep, it does," Justin answered.

"I think we need to hear from the lady, son. So, Lara?"

"How can I say no to those faces?" she said. "You win."

"Yea! You're staying!" Justin cheered. "You can sleep in my bed."

Lara's eyes widened. Ryan stifled a laugh. Justin had stolen his line. "Your bed?" she said.

Justin nodded. "Uh-huh. I have new Ernie sheets."

"Yeah, I've seen them. It's so nice of you to offer me your bed. Your little red car bed."

His son smiled proudly. Ryan almost hated to disappoint him . . . almost.

"It was really nice of you to offer Ms. Boyd your bed, Justin, but I think she might be more comfortable someplace else," Ryan said. "I think my bed will suit her needs perfectly. Don't you, Lara?"

"Yes, I do. I should be very comfortable in your bed."

Ryan grinned. This was going better than he hoped. "I know you will be."

"But if I'm in your bed, where are you going to sleep?"

Ryan blinked. Was she kidding? "I was sorta hoping
. . ."

"You could sleep on the mountain of clouds that
make up the guest bed? That's what you were about to
say, right, Ryan?"

Humor and satisfaction shone brightly in her eyes.
She had one-upped him and now all but dared him to not
follow her lead. Ryan admired her savvy. He decided to
bide his time. Lara could enjoy her victory. This was just
one battle; he had every intention of winning the war.

"How about that, Justin, Ms. Boyd can read my
mind," Ryan said. "I was just about to say I'm going to
sleep in the guest room." Ryan gave Lara his seductive
stare down. Pulse points throbbed wildly in her neck.
Her smile waned as his increased. Yes, indeed, victory
would be his.

Lara smiled down at Justin's serene face. So much for
his big plans for the evening. It was just eight and he was
sound asleep. She kissed his cheek. His soft sigh made her
heart swell. She couldn't love him more if she tried.
"Good night, precious boy."

She stepped out into the hall to hear Ryan calling her
into his room. He was supposed to be in his office
working. A nervous flutter settled in her stomach. After
that look he gave her earlier, Lara knew if she walked into
his bedroom with him still in it, she probably wouldn't
walk out for quite a while.

"Lara, come in here. I have something for you," Ryan sang.

That's what I'm afraid of. "What is it?"

"You have to come in here to get it. It's on the bed."

"Uh, Ryan—"

"Just come in here."

Lara stared at the door. She'd been in his bedroom countless times before, but tonight was different. There would be no watching movies or placing laundry this time. No, Ryan would get her in there and she'd forget a five-year-old slept a few feet away.

Cursing him for making her flesh so weak, Lara stalked into the room to demand Ryan keep his hormones in check. To her surprise, she didn't find him sprawled naked and aroused on the bed, but she did find a toothbrush, her brand of deodorant, her favorite body lotion, and a pair of red thong underwear with "Saturday" embroidered on the floss-like straps.

"Do you like your presents?" Ryan called from the bathroom.

"Mostly." She picked up the scarlet panties as if they were a used tissue. "I was going to say thank you for being so thoughtful until I saw this triangular crimson gauze amongst the toiletries. What were you thinking?"

His arms snaked around her waist. "How sexy you would look in them," he whispered in her ear.

The scent of deodorant soap and minty mouthwash overwhelmed her senses. He smelled so good, clean and fresh. Her hands trailed his strong forearms. A low groan rumbled in his throat. Needing to touch more of him, she turned to find him clad in only a low-hanging green towel. He smiled. She smiled back. And all the reasons she had for not coming into the room flew out of her mind.

Pressing her open palms against his chest, Lara's lips slid along the bulging contours. Ryan trembled under her touch. Her fingertips splayed in the blond hairs dusting his sculpted pecs. She followed the golden pathway down his torso, pausing at the knot resting just below his navel. Ryan swallowed loudly. Her gaze dropped further to find the towel protruding. She resisted the urge to rip the towel from his body. This had already gone too far.

Lara jerked her shaky hand away. "Ry . . . Ryan, we should talk."

He pressed his forefinger to her mouth. A whimpering cry escaped. "Let's make love, Lara, not conversation. I want you so much."

Ryan's soft, moist lips came crashing against hers. Their tongues engaged in a wordless conversation while his hands roamed her body in sensual exploration. The bit of willpower she clung to fell through her fingers like water. She buried her hands in his damp hair, surrendering herself to his touch.

Agonizingly slow, Ryan unbuttoned her shirt, and with the finesse of the magician he proclaimed himself to be, unhooked her lacy black bra and tossed it and the blouse to the floor. Appreciation and desire filled his eyes as he stared at her exposed breasts. Her nipples hardened as if doused by a pail of ice water. "You are so beautiful," he murmured.

A million watts of electricity shot through Lara's body and she thought she would sink to the floor in a pile of ash when his hot mouth covered first one breast and then the other. A guttural moan tore from her lips. His arms tightened around her, bringing her closer to the swell of his growing hardness. His glazed eyes bore down into hers. "I love you so much, Lara."

Her heart pounded furiously in her chest. She nodded. "I love you, too."

Their lips met in a flaming kiss. Ryan secured one arm around her waist and used the other to push the toiletries to the floor. Swooping her in his arms, he settled her in the middle of the bed. His blue eyes raked over her partially nude body. Her heart raced faster. Memories of her last time in a man's arms—Foster's arms, Foster's bed—raced to the forefront of her mind. Ryan's hand slid to the knot in the towel. The motion left Lara breathless—literally. She shot upright, struggling for breath.

Alarm wiped out the desire in Ryan's eyes. Leaving the knot intact, he raced to her side, rubbing her back. "Lara, baby, calm down. Just take it slow, take it slow," he urged, his tone anxious but calming. She nodded, doing her best to follow his instructions. "Breathe. That's it." He kissed her temple. "Just breathe. Nice and easy."

Lara closed her eyes. Ryan's soothing touch and caring words soon gained their desired effect, and normal breathing returned.

"Are you okay?"

Lara rested against the headboard. "I'm fine. A little embarrassed, but I'm fine," she answered.

"Is this something that's happened before?" Ryan retrieved her blouse from the floor and helped her into it.

"No."

"Did I scare you?"

"Not in the way you probably think. It's . . . it's been a long time for me. I guess I got a little nervous."

"Tell me about it." The shirt buttoned, he moved to the spot beside her. "I apologize if I got a little carried away."

"You didn't. I was enjoying it." She toyed with her shirttails. "It's been a *really* long time, Ryan."

"Not three years." He nudged her shoulder.

"You're right, it's been six."

Ryan's eyebrows shot up. His disbelieving gaze met hers. "Did you say it's been six?"

She nodded.

"Six years?"

"Surprise."

Ryan stayed quiet for a long time. Lara's anxiety grew. She continued to fiddle with her shirt.

"Six years, Lara?" He covered her active fingers. "You told me you dated."

"I did, but dating doesn't equate f—having sex." She gave him a pointed look. "At least not in my world."

Ryan frowned. "Lara, I wasn't an angel before I settled down with Shelly, but I wasn't Norris, either. I was honest about all that."

"Is there a point to this?"

"Yes, there is. I have a past, Lara, and I've shared it with you. Hence, your ability to make snide remarks about it. But you hyperventilated when we were about to make love. Nervousness might have played a part, but there's something inside of me saying it's something more. Was the last guy Foster?"

"Ryan, I don't—"

His shaking head silenced her. "I think you need to talk about it."

"Why? Because I haven't slept with as many men as you have women? So, I'm not a slut, shoot me!"

Lara regretted the words the minute they passed her lips. She waited for Ryan to show her to the door, but he didn't move a muscle. He just looked at her, with those blue eyes full of love and concern.

"You feel better now?"

"Not really," she mumbled, still toying with the shirt.

"I'll be your punching bag, Lara, if that's what it takes, but I'm not going to drop this, not this time. You can fumble with your shirt as long as you like, but we will talk about Foster tonight."

Anger zipped through Lara's veins at his matter-of-fact tone. Did he think she was Justin? She met Ryan with a frown, prepared to tell him a thing or two, but his determined look stopped her cold. "You're not going to drop this, are you?"

"Nope."

A defeated sigh fell from her lips. She hung her head. How would she ever find the words to explain the unexplainable? A hurt she'd never understood.

Ryan lifted her chin. "Take your time, Lara. I know this is hard for you."

"Yeah, it is, but not for the reasons you probably think." She drew a steadying breath. "I met Foster soon after I started grad school, and before too long, I was totally smitten. He was handsome, charming, and so intelligent."

"A lot like me, huh?"

Lara laughed. Ryan always knew when she needed a laugh. "Not quite," she said. "He was a corporate lawyer, on the fast track to great success. My family loved him, and I loved him. I loved him so much. We were going to have the perfect life. A new age Cliff and Claire Huxtable. The lawyer and the kindergarten teacher."

"What went wrong?"

"Everything. All through grad school Foster was there for me, reminding me of how close I was to finally achieving my goal of teaching and the plans for our life together. Everything was perfect. Too perfect. When I completed grad school, he did a total one-eighty."

"How so?"

"The first noticeable change happened the night of graduation. I . . . I was a virgin and—"

"Wait. A virgin?" Ryan's eyes roamed over her. "You? Gorgeous you? In grad school?"

"Yes. I wanted to wait until our wedding night to be together," she explained, reading all the unasked questions in his eyes. "It was only another month, but Foster didn't want to wait anymore. And because I loved him, and I wanted to make him happy, we slept together. Two weeks later, he told me I had to make a choice. I could teach or I could marry him, but I couldn't do both."

"What?" Ryan whispered.

Lara nodded. "Yeah. He said he'd thought about it, and if I really loved him there was no choice to be made. The career I've wanted since I was twelve or the man I agreed to spend my life with? Which did I want more?" She sighed. "Foster wanted an answer right then, and because I couldn't give him one, he made the choice for me. He took the ring from my finger and walked out of my apartment and my life forever. I heard he moved to New York and got married a few weeks later. I was such a fool."

"Oh, Lara."

She moved out of the reach of his open arms. "Please, Ryan, no pity."

"It's not pity, it's love. I understand your pain now. I'm sorry you had to go through that."

"It's not like I was the first woman in the world to have a broken heart and engagement. I should have seen it coming."

"You couldn't have seen that coming. He said he loved you and he supported you in your career. How could he ask you to give it up?"

"I've asked myself this question for a long time." Lara threw up her hands. "You know, it doesn't matter."

"Of course it matters. You loved him. You gave him everything. You gave him yourself, Lara. That matters."

"Maybe I didn't give him enough of myself."

"I don't understand."

"I only slept with Foster once."

"Once?"

"I felt so guilty about not waiting, so tense that . . . Let's just say I wasn't fulfilled, and I didn't want to indulge again until we were married. I never said anything to Foster, but I gathered he understood, because he never forced the issue. I thought he was being considerate of my feelings and stayed quiet so I wouldn't feel bad." She shrugged. "I thought wrong."

"It's no wonder you hyperventilated before, you're practically a virgin. I don't want you to do anything you're not ready for, and I'm sorry if I made you feel uncomfortable."

"You didn't, Ryan. You were wonderful, and I want to be with you. Hyperventilating was about my issues, not you."

"What are your issues?"

"Uncertainty," she answered. "When I heard that ultimatum from Foster, something inside me broke. He literally crushed me. I've never had regrets about teaching, but I spent the first six years wondering if I made the biggest mistake of my life by letting him walk away."

"Do you still love him?"

"It's not that, Ryan. It's not knowing what's real. After Foster, I questioned everything. If he loved me why did he hurt me, and if I loved him, why couldn't I do what he wanted? I couldn't trust my feelings anymore, and I thought I never would again, not until you and Justin walked into my classroom and changed everything.

Loving you the way I do scares me. Feeling my fears, and loving you in spite of them scares me. I want to be with you, to share myself with you, but after so many years I'm . . ."

"Petrified."

"Scared out of my mind. Ryan, I don't want the love and happiness I have with you and Justin to slip away in a heartbeat. To wake up one morning to find out it was all a lie."

"Hey." He cupped her face. "It will never happen. *Never.* You can trust in my love for you, and know I would never trifle with your emotions. We have something wonderful together." He smiled. "I think Shelly knew we would from the start."

"Shelly? Has she appeared to you again?"

"No, and I don't think she will again. I believe I've fulfilled my promise to Shelly by falling madly in love with you." Ryan held up his left hand, and after several moments of pulling and twisting, removed the ring and dropped it in the bottom drawer of his nightstand.

Lara stared at his swollen finger and tan line. "Are you sure about this?"

He claimed her lips in a kiss full of passion and promise. "I have never been more sure of anything in my life." For the second time tonight, Ryan turned his attention to loosening the buttons on her shirt. The inferno that ravaged her body earlier now sparked hotter more intense flames. "Shell's got her heaven up there, and I've got mine right here." He pushed the blouse off her shoulders and dropped it to the floor. Standing from the bed, he reached for the tuck in the towel. Lara's uneven breathing returned. Ryan dropped his hand. Concern speckled the desire darkening his blue eyes. "You all right?"

Lara moved to the edge of the bed. "I think I'll let you find out for yourself." She loosened the tie in the towel and watched it fall in a rushing swoosh to the floor. Ryan's raging length slammed against his abdomen. She cast a brazen gaze over his body, wondering exactly how that old myth went again. Ryan was a true exception to the rule if it was anything like she remembered. Sliding her hand along the underside of his member, she got lost in the warm, velvety touch. Ryan's deep groans seemed to echo in the quiet room. Feeling extremely bold all of a sudden, and encouraged by his obvious pleasure, Lara continued her slow, deliberate movement as she shimmied to the middle of the bed.

Ryan settled alongside her. His breathing grew heavier and moans deeper with every stroke of her hand. He throbbed wildly in her loose grip. Before too long, he covered her sliding hand. "Lara, babe, I think you'd better cut that out now."

"Don't you like . . ."

He brought his forefinger to her lips. "I like it a little too much." He replaced his finger with a whisper-soft kiss. "But I want to please you, and your touch on that part of my body is a little too distracting." Pinning her arms above her head, he branded her face and neck with kisses and then ventured further down. "I'll be gentle with you, I promise."

His warm tongue laved the distended tips of her aroused breasts, sending shocks of electricity shooting throughout her body. Her inability to touch him added a level of frustration to the pleasure he gave. Aflame with need, she writhed against him. "Please, Ryan," she begged, not sure if she was pleading for the chance to touch him or the fierce need she had to have him bury himself deep inside her.

Ryan's gaze met hers. "I plan to," he said, his voice deep, raspy. "I plan to please you all night long."

The unsnapping of jeans and hum of a lowering zipper joined the sound of labored breathing. Lara closed her eyes. Her heart rate increased and stomach muscles tightened as Ryan's fingers slid inside her panties, beyond her thick curls, and dipped into the liquid heat of her pulsating center.

"Mmm, Ryan," she moaned, moving against him, wanting more, needing more, as he thrust deep within her. He continued suckling her breast while his fingers moved in slow, rhythmic motions. Trapped in a prison of pleasure, unable to touch him and dying to have him touch even more of her, Lara squirmed atop the bed like an angry rattlesnake. When an exploring finger encountered her overly sensitive love bud, all bets were off. Her loud cry of pleasure startled them both.

Ryan pulled his hand away and shot up. "You're a screamer?"

"Ms. Boyd!" Justin cried.

Panicked, Lara reached to the floor for her discarded shirt and bra, now recalling her hesitation about entering the room in the first place. "I can't believe this." What she really couldn't believe was that loud sound had come from her when she hadn't even . . .

"Ms. Boyd!"

Justin's voice grew closer.

"Ryan, the door," she warned, noticing it wasn't closed and he was still very naked.

Nearly tumbling over the towel and toiletries littering the floor, Ryan closed and locked the slightly ajar door seconds before Justin twisted the knob.

"Ms. Boyd?" Justin knocked. "Daddy, are you in there with Ms. Boyd? I heard her screaming."

Ryan turned to her, his eyes pleading for assistance, but she had none to offer. Justin sounded so scared, and Ryan being aroused and naked wasn't helping matters.

Once fully clothed, Lara walked to the dresser. "You want some advice?" Ryan nodded eagerly. She tossed a pair of pajama bottoms his way. "Put those on." She sat on the bed, her hands propped under her chin. He'd have to handle this one alone.

Ryan stared at her, his mouth agape. Lara shrugged.

"Daddy?"

"Yes, son, I'm with her," he answered.

"Is Ms. Boyd all right?"

Ryan pulled on the pants. "Yeah, uh, she's . . . she's fine, Justin. I was showing her a special trick I know and she, uh—she liked it." A pleased smile covered his lips. "She liked it a lot." He managed to dodge the pillow she threw at him. "That was happiness you heard."

"She's okay?"

"She's fine. She's real fine." Ryan winked.

Lara's smiled. He made it impossible for her to get truly upset with him.

"Can I see if she's okay for myself?" Justin asked. "I wanna be sure."

Lara rushed over and opened the door. The tears in Justin's eyes broke her heart. She knelt to him. "Justin."

He dived into her open arms. "Are you all right, Ms. Boyd?"

"Yes, sweetie, I'm fine. I promise."

"I thought something hurt you."

Lara held the unsettled child close to her. "I wasn't hurt, it was just the trick your daddy showed me. I promise, I won't let him show me that trick again."

"What?" Ryan said, the word disguised in a very loud cough.

Lara eyed her miffed boyfriend. "At least, not until I'm sure I can experience it without scaring my favorite little boy," she clarified, bringing relief to Ryan's worried face.

Justin nodded. "Okay. Will you tuck me in again?"

"Absolutely." She took his hand. "Let's go."

"You don't want me to help, Justin?" Ryan asked, the thrown pillow now placed strategically in front of him.

"Ms. Boyd can do it by herself," Justin answered.

"Aren't you going to at least tell me good night?"

"Oh, yeah. G'night, Daddy." He gave Ryan a limp wave and tugged Lara's hand. "C'mon, Ms. Boyd."

"Thanks, son, I feel so special." Ryan took Lara's arm as she passed. "I'll be downstairs when you're finished up here."

Lara nodded as Justin dragged her away.

CHAPTER 13

Ryan poked the burning logs in the fireplace. Flames sparked and wood crackled as memories of what transpired in his bedroom over a half hour ago raged inside him. His loins stirred. If a near miss did this to him, he could only imagine how incredible the real deal would be.

He smiled when the scent of Lara's cherry shower gel alerted him of her arrival in the dimly lit living room. "I see you found your other presents," he said, returning the poker to the nearby stand.

Lara nuzzled his neck with kisses. "I sure did. I found the bath set, the nightshirt, and the real underwear." Her soft, slender fingers stroked his bare chest. Rock hard nipples pressed against his back through the thin material of her satin nightwear. She was driving him wild. "You're such a sweet man."

"I'm also a very horny man." He caught her roving hands before they dipped below the waistband of his pajama bottoms. "If you don't want to scare Justin again, I suggest you stop touching me and sit down on this nice comfy pallet I set up for us. I want to check out the movie you brought over. *Invitation to Life*, right?"

"Wrong," she said, crawling next to him on the thick comforter, "but I'll clear that up in a minute." She closed his hand between hers. "I'm sorry Justin heard me, and I'm so sorry we didn't—couldn't—finish what we started."

He blinked. "You didn't finish?"

"No, but I think I was pretty close."

"Wow! If that was almost, you are really great for a guy's ego." He laughed. "We will finish, Lara. That was an incredible preview, but the real deal is going to be even better."

"Promises, promises."

"That's a promise you can count on," he said with a soft kiss. "Did Justin go down okay? I looked in on him while you were in the shower and he was sleeping like a baby."

"He was out soon after his head hit the pillow. That little boy means the world to me. The way he cares about me, and is always so concerned about me. It's just—it's the best feeling in the world. Well, after tonight it's tied for the top." They both laughed. "I hope that never changes."

"It won't, because, like me, Justin will always love you. No fears." He gave her another quick kiss. "Now, where is *Invitation to Life?*"

"It's *Imitation of Life. Imitation,*" she enunciated, placing the movie in the DVD player. "It's only one of the best tearjerkers ever made."

"I should have known." He groaned. "A chick flick."

Lara settled between his legs, using his chest as a backrest. "Just watch the movie."

At the swell of the final score, Ryan clicked off the TV. "Wow, that was uh—that was something."

"Was that sniffling I heard?"

"Allergies," he lied.

Lara chuckled. "Whatever."

"I don't understand." He propped his chin on her shoulder. "How could Sarah Jane treat her mother like that?"

"Taking a moment to play devil's advocate, Sarah Jane did what she did because it was best for her. She loved her mother, but I don't think she loved herself. She didn't fit in anywhere, and she desperately wanted to fit in."

"But to deny her own mother?"

"I don't agree with what she did, but I am trying to see her side of things. This is an old movie, Ryan, but its subject matter is still relevant today. Sarah Jane's parents were black, but her father was very light and she looked white. Her life was a lot easier when she lived on the other side of the color line. You would be surprised to know the number of black people who are passing or have passed in our society."

"Passed?"

"You know what I mean."

"I do, but the term doesn't seem right. How can you pass for something you are?"

Confused eyes stared up at him. "What?"

"If I'm getting the right definition from you, passing is being black but looking white, right?"

"Yes."

"So, passing is being who you are without saying any different."

"Ryan, what are you talking about?"

"If you looked like Sarah Jane, we wouldn't get stares when we go out together, because no one would be able to look at you and tell you were black. Our being together wouldn't be frowned upon because we would be perceived as the same, even though you'd still be black."

She twirled her hand. "Keep going. I'm past Vague Street and resting at Slightly Confused Boulevard."

"What I'm saying is, if nobody can tell you're black by looking at you, and they don't ask, if you don't tell, is it still passing? Even if you had no problem with saying 'I'm black' if someone did ask."

"I see your point, and in that respect, no, it's not. You can't control this," she said, rubbing the top of her hand, "but I think denying what you are is wrong."

"You know, Lara, in the grand scheme of things, skin color doesn't matter. People are like fruit. Good and bad, bitter and sweet. If we tell this to our children and raise them with the values we grew up with, they'll be fine. They won't be anything like Sarah Jane, that's for sure."

"*Our children?*" she repeated.

Surprise shone in Lara's eyes, but she didn't seem put off by his words, which was good, because he thought about it all the time. Babies with Lara, building a life with her, it was his fondest dream. After hearing about that debacle with Foster, he wanted to share his dream with her even more.

"You said you wanted lots of children, and I think six is a good number," Ryan said. "Now, our children could be your beautiful brown, as fair as me, or a multitude of in-betweens. No matter how they look, they will be loved, and just as gorgeous as their beautiful mother. Speaking of whom," he pushed the hair from her neck and nuzzled the softly scented skin, "when are you going to make things even for us?"

Lara moaned. "I must be getting tired, because I don't know what you're talking about."

"You saw me naked, Lara, and I've only seen you half naked." His hands swept up and down her arms as he continued his neck assault. "A whole half of you is a mystery to me."

"It's not that much of a mystery. Your little encounter with that half of me is why we're down here now."

Lara mentioning that incredible moment stimulated his quiescent manhood. "Since you mentioned down." His growing erection jabbed her in the back.

"Oh, no." She wriggled out of his arms and hustled over to the fireplace. "We're not going there again. You need to get a handle on that."

"I'd rather you do it for me." Lara didn't say a word, but the scolding look she'd mastered as a teacher said a mouthful. He shrugged. "Or maybe not."

"Ryan, I love you, and I want to be with you, but with Justin here, we can't . . ."

"You're a screamer, I know."

"I think it's time we head on up."

"About that." Ryan scurried to his feet, stopping Lara before she ascended the first step. "I know we can't make love, but there's no way I can sleep alone in one bed knowing you're a few feet away in another. Let's stay down here. We have pillows and comforters, and we'll be close to the fire. I want to fall asleep with you in my arms." Seeing the hesitation in her eyes, he crossed his heart. "I promise, I'll behave."

She nodded. "All right, I'll stay down here."

Settled in the makeshift bed, Ryan snuggled spoon style against her. His fingertips combed gently through her hair. "Are you comfortable?"

Lara embraced the arm tucked securely around her waist. "Very," she said with a contented sigh.

"Me, too."

"Good night, Ryan."

He tucked his chin into the crook of her shoulder. "Good night."

Lara's eyes flew open, but it wasn't the early morning sun rays filling the room that roused her. Alarm bells sounded in her head. She felt as if she were being watched.

Light snoring confirmed Ryan was still in dreamland. She looked over her shoulder to the landing at the top of the stairs. No Justin. The feeling grew stronger. The hairs on the back of her neck stood on end. She continued her search for the source of her unease and gasped when she found Sue's angry face staring through the windowpanes.

Ryan shot up. "What's wrong? Are you hyperventilating again?"

She shook her head, pointing at the window.

Ryan's eyes widened. "What the hell?" He flung the covers from his body and stormed over to the door. Lara stayed a safe distance behind, knowing the confrontation would not be pretty. He pulled the door open. The hinges squealed from the sudden force. A chilly breeze blew inside. "Damn it, Sue! What the hell do you think you're doing?"

"I'm trying to understand what's wrong with you!" The fuming woman tossed a plastic shopping bag into the house, narrowly missing Ryan's leg. A box of pancake mix, a jug of orange juice, a pack of bacon, and a carton of eggs crashed to the floor. "I came by to prepare my grandson a nice pancake breakfast, but what do I get instead? The sight of his half-naked father entertaining some . . ."

"What?" Ryan snarled.

Sue's eyes narrowed. "Where is Justin?"

"Where do you think he'd be at seven o'clock in the morning? He's in his bed asleep."

"He's here and you have the nerve to sleep with that woman in this house? My daughter's house!"

If made of glass, Lara knew she would have been shattered to pieces from the frigidness of Sue's hateful gaze. She took a tentative step forward. "Mrs. Lomax, nothing—"

"Lara." Ryan extended his hand, halting both her words and approach. "We don't owe her an explanation."

His gaze fixed on the angry woman. "This is *my* house, Sue. I can have whomever I want, in any part of it I want, at any time I want. You have no say in that."

"I have a say as to what my grandson is exposed to, and I do not want him exposed to this or her. What you're doing is wrong!" Her quaking finger pointed at Lara. "She is wrong, and she has no place in this house, or Justin's life."

The makings of a monster headache stabbed the back of Lara's eyes. She rubbed her temples. After everything that had happened last night, listening to Sue belittle her was the last thing she needed, and she wasn't about to stick around for it. "Ryan, I'm going upstairs to shower and change. I'll check on Justin while I'm up there."

Sue eyeballed Lara's knee-length nightshirt. "Certainly not dressed like that!"

Lara closed her eyes and drew several deep breaths. This was the Lord's day, and she would not take Sue's bait. Snatching Ryan's robe from the back of the couch, she headed for the stairs.

Ryan reached her before she cleared the first step. "I'm sorry about this, sweetheart. You really don't have to go."

Lara slipped into the robe as she shot Sue a hard look. "Oh, yes, Ryan, I do."

"Hey." Tilting her chin, he kissed her deeply. "I love you."

She smiled, not feeling nearly as angry as she had moments before. "I know. I love you, too." Glancing at the still watching Sue, Lara shook her head in dismay. She patted his cheek. "Have fun, dear."

He chuckled. "Right."

Lara entered Justin's room. He slept peacefully. She kneeled at his bedside, listening to his soft breathing and watching the rise and fall of his chest. Sue's voice got louder. Justin stirred but didn't awaken. Lara sighed. He still didn't know of his grandmother's dislike for her, but if the old woman kept this up, it certainly wouldn't be a secret for much longer.

Sue wrinkled her nose. "Was that little show for my benefit?"

"Yes, Sue, whenever I get the urge to kiss Lara you're foremost in my thoughts," Ryan mocked, collecting the pillows and bedding from the floor.

"Where is your ring?"

He dumped the items on the couch. "Put away, along with the rest of my past with Shelly."

"Would this part of your past with Shelly include Justin? Where are you going to put him? You think putting away her pictures, taking off your wedding band, and having sex with that woman will get Shelly out of your heart? You'll see her whenever you look at her son."

"I see Shelly in Justin, *our* son, because he's a part of her. But I don't pine for her and long for days gone by anymore. Shelly's gone. I've accepted it and moved on. I suggest you do the same."

"Maybe you can forget Shelly, but I can't, and neither can Justin. He'll never forget his mother."

"Sue, Justin can't forget Shelly because he doesn't remember her. He was a baby when she died. His knowledge of Shelly is by way of pictures and videos you show to him *ad nauseam*. He knows Shelly loved him, but he can't remember her love." Ryan took a step forward and met Sue's gaze head-on. "What you need to understand and accept is that where Justin is concerned, Lara is the number one woman in his life. He loves her the way a son loves his mother."

Sue recoiled. "That is a lie!"

"That is the truth."

"He doesn't know that woman. You don't know her. All you see is a forbidden warm body! Justin sees you all over her and he's following your inappropriate lead."

"What's so inappropriate, Sue? What? Lara is single, and I'm single. I love her, she loves me, and we both love Justin. What is so wrong and inappropriate?"

"The woman is black."

"And that means what?" Sue squared her jaw. Ryan shook his head. *What a pathetic woman.* "It doesn't mean anything," he said. "This shouldn't come as a surprise, but I'll tell you anyway. I am crazy in love with Lara, and I see a very long and happy future for her, Justin, and me."

Sue shook her head. "No, this is not good for Justin." She clasped her hands together, as if praying for a miracle. "He's an impressionable little boy, and this kind of behavior is confusing for him."

"This kind of behavior?" Ryan grunted. "You mean exposure to deep and unconditional love? Sure, that's the stuff ruination of children is made of." Ryan rubbed his hand over his face. "Listen, Sue, you've been wonderful to Justin, and you've been a constant female influence in his life, and I would like that to continue, for his benefit, but whether it does or not is up to you."

"What does that mean?"

"It means I don't want you to drop by my house again unannounced or hear you say another disparaging word about Lara. If I *ever* find you lurking outside my home, for any reason, I will have you arrested. Do you understand me?"

"You don't mean that."

"There's only one way to find out." Ryan pointed to the door. "Go home, Sue, and pick up your breakfast on the way out."

"I want to see Justin."

"He's asleep. You'll see him next weekend."

Sue's face reddened. "This isn't done, Ryan."

"For now it is." Ryan gathered the breakfast items Sue made no attempt to retrieve, and set the bag outside. He stood by the open door. "Justin will call you later."

"Mark my words, the association you have with this woman won't last. She hasn't now, nor will she ever, take Shelly's place in Justin's life, or yours for that matter." Sue stood before him, her eyes burning with conviction. "Never!"

Ryan closed the door behind the furious woman, wondering when, if ever, she'd accept the fact Lara had already done that.

Lara held fast to Ryan's firm bottom, enjoying his expert delivery of stroke after delicious stroke. Waves of pleasure rippled through her body. She closed her legs about his waist, her hips rising and falling to his every move. "Don't stop, Ryan."

His thrusts grew faster, deeper. "I'm almost there, babe. Come on with me."

Their lips met in a fiery kiss. Probing tongues matched the frenetic pace of their joined bodies. Her back arched, bringing him deeper still. His hips bucked against hers, and with one final thrust, they crashed to ecstasy's shore.

They lay twined together. "I love you," Ryan murmured.

Lara nestled against him. Her eyes fluttered closed. "I love you, too."

"Hello, Lara."

"Foster?"

"Foster!" Lara shot upright, her heart pounding and body drenched in sweat. Pitch-blackness surrounded the room. She patted the space next to her. No Ryan. She fell back to the bed, bringing the covers to her neck. For the fifth time in two weeks, she had experienced that confusing dream. What was going on?

CHAPTER 14

"That's when I lassoed that unicorn, settled my beautiful mermaid on top of it, and we rode off together in the sunset."

"That's ni—" Ryan shook his head. *"What?"*

Norris laughed. "I'm glad you're finally paying attention."

"I'm sorry. I have a lot on my mind."

Ryan had thought taking Norris up on his offer for a beer at the local sports bar was a good idea, but not even listening to his friend ramble about his latest score or the temptation of Chandler's icy cold beer and fiery hot buffalo wings could make him unwind. Tomorrow was Thanksgiving, and the significance of that fact was taking its toll.

"So, how nervous are you?" Norris asked.

Ryan slowly turned his now-warm mug of beer. "Is there a measure for nervousness?"

"Sure. Very nervous is spending forty-five minutes letting a frosty cold mug of expensive German beer go flat as you lament over what tomorrow will bring."

"I wasn't lamenting. I'm just a bit concerned. And it's more for Lara than myself. She's petrified about tomorrow."

"And you're just a little worried?"

"I want to meet Lara's parents. I told you how I had to practically beg her to invite me to Thanksgiving dinner. I just really want it to go well for her."

"Yourself, too, right?"

"Sure, and for me. Right now Lara is over at Celeste's cooking, baking, chopping, and decorating up a storm. She wants everything to be perfect. Even Justin donated his little pinecone turkey to the cause. This is so important for her, and me, too. Lara's family means the world to her, Norris. I honestly don't know what I'll do if her parents don't like me."

Ryan raked his fingers through his hair in nervous frustration. Worry about making a good impression was keeping him awake nights. Coupled with planning a surprise birthday party for Lara while working overtime to keep it a surprise from her and Justin had him tight as a drum.

"You need to calm down. Let me order you another beer."

"I can't, I'm meeting Lara at Celeste's, and since her son Billy is coming home with Justin and me, I'll have to save room for a little pop and junk food."

Norris chuckled. "I honestly don't get why you're so worried about tomorrow when everybody gets along so well."

Sue and her endless supply of negativity sprang to mind. Ryan grunted. "Not everybody gets along."

"If you mean Sue, she doesn't count. She's a bitter old woman who wants you to mourn Shelly for the rest of your life. Lara's an incredible lady, not to mention hot as
. . ."

"Hey."

"Just an observation, pal." Norris smiled. "I'll admit, the racial difference was a concern for me."

"What do you mean, it was a concern?"

"Not like that. You know me, Ryan. A woman is a woman. I don't care what she's wrapped in, so long as she's all female when she's unwrapped. I just didn't want the prejudice of the world to throw a bucket of cold water on your happiness. From your initial reaction to Lara, I thought you were just caught up in the moment of finding a woman who made you remember you were a man, and not just a parent."

"And now?"

"I think you two are a juggernaut. If telling her your dead wife's ghost has been visiting you didn't send her screaming from your house, you know she's one of the great ones. You two are perfect together, and anyone who can't see that is either blind or stupid. Her parents are going to love you."

"You really think so? You're not just saying this to make me feel better?"

"Oh, I'm saying it to make you feel better, too," Norris said with a chuckle, "but I do mean it."

"Thanks. It helps."

"Of course it does. Norris makes everything better."

Ryan rolled his eyes. His friend's opinion of himself was way too high. "Look, I'm going to leave you and spend some time with someone a lot prettier, softer, and tons sexier than you." He pulled out his wallet to pay for the drinks.

"Put away your money, I'll handle this. Just give Lara and Justin my best. Better yet, you guys come over tomorrow for some dessert and coffee."

"Or tea and sympathy?"

"You won't need it."

Ryan looked up. "From your lips—"

"To Lara's."

Ryan frowned, putting an immediate end to Norris's laughter.

"Just kidding, pal. I'm keeping you loosened up," Norris said. "Really, try to make it over tomorrow. Mom ordered enough food to feed a small nation and there's no way Dad and I can eat all of that alone. I could invite one of my many female friends, but with my folks visiting, I wouldn't want to give the wrong impression. I love all my women, but I don't *love* any of them. And I'm perfectly happy with this arrangement."

"For now. Pretty soon the love bug is gonna bite the hell outta you, and when it does, you'll experience true happiness."

Norris grinned. "I experienced true happiness last night. And the night before that, and the night before that . . ."

"No, man, *true happiness*. Not the weak imitation that's only physical gratification. I'm talking the real deal." Ryan inched closer to the table. "I'm going to tell you something you'll have to keep to yourself."

"You haven't seen Shelly's ghost again?"

Ryan ignored the condescension in Norris's tone. "No, and I don't think I will again. I'm happy with Lara, so I think Shelly has her peace."

Norris flashed a tight smile. "Great. Is that the secretive something?" he asked.

"No, it's about Lara. I want to make a good impression with her parents tomorrow because I have very definite ideas for her future—our future together."

"Okay."

"About her surprise party Saturday . . ."

"She's really going to be surprised, pal."

"I hope so. The idea of turning thirty is bumming her out, but I think she'll really love her party. We've all been working hard to make it a wonderful surprise for her."

"Yes, we have, but I already know this."

"Here's what you don't know." Ryan reached into his pocket and showed Norris the three-carat diamond ring he had picked up for Lara earlier. "After the party, when we're alone at her place, I plan to pop the question."

"I knew it was only a matter of time." Norris gave Ryan's arm a swat. "Congratulations! That ring is as beautiful as the woman it's for. Looks like Saturday will be one great birthday for Lara, and one incredible evening for you."

Ryan had dreamt of how incredible and magical that night with Lara would be. On top of being a great help in planning Lara's surprise party, Celeste had agreed to let Justin sleep over with Billy on Saturday. There would be no interruptions this time, just Lara and him and all the privacy and time in the world. "Norris, if it goes like I plan, it will be unforgettable."

"Celeste, it's going to be horrible." Lara dropped into one of the sixteen high-back chairs at her cousin's huge dining room table. "I just know it."

"Girl, would you get a grip, please?" Celeste sat beside her. "It won't be horrible. Why are you so worried?"

"Do you want the full or condensed version?"

"It's your dime, Cuz, whichever you want to share."

"Have you ever wanted something so much the possibility of having it scared you to death?"

"Hmmm." Celeste walked over to the china closet and poured white wine into two goblets. Returning to the table, she took a long drink from one glass, and handed the other to Lara. "Have some of this and start over."

"I don't need wine." Lara pushed the glass aside. "I need for tomorrow to come and go, so I can deal with whatever happens."

"Why are you so convinced tomorrow is going to be a nightmare? Uncle Robert and Aunt Evelyn aren't ogres, and Ryan is a terrific guy."

"Yes, he's a terrific guy. He's a terrific guy, a wonderful father, and an amazing man I love with all my heart. I love him so much, Celeste, I can't even begin to describe it."

"It doesn't keep you from trying every minute you can, though, does it?" Celeste smirked. "Tell me, what's going on in your head right now?"

"You had your doubts about Ryan. You thought being with him would hurt me."

"I was worried, Lara, but I see now I had nothing to worry about. Ryan's a great guy who loves you completely, and Justin thinks you hung the moon. Your parents won't be able to find fault in that, even if Ryan's a little paler than what they expected." Celeste laughed. "You don't need to worry."

"I want to believe that."

"Then do."

The sound of little feet pounding the carpet came closer to the room. Seconds later, a breathless Justin appeared at Lara's side. "You weren't running in the house, were you, Justin?" she asked.

Justin's brown eyes widened. "Uh," he stammered, turning to Dan and Billy who entered the room behind him.

"It's okay, Lara. I told him to run in here and ask if he could go out with Billy and me for some ice cream," Dan explained, shaking his son's hand and laughing. "Justin follows directions so well."

"Yeah, he said run, Ms. Boyd," Justin said. "Can I go?"

"Can you?" Lara returned.

Justin's face scrunched as he mouthed the question he'd asked. A second later his eyes brightened. "Oh, may I?"

Lara brushed her hand through his flaxen hair. He looked so much like Ryan it should be illegal. "I don't know. Your father is going to be here pretty soon. Maybe you should—"

"We'll be back soon." His eyes worked their magic. "Please, can I go? May I?"

Rendered helpless by his powerful, pleading gaze, she consented. "Sure, you guys have fun."

"Thank you, Ms. Boyd." Justin kissed her cheek and took off with Billy and Dan.

"That's what I'm talking about," Celeste said.

Lara touched her cheek. Justin's kisses were sweeter than the finest chocolate in the world. "What?"

"Ryan trusts you completely with his most precious gift. You are so good with Justin, and he loves and respects you so much. Your parents will be just as charmed by him as we are."

"I want them to be just as charmed by his father."

"They will be." Celeste drank some wine.

"I wonder," Lara said. "I've been thinking about Foster."

Celeste lowered her wine glass, coughing. "What? Why?"

"I don't know. I just have."

"In what capacity?"

"My dreams." Lara took a sip of the wine. The taste was sweet and the river of warmth flowing from her throat to her stomach was comforting. She took another drink.

"Tell me it ain't so."

"I wish I could, but I can't. It started the night after I told Ryan about Foster and the way our relationship ended. Since then, I've been having this recurring dream. A very vivid and intense recurring dream."

"About Foster?"

"No, about Ryan and me."

Celeste scooted closer. "You're still just *dreaming* about it?" she whispered, as if they were in the middle of a funeral and not alone in her massive dining room. Her hand covered Lara's. "Is there some kind of problem or something?"

Lara snatched her hand away. "I assure you, there is absolutely nothing wrong with Ryan. And though it's been a long time, with a great lack of experience on my part, there's nothing wrong with me, either. Just an unbelievable number of bad-timing episodes." Lara took another drink of the wine. "Not much room for spontaneity with a five-year-old around."

"I can relate. Tell me about this dream."

"Well, I'm with Ryan, and we are . . ." Lara paused, her thoughts drifting to the titillating details of the dream. She pressed her hand to her neck. Pulse points pounded under her fingertips.

"Girl, are you all right?"

Lara nodded. "Yeah, I'm fine." She quenched her dry throat with more wine. "Anyway, in the dream, Ryan and I are—we are very happy. We're in each other's arms and . . ."

"I get the picture, okay?" Celeste broke in. "Go on."

"Ryan had just made the world move for me, and in the next moment I hear 'Hello, Lara,' from Foster. Right out of the blue. Then, I wake up."

"That's the dream?"

"Yep."

"And you haven't told Ryan about it?"

"No!"

"Don't you think you should?"

Lara scoffed. "Of course I should," she mocked. "I can see it now. *'Ryan, I've been having this dream of you and me making mind-numbing love, and at the conclusion of our passion, I hear my ex-fiancé's voice saying hello to me.'* Yeah, Celeste, that will go over real well."

"It was just a suggestion."

"I don't understand where Foster is coming from." Lara groaned. "I know I don't love him anymore."

"But for the longest time Foster was the only man you ever loved, and he's still the only man you've ever . . . well. I think that has a lot to do with it. And maybe it's something more."

"What more? Tell me what you think, Celeste. I really want some answers."

"Okay. I think this is some sort of defense mechanism for you." She reached for Lara's glass. "More wine?"

Lara covered the rim and shook her head. "A defense mechanism?"

"Why not? You never had your heart's desire when you were with Foster, but you were achieving it, and he wanted you to close the door on it. With Ryan you have your career, love, and a little boy who adores you. You guys are an unofficial family. Tomorrow's dinner is the test. He's meeting the folks—the whole family. Everybody loved Foster, but he turned out to be a dud. If they don't like Ryan, it's going to break your heart."

Celeste paused for a sip of wine. "Maybe you're thinking about Foster as a reminder of how things can turn out when it looks like they are going so well," she explained. "Sort of like a cushion to buffer the fall from Cloud Nine. As much as you love Ryan, you waited a long time to tell him about Foster because you were afraid to trust your feelings. I think this dream is more of the same, just on a different scale."

"I never thought of that."

"Of course not. You're too close to the situation."

"I think that's it." She gave Celeste a hug. "Thank you."

"Whatever I can do. You and Ryan won't be alone tomorrow. Dan and I are on your side. There are going to be a lot of personalities in this room, and Ryan will probably feel overwhelmed, but you guys are going to be okay." Celeste pulled out the case of silverware. "Now, I think we should finish getting this room set up."

The doorbell rang in the midst of their polishing. Lara stood. "I'll get that, it's probably Ryan." She raced to the door. Her heart skipped a beat at the sight of his smiling face. "Hey, you," she said, pulling him into a passionate kiss.

Ryan licked his lips after the fiery kiss. "That's what I call a hello." He held her closer to him. "Maybe I should go back to my car and come up to the door again."

"You don't need to leave to get seconds." Leading him inside, she pushed him against the wall and covered his mouth with hers. Ryan wasted no time taking control of the kiss. His tongue was demanding, but his lips soft and tender as they caressed hers. Moans filled the foyer while active hands and probing tongues happily explored.

"Ahem! Y'all wanna take that to a hotel? This is a big house, but we're not renting rooms," Celeste playfully chided. "All the heat is causing my paint to peel."

Lara's laughter brought an end to the kiss. "It's her fault," Ryan said, still holding her close. "She attacked me."

"Uh-huh. I see you put up one heck of a fight to get away."

"What can I say? I'm a man in love." He walked over and gave Celeste a kiss on the cheek. "How are you?"

"Not nearly as good as you. The person I like to kiss has taken Billy and Justin out for ice cream."

"That explains all the quiet I hear. Not that I would hear them anyway," he said, scanning the cavernous structure before returning to Lara's side. "Where's the rest of your brood?"

"Danny is down for what I hope is the night, and Diana's over at a friend's.

"She didn't want to hang out with a bunch of old ladies," Lara explained. "How she got a bunch out of two and old out of twenty-nine is beyond me. I can see her calling her mother old, but *moi?*"

"Unless I'm mistaken, Miss *Moi*, you have a big birthday coming up this Saturday," Celeste remarked with a broad grin.

Lara groaned. Dragging into the living room, she fell face down on the couch. "Don't I have enough on my plate without you reminding me I'm turning th—th—" She shook her head. "I can't even say it."

"Thirty," Ryan and Celeste said in unison.

"Diana's right. I am old. In three short days, my twenties are going to be over. *Over!* I'm going to be th—th—"

"Thirty," Ryan and Celeste repeated.

Lara smashed her face in the cushion, smothering her anguished moans.

"Turning thirty's not so bad, sweetheart," Ryan said. "I did it two years ago and I didn't spontaneously combust. Imagine that."

She raised her head, giving him the evil eye. His smile disappeared. "It's different for me. I'm a woman."

Celeste waved. "Yoo-hoo, I'm a woman, and I didn't spontaneously combust when I turned thirty, either."

Lara fired the same hard glare at her cousin. "Whose side are you on? Let me wallow in my self-pity for a little while."

"Wallow away, dear heart. You have five minutes to yourself before joining Ryan and me in the dining room. We need to finish setting things up."

Ryan kissed her forehead and followed Celeste out.

Lara looked around the empty room. She couldn't believe they'd abandoned her in her time of need to go polish silverware.

She shook her head. Preoccupation with Thanksgiving had put her worries about her birthday on the back burner. She knew she drove both Celeste and Ryan nuts with her "Woe is me, I'm going to be thirty" moping, but they didn't understand. They had both experienced marriage and parenthood by thirty, and she hadn't done either. She hadn't left her mark on the world, and in three short days she would reach the three-decade plateau. One score and ten. The big three-o. "Oh!" She smashed her face into the couch.

A cool, sticky hand brushed the hair from her face. "Ms. Boyd, what's wrong?"

Lara sprang upright at the sound of Justin's worried tone. "Nothing," she answered with an extra wide smile,

There was nothing worse in this world than Justin being sad. If her being happy made him happy, "Cheerful" was her new first name. "I was just being a silly old goose."

"Old goose? You're not an old goose, Ms. Boyd. You're a pretty lady who makes me this happy," he said, extending his arms as far as they could go.

"No, you make me that happy." She wrapped her arms around him and gave him a loud kiss on the cheek. Justin giggled. "That ice cream had to be really good, but it looks like you got more on your face and hands than in your stomach. Your sweet face is looking extra sweet right now."

"It was yummy in my tummy." Justin patted his stomach. "I had chocolate."

"I can tell," she said, rubbing her thumb around his chocolate-covered mouth. "What happened to Billy and Dan?"

"They saw Daddy and Ms. Celeste talking in the other room and went in there. You sounded sad so I came in here. You're not sad anymore, are you?"

"No, I'm not sad anymore. My favorite little burst of sunshine has made me feel loads better." She pressed a kiss to his forehead. "Thank you, Justin."

"For what?"

"For helping me remember what's important."

"Am I important?"

"You are very important."

"And Daddy?"

"Yes, your daddy, too. You are the two most important men in my life."

"Because you love us?"

"Yes. Very much."

Justin flung his arms around her shoulders. "I love you, too, Ms. Boyd." His arms tightened around her. "I hope Daddy makes you my mommy."

Lara squeezed Justin close to her. To hear him say those words made her realize how much she wanted that, too. Celeste had said they were an unofficial family. Lara squeezed Justin close to her. If she had one wish, it would to be to drop the "un" and make it the real thing. Tomorrow had to go well. She couldn't bear anything else.

"Is this a special Lara/Justin hug, or can daddies get in on them, too?" Ryan asked from the doorway.

Lara pressed her forehead to Justin's. "What do you think?" Justin nodded. "You got the thumbs-up, Andrews."

Ryan barreled over to the couch and threw his arms around them, raining kisses on both their necks. He stopped suddenly, his gaze on Justin. "Somebody's sticky."

"I had chocolate ice cream," the boy explained.

"What do you know, I had a little bit of that myself."

Ryan's eyes roamed over Lara's body, the intensity all but melting the clothes from her body. Her skin prickled with want. She pointed in the direction of the half bath in the far corner. "Justin, why don't you run on in and wash the ice cream off your face and hands," she suggested, her eyes fixed on Ryan's mouth. He licked his lips. Her heart pounded.

"You gonna help me?" Justin asked.

Lara nodded, but her gaze stayed on point. "Sure. You run on in and I'll be right there."

"Okay." Justin raced across the large room.

"Don't run, son," Lara and Ryan advised, neither breaking eye contact.

"Sorry."

At the sound of running water, Lara plunged into Ryan's open arms. He lay on the thickly carpeted floor, bringing her to rest on top of him. He gripped her waist. The bulge in his jeans strained against her. "Do you feel what you do to me?"

"Mmm-hmm." Her lips nuzzled his neck. "I assure you, I'm feeling every bit of the female equivalent."

His hands cupped her backside, squeezing and molding each side like sculptor's clay. "Is that so?"

"Yes, that's so." She closed her arms about his head, claiming his lips in a deep kiss.

"Ms. Boyd!" Justin shouted.

"I'm coming, sweetheart," she answered between kisses.

Ryan chuckled. "Interesting choice of words."

"Soon."

"Very soon," he mumbled against her lips before helping her to her feet.

Lara cast a final lingering glance at Ryan as she backed toward the bathroom. *Please, God, let tomorrow go well. Please.*

CHAPTER 15

Lara had gotten very little sleep. Worry about the dinner had her tossing and turning all night. And when she was finally able to sleep, she had the dream again. Last night it seemed more real than ever. Glad she decided to stay over at Celeste and Dan's, Lara rose before dawn and proceeded to the kitchen to bake some sweet potato pies.

The baking calmed her, but not nearly enough. When Ryan and Justin arrived hours later, she was still a bundle of nervous energy. "Hi, hi," she chirped, waving her hands from side to side as father and son entered the kitchen. "Where's Billy?"

"Celeste grabbed him and my cake when we came in," Ryan answered, placing a covered casserole dish on the counter. He drew a deep breath. The mouthwatering aromas of roast turkey, ham, collard greens, macaroni and cheese, and freshly baked pies filled the air. "It smells great in here."

"Wait till you taste it."

"I can't wait." He gave her lips a peck. "Good morning, beautiful."

"Good morning." She gave his cheek several light-ning-fast caresses before streaking over to Justin. "How are you this morning?"

"Good." His little eyebrows furrowed into a curious line. "Ms. Boyd, did you have too much vanilla coffee?"

"Amazingly, I haven't had a drop. Why do you ask?"

"Because you're moving around a lot. Just like Daddy when he drinks too much of his coffee. He says it makes him jump around."

"I think you mean jumpy," Ryan said.

"Yeah, that."

"I guess I'm a little jumpy," Lara confessed, "but it's not because of my vanilla coffee."

Curiosity and concern jostled for position in Ryan's eyes. He tapped Justin's shoulder. "Hey, big guy, why don't you run upstairs and help Billy put away his things."

"Okay." Justin dashed out of the kitchen.

Lara prepared herself. Twenty Questions would begin at any moment.

"Celeste assigned me salad duty, so I should get started," Ryan said, removing his sports coat and hanging it on the back of a nearby chair. Taking the assortment of fresh salad veggies from the fridge, he dropped them in the sink without a word.

"Andrews, what are you waiting for?"

He shrugged, rolling his sleeves to his elbows. "Whatever do you mean?"

"You sent Justin away so you could grill me, but you haven't started yet." She handed him a bib-style apron with "Kiss the Cook" written on the front.

"I don't want to grill you, babe. I'm just making myself available for you when you're ready to talk." He tied on the apron and ran cold water over the vegetables.

Lara joined him at the sink and kissed his cheek.

Ryan smiled. "What was that for?"

Backing against the counter, she motioned to the front of the apron.

He turned off the water. "But I'm not cooking."

"You may not be standing in front of a stove, but to me you're always cooking."

He flashed a wolfish grin. "You should check out my stirring technique."

Her cheeks, and the rest of her, burned at his naughty play on words.

"You're blushing."

"That's not all I'm doing." She draped her arms around his neck and met his lips in a lingering kiss.

"You feel better?" Ryan asked.

"Yes and no." She caressed his cheek. "Thanks to you I'm not nervous anymore, but I'm definitely something else."

He smiled. "Glad I could help. And I'll be sure to help with that other problem soon, too." His hands traveled gingerly up and down her arms, calming and exciting her all at once. "You were stressing again about my meeting your family, huh?"

"Again wouldn't be accurate. The stages of nervousness just change from time to time. Aren't you nervous?"

"Kinda, I think. I'm concerned with making a good impression. I really want them to like me."

"Me, too. Your parents totally embraced me. I want my parents to do the same to you."

"Maybe lightning will strike twice."

She buried her face in Ryan's chest, holding him tight. "I'm keeping my fingers crossed."

━━━

Ryan watched as Lara checked her watch for the tenth time in half as many minutes. His heart went out to her. She was so nervous, even more than him. On the outside she exuded total confidence, looking absolutely sensational in a black pantsuit, but on the inside, he knew she was falling apart.

He took her hand. It felt like ice. "Sweetheart, relax," he said, rubbing her hand between his. "It's going to be fine."

Lara gave him a tight smile and nodded, but practically hit the ceiling when the doorbell rang. "It's them! They're here." She leapt off the couch. Justin and Billy scattered from the cars they were playing with to make a path as she raced to the stairs. "Celeste, Dan, Diana, they're here!"

Billy bounded up the stairs. "I'll get them, Cousin Lara."

"Thanks, Billy." She returned to the living room, linking her arm with Ryan's. "They're here."

"I know." The doorbell chimed again. "I think you might want to get that."

"You're right."

"Want me to come with?"

"No, you stay here, and I'll bring them to you." She took a deep breath and headed for the door.

"There's my baby girl." Ryan shuddered at the booming male voice. The acoustics in this house were unreal. There was no way the Monroes didn't hear her calling for them. "You look wonderful, Lara."

"So do you, Daddy."

Ryan's heart pounded. *Daddy*. He drew a breath. This was really happening. He held Justin's hand as they waited for everyone to enter the room. He felt like a six-year-old waiting for his name to be called during the church Easter program.

Children's laughter grew closer and in the next moment five young people ranging in age from about four to twelve came bounding into the room. The youngest of the group, a little girl with two curly jet-black ponytails and caramel skin, approached. "Hi, who are you?"

Ryan stooped to her eye level. "I'm Ryan, and this is Justin."

"Hi," Justin said.

Hours spent looking in Lara's family albums and listening to her stories made him feel as if he knew everyone personally. The little heartbreaker before him was Lara's niece, daughter of her journalist sister, Gillian, and brother-in-law, Charles. "How are you, Miss Kayla?"

Her little mouth formed a wide "O." "How did you know my name?" she whispered.

"Magic," Ryan answered, reaching behind her ear and handing her a shiny quarter.

Her eyes sparkled like two big diamonds. "Wow!"

Ryan smiled. Kayla was impressed, and so were three of her cousins who jumped up and down shouting "Do me, do me!" He wanted this enthusiasm to spread like wildfire to the family members he had yet to meet. With the other children "done" and all smiles, the oldest, and lone holdout, had his say.

"Aw, that's an old trick." Ryan recognized the boy as T.J., son of Lara's oldest brother by two minutes, Travis. "Anybody can do that," he said.

Kayla put her hand on her hips and met her cousin with a vicious stare down. "I don't see you doing it!"

Ryan grinned. She was as sassy as Lara had described.

She turned to Ryan with a smile. "Are you Auntie Lara's boyfriend?"

"Kayla!"

Gillian entered the room and took her daughter's hand.

"I wasn't doin' nothin', Mama."

"She's right, she wasn't. And the answer to your question, pretty lady, is yes." Ryan brushed his finger against her cute button nose. Kayla giggled as he turned to her mother. "Hi, you must be Gillian."

"You must be right."

He shook his head and took her extended hand. "No, I must be Ryan, but I hope your parents think I'm right." Gillian laughed. "It's nice to finally meet you. Lara's said lots of wonderful things."

She raised a curious eyebrow. "I bet not all wonderful."

Ryan smirked. "Mostly all wonderful."

Mr. Boyd's powerful voice flowed into the living room. "So, Lara, now that all the hugging is over, where is that young man you've been talking about? I can't wait to meet him."

The slight ripples in Ryan's stomach were now full-fledged tidal waves. He sucked in a breath.

"Don't worry, his bark is worse than his bite," Gillian whispered. "Lara has said many great things about you, too, and so far they all seem true. Just be yourself. It'll be fine."

Hearing someone else say those words came as a welcome relief. "Thank you."

Lara's voice drew closer. "He's right in here," she said.

Ryan smoothed his hand along the front of his sports coat. Maybe he should have worn a tie. Lara walked in with her family. A chorus of soft but audible gasps of surprise reached his ears. Gillian didn't seem shocked by him, but it appeared everyone else was.

He studied the faces of the people surrounding Lara. He knew her father and brothers were tall, and he was no small guy, but he suddenly felt like a sapling amongst a forest of redwoods. Her parents, Evelyn and Robert, were on either side of her, and her brothers and remaining family members brought up the rear. He had a name for each and every face, but he still couldn't tell Marshall and Travis apart. One of them wore glasses today, but because neither did in the pictures, that distinction didn't help.

Lara approached. Taking Ryan and Justin's hands, she formally introduced the men in her life to her family. "Daddy, Mama, everyone, this is Ryan, and the really cute one here is his son, Justin."

"Hi," Justin said, extending his hand to the group.

Ryan watched in awe. His son was so outgoing now. Before they met Lara, Justin would have been scared to death to even walk into a room with so many people he didn't know. Now, here he was, making nice with them all.

"Hello there." Evelyn bent forward, receiving his handshake. A warm and friendly smile brightened her face. "You're as cute as Lara said."

Justin beamed. "I am?"

"Yes, you are." Evelyn straightened to normal height and offered Ryan her hand. "Mr. Andrews, it's nice to meet you."

"Ryan, please," he said, closing his hands around hers. "I assure you, the pleasure is all mine." He tried not to stare, but the resemblance between Lara and her mother was downright uncanny. At least thirty years Lara's senior, Evelyn didn't look more than forty-five.

"All right, Ryan it is." She smiled.

The tidal wave settled down. Her mom liked him. Now it was time to clear the second hurdle. Daddy. All six-foot-five, two hundred and fifty pounds of Robert Boyd. Ryan extended his hand. "Hello, sir."

Robert took Ryan's hand in an extremely firm shake. "So, you're the young man Lara's been telling us about?"

"Yes, sir, I guess that would be me." Ryan prayed the man would let go of the death grip on his hand. A barber by trade, Robert owned several shops in the Virginia area, but Ryan had never realized clippers and shears could make hands so strong.

"As much as she's told us, and she's said a lot, there's *something* she neglected to mention." His gaze shot to Lara. "Isn't that right?"

Lara flashed an uneasy smile. She had taken a page from his meet-the-parents book. Ryan hoped it wouldn't backfire.

"Hi, everybody," Celeste greeted with outstretched arms.

Mr. Boyd finally released his hand. Ryan sighed in relief. Both he and his throbbing hand owed Celeste a great big thank you.

"I'll talk more with you later, son," Robert promised, before accompanying Evelyn to say hello to Celeste.

"Are you all right?" Lara asked after everyone dispersed into several little groups.

Ryan flexed his hand. "Yeah, I'm fine."

"I forgot to warn you about the handshake," she said, massaging his aching fingers.

"You forgot to warn me about something else, too."

"I was following your lead. You're not angry, are you?"

"No. Your family is definitely surprised, but aside from a couple of broken bones in my hand, I'm okay. I should tell you I'm in love with every woman in your family. Kayla placed her stamp on my heart when she walked in here, and all the others have since grabbed their little piece and run off with it."

She smiled. "I hope they left some for me."

"Nobody can touch the part reserved for you."

Lara stopped massaging. "Does your hand feel any better?"

He hung it like a limp dishrag. "No. I think it might need a kiss."

"All right." She pecked his hand. "Now?"

"You know what, that handshake was so strong, the pain shot up my arm all the way to my lips," he said, testing just how far he could take this wounded act.

Amusement brightened her eyes. "You expect me to believe that?"

"You ever had your father's handshake?"

"Okay, you win." She gave his lips a quick smack. "There."

Ryan frowned. "That's it?"

"For now. Marshall and Travis are coming over."

"They don't have the monster handshake, do they?" The twins' respective professions as fire marshal and homicide detective sprang to mind. Fire Marshal Marshall Boyd. Ryan found that so funny when Lara told him.

"No, they don't have the handshake."

"Which one is in the glasses?"

"Marshall," she answered.

The men approached with their wives. They were carbon copies, save for the glasses Marshall wore, and as big as their father.

"I see you still like surprises, Sis," said Travis.

"It's a good thing Dad doesn't have a weak heart," Marshall added. "There's a good chance he'd be stretched out in the middle of this too-big floor of Celeste's right now."

"Marshall?" his wife, Dale, warned. "Don't pay any attention to him, Lara. You know how he can be."

"I sure do. And I never pay any attention to anything these two bozos say, anyway. At least not since I got old enough to know better." Lara rubbed the distended abdomen of the light-complexioned woman. "You sure there aren't twins in there?"

Dale patted the side of her round belly. "Bite your tongue. There's only one baby in here, and I've got a framed sonogram at home to prove it. In two and a half months you can see the *single* little darling for yourself."

"I'm counting the minutes."

"Don't try to get off the topic, Lara," said Travis, giving Ryan a once-over. "Why didn't you tell us about him?"

The muscles in Ryan's shoulders tingled. Lara secured her hands around the swell of his upper arm. His tension lessened. Her touch worked wonders on him.

"I told you all about Ryan," she said.

Travis's wife Kat nodded. "Lara's right. She did tell us all about him."

"*Please!*" Marshall drawled. "We knew he was an illustrator, a widower, and he had a little boy. Somehow, his lack of melanin went past my ears. How about you, Travis?"

"I didn't hear about it."

Lara stiffened. Sensing her rising tension, Ryan squeezed her hand. "Does it matter?" he asked neither man in particular.

"Of course it matters," the twins said in unison.

Gillian made her way over, gazing from one brother to the other. "What's going on over here?"

"Did you know about him?" Travis asked his older sister.

"Of course. Lara told us all about him."

"You women," the twins grumbled.

Marshall and Travis had the twin thing going. Their reactions weren't Ryan's first choice, but they were being up front.

"You know what he means, Gilly," said Marshall.

"I told her," Lara admitted, "and I swore her to secrecy."

"Why?" the twins wondered.

"Because I wanted honest reactions. I guess I should be careful what I ask for, huh? I didn't plan to fall in love with Ryan, but I did. I love him, and I love his son. Is it so wrong to expect my family to at least like him?"

"I don't have anything against the guy," said Marshall.

"Neither do I," Travis added.

"But?" Ryan offered.

Celeste joined the group, her hands on her hips. "You all are way too intense over here. What's the problem?"

Marshall folded his arms and eyed his cousin with a dubious scowl. "You telling me you don't see it, either?"

"What I see is Ryan makes Lara happy. That's all that matters."

"Thank you, Celeste, but I want to hear what Marshall and Travis think," Ryan said. "Speak your minds, gentlemen."

Travis scratched the corner of his mouth just above his thick moustache. "I think we want to hear from you first."

"Travis?" Lara grumbled.

Ryan rubbed her shoulder. "It's okay, Lara. What do you want to know?" he asked her brothers.

"What do you want us to know?" replied Marshall.

"I think your sister is the most beautiful, wonderful woman in the world, and I love her with all my heart." He brushed his thumb against Lara's cheek. All traces of his tension disappeared with the warmth of her smile. "I'm an open book," he said to Marshall. "Ask whatever you want, and I'll answer."

"Whoa, whoa." Celeste waved her hands. "Before the Q & A begins, dinner is about to be served. That's what I came over to say before I got sidetracked. I have two twenty-pound turkeys, as juicy as tree-ripened Florida oranges, waiting to be consumed, and I don't want them to dry up. This conversation can keep, so save it for later," she said, her words more a demand than a suggestion as she shot a warning glare at her male cousins. "You all know the way to the dining room." She motioned for them to follow her out.

While their wives trailed behind Celeste, Marshall and Travis huddled with their father, each taking sideways glances at Ryan during their brief powwow.

Lara eyed the trio as they left for the dining room. "What are they up to?"

Ryan shrugged. "Comparing notes, maybe?" He chuckled.

"How can you laugh? This is not going the way I hoped. Ryan, I'm sorry."

"Don't apologize. It's been a while since I've been on the hot seat, but I can take it. Your father and brothers aren't doing anything my father, brothers, and I haven't done. They're looking out for you. Didn't they do this with Foster, too?"

"I guess." She stared in the direction of the dining room, the look of a lamb being led to slaughter in her eyes. "This feels different."

"It is different."

Lara whimpered softly, burying her face in his chest.

Ryan wrapped his arms around her and held her close. "But it's not in the way you're thinking, at least not totally." Lara's eyes searched his for understanding. "It's different for obvious reasons for sure, but it's mostly different in that I plan to make it the last first Thanksgiving dinner you're ever going to have."

Confusion filled her eyes. "Come again?"

"Foster was a run-through. He had two back-to-back meetings and messed up royally. The third time's the charm, babe. It's my turn, and I'm not going to mess it up."

"You're really not nervous?"

"Nope, I'm hyped." He smacked a kiss on her hand. "C'mon, it's dinnertime."

CHAPTER 16

Lara stood outside the dining room with Celeste's sterling silver coffee pot filled with steaming coffee. She drew a deep breath. Though not French vanilla, the rich, aromatic brew soothed her frazzled nerves. Dinner hadn't gone too badly, considering the elephant stampeding around the table.

Discussion about the delicious food items and sports kept the conversation light and easy, but how long would this last during dessert? Lara groaned. Somebody was going mention that elephant, and soon. The question was who. Would it be her father or her brothers? They were itching to lower the boom on Ryan. She could feel it in her bones.

"Lara, where is that coffee?"

Celeste's voice shook Lara from her troublesome thoughts. Drawing a steadying breath, Lara forced on a smile and entered the room. "It's right here," she said.

Lara served the coffee and then returned to her seat to dig into a piece of Ryan's sinful German chocolate cake. Moments into her first bite, her father cleared his throat.

"I think we've avoided the issue long enough," Robert said.

Lara rolled her eyes. She managed to swallow the cake that suddenly tasted like cardboard. Ryan lowered his forkful of potato pie and directed his attention to Robert.

Her father sat on the opposite side of the table, just to the right of Ryan and herself. Far enough so he couldn't reach across the table and strike Ryan if things got out of hand, but close enough to have a discussion without shouting to be heard.

Celeste lowered her water glass. "What issue would that be, Uncle Robert?"

Lara smiled. Good old Celeste.

Robert's eyes flashed annoyance. "Celeste, you're too smart a woman to play dumb." Celeste hung her head. "I'm speaking of Lara's guest." He turned his attention to Ryan. "You've known my daughter for how long, Mr. Andrews?"

"Please, Mr. Boyd, call me Ryan."

"Are you avoiding my question?"

Ryan shook his head. "No, sir."

"Then answer it. My sons told me you said you would answer any questions they had. I hope your offer extends to me."

"Certainly."

"Good, because I have a lot of them. I've only asked one, and you already seem evasive."

"Not at all, sir. I'd just prefer you call me Ryan."

"Fine. You've known my daughter for three months, correct?"

Ryan held Lara's hand and smiled. "Fourteen weeks today."

"Ah, that's so sweet," Gillian cooed, as the other ladies nodded and smiled.

"I hear you draw pictures for a living," Robert said.

"Daddy?" Lara scolded, while her brothers gibed and laughed like matching hyenas. *What was wrong with the three of them today?*

Ryan jiggled her hand. "It's okay, sweetheart," he said. "I guess that's an apt way of putting it, sir. I illustrate children's books."

"That's your real job, not some hobby?"

"Yes, sir."

"I see." Robert took a long drink of water. "Thanksgiving is a big event for the Boyd family. It's the one time of year when we all meet under one roof. When someone invites a guest, it's a very big deal."

"I'm aware of that, and I feel honored to be here."

Lara gave Ryan's hand an encouraging squeeze. So far, he was handling himself very well.

"You must think an awful lot of yourself to accept this invitation after knowing Lara for just three months."

"Robert?" Her mother slapped a warning swat to his shoulder.

Lara smiled. Her father had that coming.

"It's okay, Mrs. Boyd," Ryan said. "I can see how you would look at it that way, Mr. Boyd. I don't suffer from delusions of grandeur, but I do think an awful lot of your daughter. I love her very much, and it makes me so proud to know she feels the same way." Ryan kissed Lara's hand, filling the quiet room with a chorus of "ahs."

"So, you're widowed?" Robert continued, seemingly unfazed by the affectionate display or the reactions to it.

"Yes, sir, just over three and a half years."

"When did you take off your wedding band? It couldn't have been too long ago, the tan line is still visible."

Ryan's face paled. Heads dropped and forks scraped dessert plates.

Lara knew the disclosure of two weeks wouldn't go over well, and if Ryan mentioned Shelly's ghost, everyone would think she'd hooked up with a whack job. She hadn't even told Celeste that little tidbit of information. This line of questioning had to stop. "Daddy?"

"He said he would answer any questions I had. That's a question I have. When did you take off the ring?"

"It's not important," she said.

"Why won't you let the man talk, Lara?" Marshall asked. "Your interruptions make me think he's hiding something."

"Yeah," Travis added. "I bet he's living off his wife's insurance policy." The hairs on Lara's neck stood on end. Audible gasps resonated around the table. "What kind of a living can he make from drawing pictures, anyway?"

Ryan's jaw clenched. He balled the linen napkin in his hand. Lara prayed he wouldn't blow as she stared at his chalk white knuckles. After several moments, he spoke.

"I make quite a good living at what I do, Travis, and before that I made an even better living as an advertiser," Ryan explained, his voice calm and tone surprisingly low and even. "I don't need insurance money to make ends meet. My ends are meeting quite well, and it's from hard work and sound financial investments. I have never used a dime of insurance money from Shelly's death. If you must know, I gave that money to her mother. She, in turn, put it in a trust for Justin."

Ryan reached for his water glass and took several small gulps. "As for Lara breaking in, I think she's trying to protect my image where you, your brother, and your father are concerned. I removed the ring two weeks ago."

Lara braced herself for the explosion.

"Two weeks ago?" Robert and the twins thundered.

"Yes," Ryan said.

"You've been widowed over three years, you've known my daughter just over three months, you say you love her—"

"I do love her, Mr. Boyd."

"Then what was the purpose of holding on to the ring? Was Lara competing with your wife's ghost and finally won you over?"

Lara slammed her eyes shut. Her father had the ghost part right, but he was way off base.

"Of course not," Ryan answered. "I've loved Lara from almost the moment I saw her. Wearing the ring didn't—"

"Let's talk about that."

"What *that*, sir?"

"What you see when you look at my daughter. Do you see what we see when we look at Lara?"

"I don't understand what you're asking."

"Neither do I," Lara added.

"Of course you do. You two need to get your heads out of the sand." Robert fixed hard, questioning eyes on Ryan. Lara braced herself. This would not be good. "My daughter is a black woman. Do you not know that?"

"Of course I know that!" Ryan sucked in a breath, then added much more softly, "Sir."

The room grew quiet. Lara shook her head. *Could this get any worse?*

Robert took a swallow of the steaming coffee and stabbed a fork into his pecan pie. "Looks like I struck a nerve," he said, eating the pie.

"I apologize for raising my voice, Mr. Boyd. I meant no disrespect." Ryan paused for a long moment. He was the loudest thinker Lara knew. If standing, she knew he would be pacing right now. "I look around this room and I see so many things, Mr. Boyd. There are people, furniture, food, plates, and glasses. But there are also things I can't see, like love, and the familial bond of care and concern. All these things are present in this room, you can feel all of them, even if you can't see them."

Travis looked down the table at his twin. "Marshall, did you bring your violin?"

"Yes, I'm playing it now." Marshall performed the mock motion before glaring at Ryan. "You want to get to the point?"

"The point is, skin color is being made an issue here, and as I look around this room, there are no two people, with the possible exception of you two funny gentlemen, who are the same color."

"But we're all the same race. Black," the twins replied.

Lara fumed. Her brothers finished each other's sentences all the time, but today she found it downright nerve-wracking, and she wanted to strangle both of them. They were going out of their way to be mean, and she couldn't understand why.

"Let's take this a step further," Ryan said. "I'm not black, but I'm human. That's a race we share. Falling in love with Lara and dating her has opened my eyes to so many things. Like how people make such a big deal out of race. My skin color has nothing to do with how I feel about her. Right now, my son is in the playroom having the time of his life. He couldn't care less that the children he's playing with don't look like him. It just doesn't matter."

Robert finished the last of his pie and said, "It's different. He's a child."

"When does it change, and why does it have to? Lara and I have had our share of disapproving whispers and glances since we got together. I never realized how full of hate and judgmental people could be. Shelly's mother is not at all happy with us, but my parents couldn't be more pleased. I've gotten mixed reactions from the crowd here, and I hope the unfavorable responses become positive, but even if they don't, I won't stop loving or wanting to be with Lara. It just won't happen."

"So, in a nutshell, you're saying you don't care what we think?"

Lara groaned. What was wrong with the men in her family today? "Daddy?"

"He said it, Lara."

"No, sir, that's not at all what I'm saying," Ryan corrected. "I do care what you think, I care very much, but what you think won't change my feelings. Lara means the world to me, and I'll withstand stares, whispers, your disapproval," his gaze shot to the twins' side of the table, "intrusive questions, and whatever else I have to if it means we'll be together. With Lara by my side, there's nothing I can't handle, and I think she feels the same way about me."

"I do," Lara answered, loving the sound of those two words.

Justin's head peeked into the room. "Ms. Boyd?"

Lara motioned him in. "What is it, Justin?"

He nudged his head to someone outside. "Come in, Billy." Billy followed his friend into the room, stopping at the outstretched arms of his grandmother.

"Did you want something?" Lara asked, hugging Justin to her side.

"Uh-huh. We want some cake, but Diana said we couldn't leave the playroom because everybody was talking in here, and we'd better keep our little—" He paused. "She said a bad word."

Celeste's eyes widened. "She did?"

"Yep," Justin said as Billy nodded in agreement.

"What did she say?"

Justin searched Lara's face for permission to speak the foul word. "It's okay to say it," she said, "but just this time."

"That's what she said!" Billy announced.

"What did she say?" Dan questioned.

"Butts," Justin said. The group snickered. He looked around. "What's so funny?"

Lara rubbed her hand over his tummy. "Nothing, sweetie, finish telling your story."

"Diana said we better keep ours in there. We wanted some cake, Ms. Boyd. So, when Diana got on the phone, Kayla, TJ, Jerry, Lindy, and Ross made sure she wouldn't look, and me and Billy came for the cake."

"We have to bring them some back," Billy said, explaining the incentive for their partners in crime.

"Can I have some cake?" Justin asked.

"Can you?"

Justin placed his head on her shoulder. His eyes worked their magic. "May I please have some cake?"

"Of course," Lara said.

"Can I . . ." Billy shook his head and started again. "May I have some cake, too, Mama?"

"Sure," Celeste answered. "I think everybody should have cake. I do believe all the grown-ups have finished talking now." She shot her uncle and cousins pointed stares. "Haven't they?"

Marshall and Travis glanced at Robert. He tilted his head slightly forward. The twins smiled and said, "We're finished."

Lara sighed. "Good!" She didn't understand the strange behavior of the men in her family, but was so glad to end the interrogation she didn't dare question it. She touched Justin's cheek. "You and Billy run and get the others and then you can have your cake," she told him.

"Okay."

She caught his arm before he got too far. "I didn't mean *run* run, Justin."

"Oops, I forgot."

"That's okay." Lara patted his bottom. "You guys go on." Lara turned back to the table. Her mother's perpetually pleasant face looked even more so. "Mama, why are you grinning?"

"You have such an amazing rapport with Justin."

"That's putting it mildly," Ryan said. "When Lara's around, I become the invisible man to my son. I'm now a close second in his eyes, and I've learned to accept that."

"All this in three months?" Robert said.

"Fourteen weeks," the group corrected.

"Right, fourteen weeks."

The squealing children came rushing into the room. "We want cake. We want cake," they sang.

"Cake you shall have. Cake you shall have," Celeste chimed in response. "Cohostess, come give me a hand."

Lara kissed Ryan's cheek. "I'll be right back."

"I'll help," he offered, standing.

Robert wiped his mouth and pulled from the table. "Let the ladies handle it, Ryan," he said, dropping the napkin to his empty dessert plate. "I'd like a word with you alone."

Panic swept through Lara's body. Her father alone with Ryan was not a good idea at all. "Daddy, uh, look, I think I . . ." Robert's raised hand ceased her words. "I said alone, baby girl. Don't worry, I'll be sure to bring him back in one piece."

"It'll be fine, Lara," Ryan said. "You go help Celeste. I won't be gone long."

Lara stared after the two men long after they left. Celeste dragged her to the sideboard. "Come on."

"Is it okay if we have a slice?" Marshall asked for himself and Travis as the women dished the cake.

Lara looked at the ceiling. "Celeste, do you hear something?"

"Don't be like that, Sis. This was planned."

She glared at Marshall, suspicious but piqued. "What was?"

"Our behavior," Travis answered. "It was a test. Ryan passed."

"What?"

Justin raced to Lara's side. "Are you all right?" he asked.

The boy's heart pounded against his chest. Lara brushed her hand against his hair. The way Justin worried about her was so sweet, but he would give himself a coronary if he kept this up. "I'm fine, honey. My brothers just—they said something that took me by surprise."

"Like the trick Daddy showed you in his room when you screamed real loud?"

Lara squeezed her eyes shut. *He did not just say that.*

"Yeah, Lara, like that trick?" her mother asked, joining them at the dessert table.

Ready for a quick exit, Lara extended the saucer to Justin. "Honey, here's another piece of cake. Why don't you and I go . . ."

"Go share the cake with Billy instead, Justin," Celeste broke in. "I think he'd really like another piece."

"Okay." Justin dashed off to his friend.

A slow death from embarrassment ravaged Lara's body, but her family refused to let her succumb in peace. Four pairs of eyes burned holes through her.

"So, Ryan showed you a trick in his room?" Evelyn said with a smirk. "I'm no prude, Lara. Which trick was it?"

Lara hugged her arms around her trembling body, desperate to ward off the discomfort she found in this particular conversation. "Mama, please, this is not a conversation for mixed company." *Or the kind you had with your mother.* Her gaze drifted to her brothers. "Besides, I want to know what you guys were talking about before Justin shot over here."

Marshall nibbled a few bite-size morsels of cake from the crystal stand. "It's just what we said. It was a test." He licked his fingers. "This is delicious cake."

"Ryan baked it," Celeste shared.

"He did?" the twins marveled.

Lara nodded. "Yes, he did. But enough about cake, tell me about this test."

"Oh, that." Travis snatched up the last piece of cake before Marshall could reach it. He gave his brother a triumphant grin. "I'll always be first and fastest, never forget."

Marshall gave his brother a disgusted frown. "Two minutes," he grumbled. "Since *he's* going to have his mouth full, I'll explain. You told Gillian about Ryan. She told Charles, who let it slip to Travis. Travis told me, we told Dad, and together we devised this plan. Lara, the way you talked about Ryan was unbelievable, and up until a few months ago, Foster was still an unresolved issue for you."

"We didn't want you hurt again," Travis added between bites of cake. "We were glad you finally found someone new to care about, but Ryan being white gave us a moment's pause, so we decided to test him. How he reacted to our worst behavior, meddlesome questions, and the issue of race in your relationship. Any and everything you could encounter being with him, and even things you wouldn't, we wanted him to experience. He couldn't be too sensitive, because if he was, he wouldn't be right for you. Ryan did very well, and we tried our best to shake him up."

"Uh-huh." Marshall nodded in agreement.

Lara gazed from one brother to the other, searching their faces for confirmation. "So, all of that in the living room and in here with the violin thing was a test?"

Marshall nodded. "Yep."

"Mama, did you know about this?"

"No, I was completely in the dark," Evelyn answered, "and if anyone should have known about this, it's me. I didn't know my family was so good at keeping secrets."

"I would have told you, Mama, but I wanted honest reactions to Ryan and our relationship. It seems yours was the only one."

Travis finished the cake in record time. "Here's our honest reaction," he said, licking his fingers. "Ryan's a nice guy and a great cook. Didn't he do that bean casserole?"

"Yeah."

"And the way you are with his son." Evelyn smiled as she watched Justin play with Billy and the other kids. "Lara, that boy is totally in love with you. I can see you feel the same."

Lara sighed. "I do, Mama. I didn't give birth to Justin, but I couldn't love him more if I did. He feels like mine."

"You're in love with his father, so of course you would love him, too. Come with me." Evelyn took Lara's hand and led her to the table. "It's good to see you so happy, Lara."

"It's good to feel this happy." They pulled out two chairs and sat. "I never thought I'd fall in love again, much less with someone so unlikely, but Ryan walked into my classroom one afternoon, stunned, nervous, and smelling like furniture polish, and I was struck. Not only by how incredibly attracted I was to him, but the way he was with Justin. He's a wonderful father and the most gentle and caring man. I love him so much, Mama. He and Justin mean everything to me."

"As well I see." She pressed her hand to Lara's cheek. "Your happiness is all your father and I want for you."

"Daddy." Lara checked her watch. "He and Ryan should have been back by now." She sighed. "I hope everything is okay."

"So, you understand why I did what I did?" A soft hiss filled the conversation lapse as Robert twisted the cap from a mini-bottle of sparkling water.

"Yes, sir, I do understand," Ryan answered, surprised to learn the behavior of the three Boyd men had been part of a test, but pleased he'd passed it. In the half hour they'd spent in Dan's study, Lara's father had said quite a lot, and every word showed how much he loved his daughter.

"I'm still worried about you two, especially with Justin." Robert returned to the couch across from Ryan and sat. "His way with Lara is just so . . ."

"Natural?" Ryan offered. Robert nodded, taking a drink from the bottle. "My son loves Lara as much as I do. He's very protective of her, and there's nothing he wouldn't do for her."

"Appears my daughter feels the same way about him. Ryan, I'm concerned for you and Lara. I could have been a lot harder on you in there, but you cut me clean off before I could give you my full treatment."

"That wasn't the full treatment?"

"No. It could be so much harder for you two, and the world won't pull back. I know interracial couples aren't uncommon, but the stigma and the problems still exist."

"You don't have to tell me, Mr. Boyd, but I'm not going to stop loving your daughter because some people in the world have a problem with us. It's their problem, not ours. Lara and I have faced every challenge that's come our way, and we'll continue to do so as a united front." Ryan paused for a moment and said, "Sir, it's my wish to make this union legal."

Robert lowered the bottle from his lips, loudly swallowing the water in his mouth. "Are you trying to ask me a question?"

"Actually, I want to ask the question to your daughter. What I want from you is your permission to ask it."

"Does Lara know about this?"

"No, sir. I'm throwing a surprise birthday party for her on Saturday, and afterward I want to ask for her hand. She'll be surprised, but I think she'll say yes."

Robert grunted. "Me, too." He finished the bottle and tossed it in the waste can.

Ryan couldn't suppress his smile. "Really?" he said.

"I'm willing to bet on it."

"Does this mean I have your permission?"

"Hmm. Well, I—uh . . ." Hemming and hawing, Robert rubbed his hands over his graying moustache. He met Ryan's gaze. "If I said no, would you still ask her?"

"Yes, sir, I would. I want to spend my life with her."

"You've only known my daughter three mon—fourteen weeks."

"I know it seems sudden, but I'm certain of this."

"This does indeed seem sudden, but you have my permission." Robert managed a smile. "You can ask my daughter to marry you."

"Thank you, sir." Ryan took Robert's hand in a grateful shake. "I promise to take care of Lara and do all I can to make her happy."

"You see to that," Robert said, his stern look only half teasing.

"You don't have to worry. I wish you could stay for her party."

"Me, too, but T.J. has his first basketball game that night, and we all promised to be there and take him out after." Robert held up a finger. "I'll expect a call when you get your answer, whatever it may be. Leave a message if we're not in."

"You'll be the first person I contact." Ryan placed a cordial hand on Robert's shoulder. "I bet Lara's thinking the worst right now. We better get back in there, Dad."

"Let's not get carried away."

Ryan smiled. "Just getting used to the sound of it, sir."

Lara pulled her coat together, braving the cool, windy weather she, Ryan, and Justin encountered at the steps of Norris's condo. Ryan's hand moved in circular motions on the small of her back. Suddenly the cool air wasn't a factor, as the heat of his touch warmed her entire body.

"You sure you up to this, Lara?" Ryan asked. "We had a very exciting day, and you've been up since before daybreak. I'm sure if we left now, Norris would understand. You must be exhausted."

"Uh-uhm, I'm exhilarated," she said, still flying sky high from how well things went. She'd practically dragged Ryan away to get him here. "Besides, I'm curious to see what kind of people can create a guy like Norris, and I promised Justin a little more cake. Right, Justin?"

He tilted his head to look up at her. "Yep."

Ryan checked his watch. "Okay, it's six now, we can stay about an hour or so." He eased close behind her, slipping his arms around her waist. Surges of desire swept through her body as his soft lips trailed a path along her neck. "Then, I'm going to take you home and—"

"And what, Daddy?" Justin asked, his brown eyes wide-open and curious.

Ryan cleared his throat. "I'm going to heat up the leftovers we dropped off on our way over and make myself a nice turkey sandwich." He tweaked Justin's nose. "I might even make a mini-sandwich just for you."

Lara smirked. Ryan was so quick on his feet.

The door to the apartment creaked opened. "Lara, I thought I heard your voice." Norris pulled her inside, holding her close. "Tell me you've come to your senses and decided to leave what's-his-face," he said, jerking his head at Ryan.

Lara laughed. "Nah, I think I'll keep him."

Norris kissed her cheek. "Oh, well, I'll take what I can get."

"Don't I know it," Ryan said as he and Justin joined them inside. "Happy Thanksgiving, Norris."

"From the bright smiles on all your faces, I think I'm correct in assuming yours was happy and then some."

Lara's fingers twined with Ryan's. Her smile grew wider. "Extremely happy," she shared, scanning the apartment. Norris had two new art pieces and his tan leather living room group was now ecru. No matter how often she came over, something was different every time. "So, where are your parents?"

"They're right—"

The approaching sound of a woman's voice interrupted Norris's words. "We heard a gorgeous little feminine voice out here and knew it had to be Ryan with his—oh." The dark-haired woman stopped speaking when she entered the room. The tall man behind her with equally dark hair stopped in his tracks.

Norris waved them over. "Mom, Dad, I want you to meet the incredible lady who had the misfortune of falling in love with Ryan. Can you believe someone this beautiful wants him?"

"I—uh, uh, no, I can't believe it," the woman stammered.

Lara's happy buzz sobered. If the Converses were trying to put up a pleasant front, they were failing miserably. After a very strained introduction, Genevieve and Harold retreated to the kitchen to get the dessert.

Oblivious to the tension, and anxious for his cake, Justin followed the elder Converses into the kitchen when they took too long coming back. A few minutes later he returned, his little face downcast.

Lara held her hand out to him. "Justin, sweetie, what's wrong?"

"I don't feel good."

She touched his forehead. "You don't feel hot."

"It's my tummy."

Lara brushed crumbs from his mouth. "Too much cake?"

He hunched his shoulder. "I dunno, it just hurts. Can we go home?"

Lara enjoyed Norris's company, but she'd be lying if she said the idea of leaving upset her.

She glanced over at Ryan, who stood immediately. "Yeah, buddy, we can go home," he said.

Norris helped Ryan gather the coats and walked them to the door. "I'm sorry you're not feeling well, Justin. A little of the pink stuff and some rest will have you better in no time."

Justin nodded. "Okay."

"I'm really sorry about all this, guys." Norris glanced in the direction of the kitchen, where after twenty minutes, his parents still remained. "This is not how I wanted the evening to turn out."

Lara rubbed his shoulder. "It's okay, Norris. It's not your fault your parents aren't feeling very sociable this evening. Your wonderful hospitality more than made up for it."

"She's right," Ryan agreed.

"You're being kind, thank you," said Norris. "Let's all do dinner on Monday—my treat. We can celebrate the wonderful turnout of the Boyd Thanksgiving dinner meeting."

"Sounds like a plan. You game, babe?"

"Free dinner?" Lara smiled. "Absolutely."

"That seals it," Norris said. "I'll swing by around six."

Norris smiled, but misery flickered in his eyes. Lara's heart went out to him. On her way out the door with the ailing Justin, she kissed Norris's cheek.

He touched the spot on his face. "What was that for?"

"It's for being a great friend to us."

The mischievous glint returned to Norris's eyes. He pressed a kiss to Lara's hand. "Well, you know, I can be a *really* good friend to you if Ryan here ever —"

"He's back," Ryan announced, leading Lara and Justin out the door as his friend laughed. "Good night, Norris."

"I'll be right up, sweetie, okay?" Lara called out to Justin as he ambled slowly up the stairs to his bedroom.

"Yes, ma'am," was his solemn reply.

Lara turned to Ryan. "I'm staying the night," she informed him, handing over her coat. "I can't stand to see my poor baby like this."

Ryan smiled. Lara's mother hen worry endeared her to him all the more. "It's just a stomachache, Lara," he said, hanging up their coats. "He'll be fine."

"I don't care. I'm staying."

"You won't get an argument from me." Ryan leaned in for a kiss, but she turned to the stairs before their lips connected.

"Good. You can keep me company in Justin's room." Lara ascended the stairs. "That's where we'll be sleeping."

"All night?"

"Yes!" she answered from the top of the stairs.

Ryan frowned as he raced up behind her. "Babe, it's just a stomachache."

CHAPTER 17

Just before noon on Saturday, Lara opened her door to find Celeste with a brightly wrapped gift.

"You're still in one piece. I'll take this to mean the clock striking twelve didn't do you in," Celeste said with a hearty laugh, extending the box as she walked in. "Happy Birthday, Cuz."

Lara shook the present to her ear. "It is so far." She motioned to the coffee table at the huge bouquet of red, yellow, and peach roses that filled the room with a wonderful scent.

"What gorgeous flowers." Celeste hung up her coat and walked over to the bountiful display, inhaling their soft fragrance. "I guess I don't have to wonder who gave you these."

"Nope." Lara dropped the gift by the vase and extended the memorized card to her cousin. "Thirty beautiful roses for my thirty-year-old Lara Rose. All my love, Ryan," she recited.

"That's so sweet."

"I woke up this morning to the smell of frying bacon and Justin jumping up and down on my bed. My two guys came over with flowers, breakfast, and a huge basket of bath and shower goodies." She smiled. "They are going to spoil me. I didn't want a big fuss over my birthday, especially this birthday, but coming from them, I can't complain."

"Where are they?"

"Out doing something. Justin was about to tell me what, but Ryan covered his mouth before he could spill the beans." Lara moved to the couch and sat. "Now I have to wait."

Celeste joined her. "I bet you wish you'd covered Justin's mouth before he mentioned the trick Ryan showed you in his room," she said, laughing. "Why is it I didn't hear about this little trick from you?"

"Where is it written I have to tell you everything?"

"Page ten of *The Best Friend/Cousin Handbook*. So, what happened?"

"Nothing."

"You were screaming in Ryan's bedroom and you expect me to believe nothing happened?"

"Yes, I do. Nothing happened."

Celeste shook her head. Doubt filled her dark eyes.

"Okay, it almost happened," Lara confessed. "It was dangerously close to happening, but Justin overheard my enthusiasm over the preliminaries, got scared, and came rushing to the room to my aid, effectively ending things before they got started. Satisfied?"

Celeste smirked. "Apparently you and Ryan aren't. With Justin at my house tonight, perhaps that little problem can be rectified. I take it he's feeling better."

"Yes, he is, although he's been a little overly concerned about Ryan and me being too hot, and offering us lots of water. I thought it might be a temperature, but it's been normal. I got him to ease up by promising to tell him if I got too hot or thirsty. I think Justin's one of those naturally hot-blooded people, because, lately, he's been asking for the thermostat to be turned down."

"I'll keep this in mind, and let Millie know, too."

"That's right, she's going to be in charge while you and Dan are at that dinner."

"Yes, the post-Thanksgiving feast for his law firm. All the partners have to be there. Does Ryan have big plans for you this evening?"

"He's taking me to Martin's, but I have big plans for us when we come back here."

"Really?"

"Yes, really. Tonight is going to be our night, no more waiting." Lara paused for a moment. "You know what's weird?"

"What?"

"Remember the dream I told you about?"

Celeste nodded. "Have you had it again?"

"Yes. It seems your guess on the cause of the dream was wrong. Things were shaky at Thanksgiving, but it turned out so well. Yet I'm still having the dream."

"You still haven't told Ryan?"

"No, but last night it seemed more real than ever."

"And Foster?"

"His voice is still there. I think moving on to the next level with Ryan is the crux of the dream. Foster saying hello is strange, but maybe the hello is really a good-bye."

"A good-bye to your celibacy?"

"Why not? That's what it is, and good riddance. The best of this dream will become a reality tonight, and I am counting the minutes." Lara frowned. "Does that make me a hussy?"

Celeste laughed. "Of course not. It makes you human. You're a young, vibrant woman with needs. It's so good to hear you talk like this." Smiling wickedly, Celeste picked up the wrapped box. "I think now is a good time to open your present."

Lara eyed the gift. "The look on your face worries me."

"Don't be worried, because what's in this box can cure what ails you, or at least make you forget you what troubled you in the first place. Go on, open it."

Lara opened the box to find a lacy black negligee. "Oh, my." She pressed the sheer garment against her chest. "Happy birthday to me."

An Arctic blast rivaling the cool temperatures outside welcomed Ryan when he stepped inside his house. He blew on his hands and rubbed them together. "Keep your coat and gloves on, Justin. It's freezing." He approached the thermostat to find the air-conditioning turned on. Maybe he'd flipped the switch in his rush to get to Lara's. Justin liked it a lot cooler lately, but he couldn't reach that high. "It should be warming up in no time, big guy."

Justin trembled on the couch. "Daddy, it's not too cold. I think it feels good," he said, his teeth chattering.

"Are you kidding?" Ryan sat on the couch and propped Justin on his knee, rubbing the boy's arms. "You're shivering."

"I think it's better to be too cold than too hot. You don't want us to burn up."

Ryan didn't understand Justin's sudden obsession with the cold, but he hoped this phase wouldn't last long. "I promise, son, I won't let us burn up, just warm up." He kissed Justin's forehead and sat him on the couch. "I'll be right back."

"Daddy, do people hurt when they burn in hell?"

Halfway off the couch, Justin's question propelled Ryan back down. "Why would you ask that?"

"Rev. Stealth talks about hell a lot at church, and I wanted to know if when people do bad things they hurt a whole lot 'cause of the fire."

"Hell isn't a fun place. That's why bad people are sent there, and yes, they hurt a lot. Remember a couple of weeks ago when you burned your tongue because you didn't wait to drink your cocoa like I asked?"

Justin nodded.

"Hell is sorta like that, but this many times worse," Ryan explained, opening and closing his hands in rapid succession.

Justin gulped. "Are good people sent there?"

"Not usually. Hell is for bad people."

"Can good people be sent there? Maybe they're always good, but then they do something that's not good."

"I guess they could." Figuring Justin and Billy had plans to torture Diana and their sitter, Millie, this evening, Ryan added, "The best thing would be for them not to do the bad thing. That way they won't have to go to hell for doing it. It's like the cocoa. If you had waited to drink it when it was cooler like I'd asked, you wouldn't have gotten burned. Does this answer your question?"

"Uh-huh."

"Okay. You get the picture you drew for Lara's birthday and I'll get her other presents and your bag for the sleepover. When that's done, we'll leave to have the party you almost told her about." Ryan tapped Justin's nose.

"Sorry, Daddy."

"That's okay, I caught you before you said too much." This party was only for the two of them and Lara and Justin almost spilled, but if he knew about the adults-only surprise party planned for later at Martin's, it would be anything but a surprise. Ryan wasn't present, but he shuddered at the thought of the reactions to the screaming trick Justin had dropped at Thanksgiving.

"I didn't mean to almost tell her," Justin said. "I love her, that's why I almost told her. I want her to be happy."

"I know. That's why it's okay. I love Ms. Boyd, too."

"You love her a lot." Justin giggled. "I see you kissing her sometimes when you think I'm not looking."

Ryan smiled. "You're sneaky." He wanted to share his plans to propose, but the minute they got back to Lara's it would be the first thing Justin would say. *"Guess what, Ms. Boyd? Daddy is gonna marry you."* Uh-uh. He couldn't risk it. "Go on and get your picture, we'll leave in a bit."

"Okay. Ms. Boyd is gonna like her surprise."

Ryan fingered the ring box in his pocket. "I sure hope she likes her surprise, son. I hope she loves it."

~

Lara tugged Ryan's hand before they walked into Martin's. "Do we have to go in there?" She slipped her hands inside his full-length tweed coat, skimming the muscular contours of his back. "I'd rather we celebrate at my place." She kissed his neck. "I have a special birthday suit I'm dying to show you."

Ryan swallowed. "Hold on to that thought, babe, please. You look like a million bucks in your green dress, and I want to show you off. We'll go back to your place right after we eat."

"Huh-uhm," Lara murmured. "I'm not hungry for food, but I am starving for you." She kissed him deeply, thrusting her tongue in his mouth. Ryan cupped her bottom. Through the thick barrier of her overcoat, she felt him stir to life. Lara swiveled her hips. A deep moan rumbled in his throat. "Let's go, Ryan, please."

After several moments he nodded. "Okay." They were almost to his SUV when Ryan's cell phone rang. He checked the number and groaned. "Sweetheart, I have to take this." He turned his back. "Yes? I know. Look, I know. I am. I will. Give me one second." Ryan lowered the phone to his side. "Lara, this might take a minute."

Lara pulled her coat around her, the November air suddenly a lot colder. "Ryan, do you have to do this now? It is my birthday, and I thought we were leaving."

"I know, but if this call wasn't important, I wouldn't take it. You know that."

"Yes, I do know," she grumbled. "Work?"

"It's definitely work." He cast a glance at the restaurant. "Since we're here, we might as well eat." He kissed her forehead. "Go in and get our table, and I'll be right there."

Lara walked into the restaurant. The aroma of baking bread greeted her. Her stomach rumbled in anticipation. Maybe staying wasn't such a bad idea after all. She just hoped they didn't get Felipe as a waiter.

After Lara waited briefly at the podium, the hostess arrived. "I apologize for the delay," said the brunette. "We're short-staffed tonight."

"No problem. I'm actually still waiting for my boyfriend to finish a call outside. Andrews," Lara said. "Six o'clock."

The woman scanned the book. "Yes, a table for two. Right this way." As she led Lara to the dining room, the phone at the podium rang. The woman looked over her shoulder.

"It's okay. I can show myself," Lara offered.

"Thank you so much. Your table is straight ahead, third on the right. A waiter will be with you shortly, and I do hope you enjoy your evening at Martin's."

"I'm sure we will."

Lara stepped into the dimly lit dining room to a collective cry of "Surprise!" She covered her racing heart. Tears flowed freely.

Moving out of the shadows, Ryan led the voices in "Happy Birthday." His soft kiss and warm embrace greeted her at the end of the familiar tune. Smiling, he brushed away her tears. "Happy Birthday, sweetheart. Surprise."

After receiving birthday greetings from everyone, Lara got hustled into a corner by Celeste.

"Do you realize you almost ruined your surprise party? I practically had to close my eyes from the show you and Ryan put on out there." Celeste shook her head. "I'm surprised he even answered his phone."

"That was you?" Lara's eyes widened. "And you saw all that?"

"Yes, and Norris, too. The party was Ryan's idea, and you had him ready to leave before it started."

"This party is wonderful, and I truly appreciate it, but I wouldn't have cried a river if I missed it." She spotted Ryan across the room with Dan and Norris. She couldn't wait to be alone with him. "Don't be upset if this party ends early."

"Did you like your party?"

Lara smiled brightly as Ryan hung up their coats. "Nope, I *loved* it. How did you manage to keep it from me?"

"It was a surprise party, sweetheart. If I told you, it would have lost an important element."

"You didn't tell Justin?"

"Uh, no," Ryan said laughing. "That's why it was still a surprise." He rubbed his hands together. "Are you cold?"

So caught up in the excitement of the evening and the anticipation of what it still promised to hold, Lara didn't realize it was freezing. "Yes, I am."

Ryan walked to her thermostat. "It's off."

"I lowered the setting earlier because Justin felt too warm, but I don't remember turning it off before we all left. He's been a bit preoccupied with temperature lately, hasn't he?"

"Yes, he has." Ryan flipped the switch and returned to her side. "But I'm sure he's toasty warm at Celeste and Dan's right now. And in a few minutes, we'll be nice and warm, too."

"Oh, Ryan." She gave him a big hug. "Thank you."

"For turning on the heat?"

"No." She laughed. "The prospect of turning thirty was—"

"Causing you to pull this lovely hair out." He gently tugged a few dangling strands from her updo. "I wanted to make this an unforgettable and very happy day for you."

"You did. This has been my best birthday ever."

"It's not over yet. There's over two hours left of your very special day, and I have a couple of surprises left."

"More surprises?"

"You're thirty today, and I think you should have thirty gifts and surprises. You got the first fourteen during breakfast and your party with Justin and me. Presents fifteen through twenty-eight are among the pile of brightly wrapped boxes and colorful gifts bags over there." He motioned to her huge stack of gifts against the wall. "Presents twenty-nine and thirty are a lot closer, and I'm ready to give them both to you. A little fair warning, these are very, very, big presents." He wriggled his eyebrows. "Very big."

His innuendo not lost on her, Lara smiled. "Bring 'em on."

Ryan led her to the couch. An uneasy laugh followed his prolonged silence. "I rehearsed this so many times, but now I can't—I can't remember what I was going to say."

"Just say it. You don't have to rehearse yourself for me."

"I know, but I want this to be just right for you. Lara, I love you so much. You're sweet, funny, kind, caring, intelligent, so very beautiful . . . I don't think there are enough adjectives to describe how incredible I think you are. So what if you can't sing." They both laughed. "Justin and I think you're perfect, and I want you in our lives forever." Ryan dropped to one knee.

A soft gasp passed Lara's lips. Tears flowed. "Ryan."

"Your love is the most wonderfully unexpected gift I've ever received, and I never want to lose it. I promise to honor you, hold you, cherish and keep you every day of my life, if you allow me the opportunity to do so." Ryan reached into his pocket and pulled out the most beautiful diamond ring. "Lara Rose Boyd, will you marry me?"

"Will I marry you?" she repeated softly.

He brushed away her tears. "I know it might seem too soon, but—"

Lara silenced him with a kiss. "I had two birthday cakes today, but only one wish. You just made it possible for my wish to come true. Yes, Ryan, I will marry you."

"You will?"

"I will."

Ryan slipped the ring on her finger, and after a too quick kiss, leapt to his feet and pulled out his cell phone. "I have to call your father. He told me to call when I got an answer."

"Daddy knew?"

"I asked his permission when we talked alone on Thanksgiving." He pressed two buttons on the phone, hugging her against him as he waited. "Voice mail." After leaving a short, but enthusiastic message, he tossed the phone to the couch and lifted Lara into his arms, spinning her round and round.

"Ryan, you're making me dizzy." She laughed.

"Sorry." He lowered her to the floor. "Are you all right?"

"I'm better than all right." She admired her newly adorned finger. "We're getting married."

"Yes, we are. Justin is going to be thrilled."

"Justin! We should call and tell him the news."

"No, no, no." Ryan shook his head. "Tomorrow. He's probably already asleep, and there's still one more present for you."

His eyes raked hungrily over her. A ripple of excitement flashed through Lara's body. "Another present?" she said.

"Uh-huh. One more." He kissed her softly and settled her on the couch. "Sit tight. I'll be right back."

While Ryan took off down the hall, Lara removed the pins from her hair and worked on a present for him. One she was sure he'd love as much as the ones she'd received all day.

Minutes later, Ryan returned. "Okay, Lara, the scene is set, your . . . Holy moly!"

Lara stood from the couch and did a slow turn, allowing Ryan a complete view of her newest ensemble. The emerald green push-up bra and panty set left very little to the imagination, and Ryan's wide-eyed, slack-jawed expression made the provocative satin and lace purchase worth every penny. With tempting, slow strides, she sauntered over. "You like?"

Ryan's eyes twinkled like the brightest stars as his gaze swept up and down her body. "I love." His fingers twined in the hair framing her face. "You are so beautiful."

"You make me feel that way. Ryan, you make me feel so many things." She linked her arms around his neck and brushed his lips with a tender kiss. "I love you so much."

"I love you, too."

No further words needed, Ryan swept her in his arms and carried her to the bedroom where Lara found the scene he had set. Dozens of candles cast a warm glow and soulful words of forever love played softly in the background. Ryan lowered her to the bed, shed his clothes, and settled alongside her.

Lara closed her eyes, breathing in the intensely masculine scent of him, enjoying the feel of his hot, bare skin against her body. She moaned softly as his lips trailed along her neck, across her shoulders, and over the swell of her breasts. Exploring hands glided from her ankles to her hips to just below her breastbone and back again. Her body tingled with thoughts of the other more sensitive places she wanted those lips and hands to venture. Liquid heat settled between her thighs. Her nipples grew hard, straining against the thin fabric of her bra, aching for his touch, puckering in wait for his kiss.

Ryan unloosened her bra and tossed it over his shoulder. Wasting no time, he lowered his head and pulled one hard, achy tip into his mouth. Squeezing and caressing the fleshy mounds, Ryan suckled her like a starving newborn. Moans rumbled deep in Lara's throat as he tasted and tormented one taut nub and then the other.

Fire raged inside Lara's belly with every stroke of Ryan's tongue. His throbbing arousal pressed against her thigh. She grew hotter, her panties wetter. Sliding her hand between them, Lara reached for his straining hardness. She needed to feel him. To hold him.

Ryan released her breast with a soft plop and grabbed her creeping hand. "Uh-uh. This night is about you," he said with a kiss. "I'm going to make it one you'll never forget."

She combed her fingers through his golden hair. Her shiny new ring sparkled. "You've already made that happen."

"No, lady, I've barely gotten started."

Kissing his way down the center of her body, Ryan stopped when he reached her belly button. Her stomach muscles tightened when his tongue dipped inside her navel. His hands at her hips, Ryan peeled away the panties and dropped them to the floor. He lowered his head, breathing in her scent. "You smell so good." He lifted her legs and spread her thighs. "I bet you taste even better."

Taste? Cries of pleasure squeezed from Lara's throat as Ryan's lips and tongue became intimately acquainted with the once-mysterious half of her. Poised and concentrated, he lapped at her femininity like a starving kitten before a bowl of warm milk. Her fingers buried in Ryan's hair, she held him fast, calling his name as he continued to please her. He kissed her deeply and thoroughly, laving her delicate folds and nipping and sucking her sensitive love bud.

Lara writhed on the twisted sheets, a boiling cauldron of sexual frustration. Never had she come so close to total fulfillment only to be dragged from the edge and brought back time and again without achieving the satisfaction her body craved. When she thought she could take no more of his decadent pleasure, Ryan slipped in a finger, and explored her even deeper.

The delicious pressure in the center of her belly built more and more. Ryan slipped in another finger. Lara's cries grew louder, her desperation more intense. She held him closer. If she didn't get some relief soon, she would go absolutely crazy. As if sensing her needs, Ryan's suckling grew louder, his movements faster.

Lara's legs trembled as the building pressure reached a pinnacle. She closed her eyes and cried out, yielding to the incredible release. Ryan stayed with her, stroking her, kissing her, loving her until she descended from her first trip to the mountaintop. When her movements stilled, and her breathing returned to normal, she met his smiling face with a smile of her own. "Thank you," she said.

"You're more than welcome. It only gets better from here."

Better? Lara couldn't imagine anything being better than that, but she couldn't wait to be proven wrong. It was a good thing she had soundproof walls, because if the neighbors could hear . . .

Keeping one hand secure between her thighs, Ryan kissed his way up her body while the other hand squeezed and caressed. He came to a stop at her breasts. His tongue laved her erect nipples. Sensual bites teased and engaged them. Before too long the sweet tightening in her loins returned. Every brush of his thumb against her aroused and well-lubricated nub sent shock waves racing up and down her spine. She could feel his hardness straining against her upper thigh, pounding, pulsing, aching for a tight, warm place to rest.

Snaking her arm between their meshed bodies, she took possession of his throbbing arousal. His movements inside her paused as she glided her fingers up and down his length. He pressed himself against her hand, moaning his approval.

That sound all the motivation she needed, Lara applied more pressure, moving her fingers up and down his steely shaft. She nibbled his neck and shoulders before moving to his chin and lips. Their tongues met. She plundered his mouth, tasting and exploring every nook and cranny in much the same way she wanted him to explore her when their bodies became one. Ryan's moans grew louder.

Throbbing wildly in her hand, Ryan broke the kiss, and stared deeply in her eyes. "I need you now, Lara." Grabbing the box of condoms from her nightstand, Ryan ripped open a foil pack and sheathed his length with the extra-sensitive sheepskin. "I'll be so gentle with you," he promised, guiding himself inside her, inch by inch. "So gentle."

She whimpered softly, as six years brought some resistance, but Ryan was true to his word and gentle. As he paused to give her time to accept what he had to offer before giving more, the initial pain soon made way for pleasure. With complete penetration achieved, she adjusted to his dimensions, clamping down around him.

Ryan began to move. She pulled him in deeper and deeper still as his hips ground against hers. Dueling tongues moved in time to the gyration of their hips as they searched for and found their perfect rhythm.

Lara didn't know intimacy could be like this. So enticing, so liberating, so incredibly fulfilling. There were no doubts with Ryan, no inhibitions. She wanted him as much as he wanted her, and she wanted to please him as much as he'd already pleased her.

Turning Ryan over, she straddled his waist, rocking back and forth. A loud curse, or maybe it was a demand, flew from his mouth as he groaned.

Lara threw her shoulders back and smiled. "If you insist," she replied saucily as she increased her pace. He held fast to her bucking hips. She leaned forward, laving his hard nipples, enjoying the salty taste of his sweat-glistened skin and deep moans of satisfaction her pleasure gave him.

Ryan flipped her beneath him. A soft grunt fell from her lips as he buried himself inside her and delivered a series of deep thrusts. Lara wrapped her legs around his waist and cupped his backside, riding the waves he stirred within her as his lips reclaimed hers. The intense pressure returned, but she didn't want the journey to end. Not yet. She sensed the same from Ryan as he slowed his frenetic pace.

Holding her legs against his waist, he eased in and out at a snail's crawl—staving off the inevitable for a while longer. Lara watched through passion-filled eyes as their bodies moved together as one—his slow retreat and swift reentry—over and over and over again. Her fire burned hotter. Their lovemaking was a beautiful and incredibly erotic sight to behold.

Soon, Ryan's thrusts went back into overdrive. He tried to ease out, but Lara closed tighter around him, arching her back, keeping him in place. She was too close to turn around and determined to take him along this time. Following another deep thrust, her body tensed as her passion reached its crescendo for the second time tonight. She screamed as wave after wave of pleasure overtook her. The rumble in Ryan's voice when he called her name left no doubt of his arrival. He fell atop her, his body seizing with orgasmic jerks.

When his movements ceased, Ryan rolled over to his back, bringing Lara with him. "See, exploding on your birthday isn't such a bad thing, is it?" He draped the covers around them and hugged her close to his chest, his softening member still inside her. "I take it you finished this time?"

"Most definitely," she answered, nuzzling against him.

"How do you feel?"

She purred. "Incredible."

"Me, too. You were amazing, Lara. I swear, the earth moved." He kissed her softly. "I love you so much."

"I love you, too."

"I don't want to wait to get married, at least not long. I'm thinking Christmas."

"Christmas?" She sat up, disengaging their bodies. "The one coming up twenty-six days from now?"

"Not soon enough for you?" He grinned.

"That's soon. Can we get a wedding together that fast?"

"We can do anything. Unless . . . do you want to wait?"

"No, I don't." She smiled. "I think we can do this."

"I know we can," he said with a kiss. "We will need to find a house."

"Why? You have a house."

He eased up. "You're okay with living there?"

"I practically live there now." She laughed. "Besides, it's your home, and I feel very much at home there."

"You mean that?"

She kissed him. "Absolutely."

"Feel free to redecorate however you like."

"I wouldn't want to change anything." She tilted her head. "Well, except maybe put in some browns and add a few plants, but nothing major."

"Do whatever you want, Lara. My home is yours." Ryan kissed her forehead. "I just want you to be my wife."

Lara nestled contentedly in his arms. "In twenty-six days I will be."

The smell of sizzling bacon, eggs, toast, and brewing French vanilla coffee teased Lara's empty stomach, while Ryan standing at the stove in only a pair of black boxer briefs teased the rest of her. She tapped his backside and propped her chin on his shoulder. "How much longer will I have to wait for breakfast?" She stole a bacon strip, devouring it in seconds. "It looks done to me."

"It is done," he said, turning off the burner for the eggs, "and somebody doesn't know what 'breakfast in bed' means."

"I got lonely in there. Besides, I've been lying down a little too long. I think I'd like to sit in chair."

"Whatever your heart desires. You go to the table and fill our glasses with juice. By the time you're done, I'll be out with two loaded plates, okay?"

"Will do." She saluted.

"Could you grab the paper, too? I think I heard it hit the door."

"You and your Sunday comics," she said, well aware of why he wanted the paper. "Yes, I can do that, too."

He kissed her cheek. "Thanks, babe."

"Yeah, yeah. Just get my food together."

Lara placed the juice on the table and then went to retrieve the paper. Since the neighbors never ventured out before ten on Sunday mornings, she had no worries about being seen in only Ryan's dress shirt. When she stooped to pick up the paper, a pair of shiny, black shoes came into view. A sense of foreboding washed over her. She grabbed the paper and stood to her full height.

"Hello, Lara."

The paper dropped to the floor. She pinched her hand. It hurt. She wasn't dreaming. This was real.

"Foster."

CHAPTER 18

"Lara, I have your food and your coffee, but I don't see you or the pa—" Ryan stopped talking when he entered the living room to discover Lara wasn't alone. He hadn't seen Shelly in months, but Lara looked like she'd just seen a ghost. He joined her at the door. "I'm sorry, I didn't know we had company."

"We don't," Lara answered, her voice shaky. "He was just leaving."

"Who is that?" the man huffed. His hazel eyes flashed with contempt as he took in Ryan's state of undress.

Ryan observed the miffed stranger. A thin beard framed the pecan-tan face of the six-foot man. Close-cropped dark hair covered his head, and his trench coat and Italian loafers reeked of privilege. Ryan supposed women would find the guy attractive, but his arrogance and haughty tone could be major turnoffs. "I'm Ryan," he answered, not happy with being called "that." "Who are you?"

"Foster Grayson."

That explained Lara's ashen look. Ryan draped his arm around her shoulders, in as much a show of support as it was to make a point to Foster. "What do you want?"

"I want to talk to Lara."

"She doesn't want to talk to you."

Foster grunted. "Lara, who is this person?" He waved at Ryan as one would an annoying fly. "And since when does he speak for you?"

"He's my fiancé, and he's not speaking for me, he's reiterating what I already said. You *are* leaving."

Foster eyed Ryan in disbelief. "Fiancé?"

Lara lifted her left hand and wrapped her right arm around Ryan's waist. "That's what I said. There's nothing here for you, so you can go back to wherever you came from."

"I can't. I have a lot to say to you, Lara." Foster's gaze roamed over her body, undressing her with his eyes. "You're still as beautiful as ever."

Ryan balled his fist, fighting the intense desire to punch Foster's lights out. "Are you done?" he barked.

Reaching inside his breast pocket, Foster extended a business card. "I'm staying at the Denburg Inn, the room number is written on the back of the card. Please, call me. I'm not leaving town until we talk. Take the card, Lara."

Ryan snatched the card from his hand. "She has it, now go."

Foster turned to Lara with a sweet smile. "Happy belated birthday. Thirty looks good on you." His eyes cut to Ryan. "And do me a favor, Lara. When you come over, leave the watchdog at home." He scowled.

Ryan slammed the door in Foster's face. *Jackass!* Picking up the paper, he ushered Lara to the couch. "Are you okay?"

"I'm in shock."

"I imagine so." He dropped the card and paper to the table and held Lara's trembling hands. "Foster had to be the last person you expected to see."

"Yes and no. It's like my dream, only worse."

"What dream?"

"This dream I've been having for the past couple of weeks. We're making love and so happy."

He smiled. "That sounds like a wonderful dream."

"It is, until the end." She sighed. "We're basking in afterglow when I hear Foster say 'Hello, Lara,' and then . . . and then the dream ends. It's over."

Ryan sensed where this was going. "Look, Lara . . ."

"Last night was perfect, and this morning was more of the same. Then I go to that door and there's Foster saying exactly what he said in the dream." Tears filled her eyes. "Is this some sort of sign, Ryan? Is our dream going to end?"

"Absolutely not." Ryan held her head against him, comforting her as she cried. "Nothing and no one is ever going to come between us, Lara." He eyed the business card on the table. "I won't let it."

"Ms. Boyd's gonna be my mommy!"

Lara watched Justin race across the lawn to his grandfather. His elation about their impending nuptials worked wonders on her worry about the dream, almost as much as Ryan's lovemaking did after Foster left. She still didn't know what the dream meant, but one thing was certain: Foster couldn't touch what she had with Ryan and Justin.

Carl stopped stringing his bushes with colorful lights to greet the happy boy. "Daddy's gonna marry Ms. Boyd on Christmas, Grandpa. I can't wait to tell Grandma!"

Lara squirmed as Justin rushed off like a jackrabbit. No way would Sue be as thrilled by Justin's news as he was.

"Somebody got a Christmas present early," Carl said after Justin dashed into the house shouting his happy news.

Ryan kissed Lara's forehead. "A couple of some-bodies," he replied.

Sincere happiness brightened Carl's dancing gray eyes. Lara was constantly amazed that a man as nice as Carl Lomax could be married to a woman like Sue. The tall, robust man always had a nice word and warm smile for her, the exact opposite of his loving wife.

"Congratulations to you both." He bussed Lara's cheek and gave Ryan's hand a firm shake. "I know Sue's not happy with this relationship, but I'm glad you and Justin are finally happy again, Ryan. It's been a long time coming."

"Thank you, Carl. That means a lot," Ryan said.

"To both of us," Lara concurred.

Carl rubbed his arms. "I'm not quite done, but it's a bit nippy out here. You want to come in for some coffee?"

Lara smirked. *Was he kidding?* She appreciated Carl's hospitality, but was in too good a mood, especially after everything with Foster, to subject herself to Sue. "Thanks for the invitation, but we just had breakfast with Justin, and we—"

"We have *lots* of wedding plans to make," Ryan said, drawing slow lazy circles along her side. "Lots and lots of wedding plans." A devilish smile curled his lips. He wanted to make something all right, but Lara knew wedding plans didn't top his list.

Ryan told Carl he'd be back for Justin around five, and then drove Lara back to his house where they spent the rest of the day in bed and actually managed to make some wedding plans before all was said and done. Deciding on an intimate gathering with family and close friends, they chose the wedding party, menu, arranged for the use of her church and pastor for the ceremony, the social hall for the reception, and even found time to call their surprised but happy parents with the details.

Their wedding was shaping up nicely.

Later that evening, after Ryan dropped Lara back home, Celeste arrived to help search bridal magazines for the perfect dress. With the ideal gown chosen, and a prayer they could get it delivered in time, Lara shared the details about Foster's surprise visit.

"You're telling me Foster showed up at this apartment?"

Lara settled in the corner of her comfy couch, hugging a throw pillow to her chest. "That's what I'm telling you."

"Just like the dream. So, how did Ryan take it?"

"Pretty well. He was a little possessive, but I liked it." Lara smiled. "Of course, Foster behaved like a total jerk."

"What did he want?"

"To talk, he said."

"About what?"

"That's a good question, and one I plan to get the answer to. Want some apple juice?" she asked, walking into the kitchen.

Celeste followed. "Sure."

Lara poured two glasses and joined Celeste at the table.

"How do you plan to find out what Foster wanted?"

"I'm going to see him," Lara answered, taking a swallow of juice.

"You're going to see him?"

"Yes. I was stunned when he showed up unannounced at my door this morning, but with Ryan's help, I've been able to work through all of my Foster issues. I'm free at last, and I'm *so* happy."

Celeste drank some juice and gave Lara a knowing grin. "You had a good time last night, didn't you?"

Lara smiled at the thought of the good time she'd indulged in last night, this morning, and this afternoon. She knew she should feel ashamed for missing church and fornicating on the Lord's day, but was too happy to give in to it. "I had the best time. I thought the proposal was wonderful, but afterward. . . Celeste, last night was the most amazing experience of my life."

"Say no more. The way you're *skinnin'* and *grinnin'* is telling me plenty, thank you very much." Celeste's expression turned serious. "Lara, are you sure you want to visit Foster? You said it yourself, you're happy. What could he have to say now that you need to hear?"

"Nothing, but I want to hear it, anyway. Ryan probably threw away his card, but Foster's staying at the Inn, and I plan to see him tomorrow."

＝

Norris lowered his empty beer bottle to the table. "I can't believe Lara's ex showed up at her place the morning after you proposed."

Ryan had invited Norris over for a celebratory engagement drink, and the wedding talk had segued into Foster's surprise visit. "It wasn't expected, but we dealt with it," he said, eyeing the man's business card on the coffee table. "The guy is so arrogant. I can't believe Lara was going to marry him."

"You're not a little worried he could slip back into her heart and try to steal her away?"

Ryan shook his head. "No. I trust Lara, and I know she loves me. I don't think Foster gets that, though. The way he looked at her . . ." Ryan finished his beer. "Nobody looks at my woman like that but me."

"And me." Norris laughed, but Ryan wasn't amused. "I'm kidding. Geez."

"He has something to say to Lara." Ryan lowered the bottle to the table and pocketed the card. "She doesn't want to hear it, but I do."

"Does she know you do?"

"I didn't tell her, but I will. I'm just going to have a nice man-to-man talk with him."

"Good luck with that." Norris stood from the couch and pulled on his jacket. "I have an early meeting tomorrow, so I'm heading out. Give Lara my best wishes on your happy news, and rest assured, I'll do my best man duties with the usual aplomb with which I do everything else. I won't bother to tell my parents the news." Norris grunted. "I'm still floored by what happened at Thanksgiving. Later on, they mentioned every crazy stereotype ever made. They said Lara sounded white. Can you believe that?"

"Actually, yes, I can. It's easy to be tolerable about things like race from a distance. Maybe they'll come around."

"You have to be around to come around, and they stayed in the kitchen."

"Try to look at the bright side. At least they didn't come out of the kitchen and demand Lara go in." Ryan laughed.

"How can you joke about this? Doesn't it make you want to hit something?"

"It used to, but not anymore. If I get crazy over every unkind word, or too long a stare, I'll become a bitter man. I'm about to marry the most wonderful woman on the planet—a woman who loves my son as much as she does me. I won't let the narrow minds of the world take that away from me."

Ryan walked Norris out, and then gathered the two empty beer bottles from the table.

"It's good to see you in such good spirits, Ryan."

He turned to the familiar voice and smiled. "Shell. I thought I'd seen the last of you."

"I was away because you didn't need me, but now you do."

"I think you're a little confused." He lowered the bottles and held up his left hand. "No ring. You're at peace now, and Lara and I are getting married."

"Are you sure?"

"What do you mean, am I sure? Of course I'm sure. We got engaged last night. We . . ."

"I know what happened last night and today, Ryan. I'm discreet, but aware."

"Then you know we're very happy. This is what you wanted for me, remember? Are you now telling me it's not?"

"Not at all. I do want you and Lara together, but there are things going on that aren't what they appear."

"Not what they appear? Is this about Foster? Why are you back with these riddles now, Shell? I did what you wanted. You have your peace."

"If I had my peace, would I be here?" Shelly turned her back. "There're still no wings back there." She faced him again. "Turmoil is coming, Ryan. Look closer and remember."

"Look closer and remember?" Shelly's form faded. Why was she leaving him with a cryptic message like that? "Shell? Shell!" She had disappeared completely. "Damn!" Primed to kick the hell out of the coffee table, Ryan was interrupted by the ringing phone. He jammed the receiver to his ear. "What!"

"Did you and the woman have a fight?" said Sue.

Ryan groaned. *Why was this happening?* "If you're referring to Lara, no, we didn't have a fight."

"Something's got you on a tear."

"And, of course, you'd hope it's a fight with Lara." He blew out a breath. "What do you want, Sue?"

"I heard about your wedding plans. Is there a reason for this rush?"

Ryan shook his head. They didn't make tape less transparent than this woman. "Yes, actually. It's because I love her, and don't want to wait to make her my wife," he answered.

"You really need to give this more thought. I think you're making a big mistake."

"Tell me something I don't already know. For instance, what happened at your place today? Justin's not the happy kid I dropped off this morning. Did you say something to upset him?"

"Like what?"

"You know very well what."

"I haven't put any ideas in his head, if that's what you're suggesting. Maybe Justin isn't as happy about this wedding as you. Ever thought of that?"

"Not once. Good night, Sue."

Ryan ended the call and made fast work of his cleanup. While heading upstairs, he noted an acute drop in the temperature and spotted a chair against the wall by the thermostat. He sighed. Justin was taking this preoccupation with temperature too far. After returning the setting to normal, Ryan entered his son's room.

Justin slept huddled under the covers in a shivering ball. Ryan smoothed the boy's hair and rubbed his back. Justin's small body continued to tremble. "What is going on with you?" he said, kissing a shaky shoulder.

When the room grew warmer and Justin's teeth stopped chattering, Ryan took a hot shower and gave Lara a call. Her sweet hello was like a lullaby for his restless soul after the crazy evening he'd endured. "You sound *so* good," he said.

"You don't," Lara said. "Are you all right?"

"It's been a strange night." Ryan tucked a pillow behind his head and rested against the headboard. "I saw Shelly."

"Shelly?"

"I was surprised, too."

"What did she want?"

"To warn me of coming turmoil."

"Coming turmoil? What do you make of that?"

"To be honest, Foster was my first thought."

"Ryan, seeing Foster shook me up, but that initial shock is the extent of any turmoil he can cause. My heart is with you."

He smiled. "I never doubted you, Lara. I trust you completely, and I love you even more, but Foster is a different story. I want to talk to him. He may not be able to cause turmoil in our life, but I don't think he's above trying."

"Me, either," Lara said. "I changed my mind about seeing him, and I want you to come with me. Will you?"

"Yes," he readily answered. "I think our seeing him together is a great idea."

"Then it's settled. Now, enough with this Foster talk. Did Justin get to sleep okay, or was he too excited about the wedding?"

"Actually, he was pretty quiet when he came back from his visit with Sue. When I checked on him after Shelly's appearance, I discovered a chair at the wall by the thermostat and the air-conditioning turned on."

"What?"

"It was fifty-five degrees, Lara. Justin was shaking like a leaf. He asked me about hell yesterday, and it was freezing then, too."

"He's always asking if we feel hot or need water, and my apartment was chilly when we got back last night. What do you think this is about?"

"I don't know. Maybe he heard Norris say you were hot one too many times." He laughed. "I'll ask Justin in the morning. He's the only one who can make any sense of this."

CHAPTER 19

"Good morning, Justin," Lara happily greeted when he and Ryan entered her classroom the next morning.

"Mornin', Ms. Boyd," Justin muttered, traipsing to the coatrack and removing his outerwear.

No hug and no smile. Totally atypical Justin behavior. Lara turned to Ryan. "Did you find out anything?"

"Not much," he answered. "He did admit to changing the thermostat at your place and mine because it was too hot, but said nothing was wrong. At least nothing he couldn't fix."

"Nothing he couldn't fix?" Lara watched Justin join the other children and Penny at the round reading table and open a book. Her gaze met Ryan's. "What does he think is broken?"

Ryan leaned against the doorjamb and shrugged. "He had that stomachache the other day, and he's been complaining about it being too hot ever since. Maybe it's some bug or something."

"But he didn't have a fever." Lara sighed. "I'll try to talk to him a little later. Maybe he'll open up some more."

"It couldn't hurt. You can get him to do anything. Nobody's like Ms. Boyd." After checking to make sure the children weren't looking, Ryan gave her a quick kiss.

She smoothed the lipstick from his lips. "Are you free this afternoon?"

"Why? You want to take me to your place and have your way with me?" He smiled. "I really missed you last night."

"Actually, I want to take you to a hotel, but not for that. I thought we could find out what Foster has to say."

"Oh, *that*. I'm available, but I'll need to arrange a sitter for Justin. I'll ask Mrs. Borden from next door. It shouldn't take too long, right? I'm mean, how long does it take somebody to say 'I'm a stupid, smug bastard jerk'?"

Lara laughed. "Not too long."

Ryan walked to the table and kissed the top of Justin's head. "I'll see you later, buddy."

"Bye, Daddy." Justin sounded a lot happier than he did when he first walked in. Lara decided she'd try talking to him at lunch. PB&J had a way of making him sing like a canary.

Lara walked over. "Penny, I'm going to walk Ryan out. I'll be right back, okay?" she said.

"No problem," Penny replied. "By the way, I wanted to say the party was great, and congratulations on the engagement." She smiled. "I know you'll have years of happiness together."

"Thanks, Penny." Ryan hugged Lara to his side, and pressed her adorned hand to his lips. "I know we'll have years of happiness, too." Once outside, away from pairs of curious, smiling little eyes, Ryan pulled her close, kissing her hard and deep. "Have a great day, sweetheart. I love you."

Fanning her face after Ryan's passionate departure, Lara spotted Justin watching from the door. "Hi," she said.

"Are you hot?" he asked.

"Excuse me?"

Justin took a few steps out. "You fanned your face after Daddy kissed you. Does he make you feel hot?"

She grinned. "Yeah, pretty much all the time."

"Oh," Justin murmured. "Do you want some water?"

"No, but, thank you. Are you thirsty?"

He stared at her for a long moment before dropping his head. "Huh-uh. I'm gonna go finish looking at my book." He stopped just inside the door and turned around. "Ms. Boyd?"

"Yes, sweetie?"

"I love you."

Lara smiled. Justin's solemn mood troubled her, but she never tired of hearing those words from him. "I love you, too. Are you sure everything is okay?"

"Yes, ma'am. Everything is going to be okay."

"I see you are truly in your element around here."

Lara groaned. First, Justin didn't want to eat with her, in fact, he'd gotten a lot quieter over the course of the day, and now she had to deal with this. She looked up from her lesson plan to find Foster all smiles. "Why are you here?"

"I told you we needed to talk." He looked around the empty classroom. "Where are the children?"

"They're having lunch."

"You don't want to have lunch? We could go . . ."

Her impatient grunt ended his words. "Foster, I'm not going anywhere with you." She closed her eyes and rubbed her throbbing temples. "How did you even know I was in South Carolina? And how did you find my apartment?"

"I know people. I needed to see you, to talk to you."

He wanted to talk, and she wanted this over. When she left school, the only person she wanted to concentrate on was Justin. "You said you have a lot to say. I'm giving you five of the twenty minutes left of my break to spill it. Talk fast."

Foster removed his coat and sat. "You've changed, Lara," he said, trying to get comfortable in the small wooden chair.

"Six years will do that." The chair squeaked under his weight like floorboards in a haunted house. How nice it would be to see him fall flat on his backside. "I know you didn't come all the way from New York to tell me I've changed."

Foster stopped moving and smiled. "You kept tabs?"

"I heard you got married soon after we ended. New York is where you moved. I assumed it's where you stayed. After six years, I'd hardly call that keeping tabs."

"I never stopped thinking about you, Lara. Every day . . ."

She held up her hand. "Don't go there."

"I can't stay away from it."

"Are you kidding me?" She retreated to the other side of the room, certain she'd scratch his eyes out if she stayed close to him. "Do you not remember what happened between us?"

"I want to explain."

"Can you?"

"I'm sorry, Lara."

She rolled her eyes.

"I did love you," he said. "I still love you."

"You have no concept of the word!" Lara lowered her tone. "If you loved me, you would have never done—" She paused, willing herself not to cry. "The career I'd wanted since I was a child, or the man I gave my virginity to and agreed to spend my life with. Which did I want more? *That* was your love, Foster. And when I couldn't choose, you walked away from me. For years, *years*, I second-guessed myself. I loved my work, it was everything I hoped it would be, but still I had doubts. Was wanting a rewarding career worth losing the man I loved? I ached for you, Foster. I lost count of how many times I cried myself to sleep."

"You hurt because you knew what we had. It was real, Lara. It was real, but I let the success I'd achieved go to my head. The partners at the firm they—they made me feel like a god. Power is heady. It made me want to have things my way. And being the big man I was, I decided my way was a wife at home, not one working with little children."

"You decided?"

"Yes, I decided." He moved to within a few feet of her. "And because I said it, it was law. After waiting almost two years, a month before our wedding, I got you to sleep with me. If I could get you to do that . . . I pushed the envelope with the ultimatum, and I regret it more than you'll ever know, but it's not too late for us. You even said you had doubts."

"Yes. Doubts. I had doubts, but I never had regret. It was because of my work I discovered the true love of my life. Even as much as I loved you, and I did love you, you weren't my heart's desire. I think that's why I was so hesitant about sleeping with you. If I have a regret, it's that I didn't say no. You weren't the one. It took meeting Ryan to finally make me see that and get over you."

"Lara, please, stop talking like that. You don't love that man." He took her hands in his. "I'm divorced now, and my ex and I never had children. You and I, we can have the life together we always wanted. I'll let you teach."

Lara jerked her hands away. "You'll *let* me teach?" Her mocking laughter filled the room. "How big of you."

"You know what I mean. Come on, Lara, you still love me." Foster slipped his arms around her waist and pulled her close.

His designer cologne filled her nostrils. Six months ago, she'd have probably been all over him like a cheap suit, but today it took all she had not to laugh in his face at his attempt at seduction.

"I'll never believe you don't love me," he said with confidence.

Lara freed herself from his loose grip. "I guess you'll be living the rest of your life in a fog of delusion, because I'm in love with Ryan, and my life is with him and his son."

"Lara, baby, don't—"

"Foster, save your dignity and stop the sweet talk. This conversation is over. I'm glad we talked. I really am. I needed to hear your side of things, and it gave me some understanding I otherwise wouldn't have had, but it doesn't change anything. I sincerely hope you find what you're looking for, but it won't be with me."

"So that's it. We're over?"

"We've been over for a long time. I'm finally going to be a mother and a wife, and I still get to be a teacher. I wasn't looking for love when Ryan came into my life, but I found just that when he walked through those doors with Justin. Real and true love, and it was the best thing to ever happen to me."

"You really look wonderful, Lara."

"It's called happiness. I recommend it to everyone, even you." Lara kissed his cheek. "Good-bye, Foster."

Foster picked up his coat from the tiny chair and made his way to the door. He watched her for several moments without saying a word. Then he waved good-bye and was gone.

Lara's attempts to get Justin to talk fell flat. His only utterance on the ride home was his request she turn down the heater in the car. When they made it to Ryan's, he raced up to his room and closed the door.

Lara's gaze stayed trained on the staircase as Ryan massaged her knotted shoulders. "You didn't have any luck, huh?"

"No." She buried her face in Ryan's chest. Justin's silence worried her, but the sadness in his eyes on the few occasions he looked her way broke her heart. She sniffled. "I don't want him upset with me."

"He's not upset with you. Hey." Ryan lifted her chin and smoothed away her tears. "He loves you. There's something upsetting him, but it's not you. Don't worry, we'll get to the bottom of this." He snapped his fingers. "I have something that will cheer you up."

"You do?"

"Yep." He walked to the coffee table and picked up several colorful, glossy brochures. "I went to the travel agent today. How does a honeymoon in the tropics sound?"

"The tropics?" she said, glancing back at the stairs.

"Lara, you aren't paying attention."

"The tropics, I heard you."

"Lara?"

"I'm sorry. I'm worried about him."

"I know, but a little alone time surrounded by Ernie and his cars will do him good." The doorbell rang. "That's probably Mrs. Borden."

"I'll get it," Lara said. "We don't need her now."

"We don't? Why not?"

"I'll explain." After sending Mrs. Borden on her way, Lara returned her attention to the stairs. Details about her encounter with Foster would have to wait. "Let's go talk to Justin." They entered the room to find him lying in bed with his back to the door. Lara hastened over and stroked his shoulder. "Justin, sweetie, look at me."

He turned around. Her chest tightened when she saw the tears streaming down his rounded cheeks. "Oh, Justin." Lara gathered him in her arms, rocking him as he cried. "Baby, what's wrong?"

Justin peeled his tearstained face from her chest. "You love me, Ms. Boyd, right?"

"Yes." She smoothed away his tears. "So very much."

"And you'll do anything for me?"

"Anything at all. Just tell me and I'll do it."

"Don't marry Daddy," he said, his voice low and quaky, but peppered with urgency. "Please, please, don't marry him."

A breath lodged in Lara's throat. Tears filled her eyes. Did she hear him right? *Don't marry Daddy?*

Ryan sat next to her on the bed. His hand closed around Justin's shoulder. "What did you say?"

"I don't want Ms. Boyd to marry you."

"Justin, what's wrong?" Desperation shook Ryan's now slightly elevated voice. "You want me to marry Lara. You want her to be your mommy. I heard you tell her so at the Monroes'."

"Uh-uh, Daddy. You can't marry Ms. Boyd. You can't marry Ms. Boyd. You can't, you can't, you can't." He dissolved on the bed in a mass of hysterical sobs.

The knot in Lara's chest tightened and tears streamed from her eyes. Her dream had turned into a living nightmare. Justin was inconsolable, and the confusion in Ryan's tear-filled eyes as he looked from her to his son showed he didn't know whom to comfort first. Lara stood, making the decision for him. "You tend to Justin, I'm going home."

Ryan shot up and grabbed her arm. *"NO!"* With trembling hands he wiped the tears raining down her cheeks. He lowered his voice. "We can settle this. Lara, this is Sue. Justin doesn't mean what he's saying."

"No, he means it. Look at him." Sobs wracked Justin's body. Steady chants of "You can't" accompanied his tears. Sue didn't like her, but this was about Justin. His upset told her so. "Your son needs you."

"My son? He's *ours*, Lara. He needs both of us."

Lara shook her head. What Justin needed was her not to marry Ryan. In every way that mattered, he was her son. As such, his needs came first. It was good she'd waited to talk about Foster. She prayed Ryan wouldn't always hate her for what she was about to do.

"This is my fault," she said.

"What?"

"Let's step outside." Lara walked to the door and cast a final glance at Justin. She ached to run to him, to hold him until his tears stopped. She couldn't do that for him, but there was something she could do. *Not marry Ryan.* She left the room.

Ryan closed the door and walked the few steps to Lara. "We really need to go back to him."

"Not me. I think—I think Justin saw me with Foster."

"Saw you with Foster?"

"He came to my classroom today and we talked. Ryan, things have changed."

"Changed how?"

Fingernails cut into her skin from the tight ball she made of her fist. It killed her to lie to him, but this had to be authentic, convincing. *Lord, give me strength.* "You asked me before if I still loved him. Today, I realized I still do. He explained everything and apologized. He's divorced now, Ryan. He asked me to come back to him, and I . . ."

"Stop! Just stop it. You're lying!"

"I'm sorry this hurts you."

"This doesn't hurt me. This infuriates me!" He paced a few steps and turned to her. "You expect me to believe you're leaving me for Foster Grayson, minutes after Justin asked you not to marry me?" He held her shoulders. "Lara, I know you love Justin, but you don't have to do this."

She wished she didn't, but Justin's plea to her wasn't idle. If this gave him the slightest bit of peace, relieved his obvious pain just a little, she had to do it. Regardless of what it did to her, and sadly, to Ryan. They were adults, but Justin was a little boy. Her little boy.

"Ryan, why do you think I told you we didn't need Mrs. Borden? Foster showed up at lunchtime and we settled everything. Being alone with him, kissing him, I couldn't deny—"

"Kissing him?" Ryan backed away, shaking his head. "I can't listen to this."

"I'm sorry, but Foster is my first love."

"And I'm your *true* love! Are you going to deny that?"

"We rushed into this. It was attraction we took too far, too fast. It wasn't real."

"It was a lot more than attraction, and it *is* very real. It's real in the way your eyes light up when I walk into a room. It's real in the way my heart expands whenever I see you, and it's real in the way we touch each other when we make love. You wouldn't be able to give yourself to me so completely if it wasn't real. That ring on your finger. That's real, Lara! You agreed to be my wife, to spend your life with Justin and me, and now you're walking away because some guy said he was sorry? No! I won't let you walk away from me and all we have. I won't let you do it."

Ryan pulled her to him, kissing her hard, desperately. His lips so soft, but his tongue rough, demanding, as it raked against hers. His arms closed tight around her, his hands squeezing, molding, exploring the body he'd come to know so well. Succumbing to him would be so easy . . . too easy. She had to be strong, to think of Justin. Summoning every ounce of strength, she pushed him away.

Ryan's strangled sob shattered the tiny shard left of her broken heart. "Lara."

Emotion knotted so tightly in Lara's throat, she feared she might explode. How was she going to talk when all she wanted to do was run out of there and cry? "You can't change this, Ryan," she managed to say, "it's over." She pulled the ring from her finger. "I'm moving to New York to be with Foster. Years ago I couldn't make a choice, and I won't make the same mistake twice." She extended the ring. "Take it."

"No."

"Take the ring."

Ryan shook his head. His tears flowed.

Seconds from cracking, Lara jammed the ring in his hand and raced down the stairs, nearly stumbling on her legs of lead.

Ryan followed. "Lara, please, don't go. Lara!"

Ignoring Ryan's cries, she grabbed her coat and purse and dashed out of the house. The cold December air whipped unceremoniously at her face, chilling the warm tears that filled her eyes. Sliding behind the wheel of her car, she managed to make it to the end of the street before the blinding tears made driving impossible. With only the soft whir of the heater to keep her company, she hung her head and cried.

CHAPTER 20

"Lara, for God's sake, go back over there," Celeste implored. Her cousin had raced over when Lara called in the midst of her hysterical tears, and after hearing the story, she was staunch in her opinion. "You need to work this out."

"There's nothing to work out." Lara walked to the closet and pulled out her wardrobe bag. "Justin doesn't want me to marry Ryan." She brushed away the droplets glistening her lashes. "What Justin wants is the most important thing."

Celeste snatched the luggage away. "What are you doing?"

Lara grabbed the bag back and tossed it on the bed. "What does it look like?"

"It looks like you're running away."

"No, I'm *going* away. I can't stay here."

"What are you talking about?"

"Justin is in my class." She unzipped the bag and flipped it open. "I can't see him every day, feeling the way I do about him, and know I'm hurting him."

"You're not hurting him. Lara, he loves you, and you love teaching. This is crazy. Justin was on top of the world yesterday. Now he doesn't want you to marry Ryan, and you're taking it at face value and leaving everything you care about?"

"You didn't see him. He doesn't want me to marry Ryan, and he means it. I don't know what changed, but something did."

"You didn't want an explanation? This is your life, too."

"Ryan is Justin's father, and I'm just . . ."

"The only mother he's ever known." Celeste huffed. "You're starting to sound like Sue. That old bird has done something to him."

"Ryan thinks so, too. As much as I would love to blame this on Sue, I can't. She dislikes me, but she wouldn't slam me in front of Justin. She'll do it in front of Ryan and me in a heartbeat, but not him. She doesn't want to look bad in his eyes." She continued her packing. "Besides, Justin's been acting differently since before his visit with Sue. This is his decision, and I love him enough to give him whatever he needs."

"What about you and Ryan, and what you two need? Lara, you've finally found the man of your dreams. How can you just walk away from him?"

"I can't be selfish, Celeste. This is not just about Ryan and me. Justin is as much a part of this as we are. I love Ryan, and I thought I would spend the rest of my life with him, but it's not to be. Justin's happiness is more important than mine, or even Ryan's."

"If that's how you feel, how can you leave him?"

More tears fell. "Because staying is too hard." Tossing in some undergarments and her travel tote of toiletries, Lara placed Justin's framed crayon "family" picture, her beloved birthday present, on top, zipped and folded the bag, and headed for the door.

Celeste followed. "Where are you going?" she asked.

"I don't know. Ryan thinks I'm going to New York to be with Foster. I guess I could go to Virginia, but the family would just send me back here." She managed a smile as her heart continued to break. "They love Ryan." Her mind flashed to his devastated expression when she left. Tears refreshed. "Even if I knew where I was going, I wouldn't tell you."

"Why not?"

"Because you would tell Ryan, and I can't see him. Unlike the ultimatum from Foster, this choice was easy to make because I did it for Justin, but living with it and without Ryan is the hard part. He needs to take care of his son and believe I'm with Foster."

"Lara, Ryan's already left half a dozen messages on my cell. I can only imagine how many times he's called the house. What am I supposed to tell him?"

"Nothing."

"Please, don't do this."

"I'm sorry, Celeste, but it's already done."

Ryan raced to the Denburg Inn the moment Norris arrived at his place. He'd forgotten all about their dinner plans, but was grateful to have a sitter he didn't mind leaving with Justin when the boy was still so upset. In a barely controlled rage, Ryan rode the elevator to Foster's room.

Shelly's ghost appeared. "You don't want to do this."

"The hell I don't! This is your fault. If you hadn't insisted I go after Lara, I wouldn't be . . ." He choked back a sob. "I love her. How could she do this to me? Damn it! How could I be so blind? I thought she loved me. I knew she loved me!"

"Ryan, you need to calm down and remember what I said."

"Oh, I remember what you said," he snapped. "*'Turmoil is coming.'* Well, it came! You asked if I was sure I was going to marry Lara. I thought I was, but looks like I was wrong. I don't want to talk anymore, Shelly. What I want is to smash the hell out of Foster Grayson's face."

"To what end?"

"I'll feel better."

Ryan stepped off the elevator and pounded furiously on the door of Room 209. Curious guests peeked out of their rooms, but Ryan's angry scowl sent them scrambling back inside.

He continued to pound. "Grayson, open this damn door!" His arm went flying through the air as the door flew open with a jerk. Foster answered wearing only a blue terry cloth robe. Thoughts of Lara waiting in the man's bed filled Ryan's head and fueled his rage. An angry nerve flickered above Ryan's lip.

"What is your problem, man?" Foster barked.

"You, you bastard!" Ryan's fist connected to Foster's jaw with a loud smack. The force sent his foe stumbling backward. Ignoring the pain in his hand, Ryan stomped inside, pushing Foster out of his way. "Where is Lara?"

"What the hell?" Foster shifted his jaw.

Ryan grunted. Too bad it wasn't broken.

"Why would you think Lara's here?" Foster asked.

"I'm in no mood for games, Grayson," Ryan said, flexing his throbbing hand. "I know you saw Lara today, and I know what happened."

"If that's so, why are you here?"

Fury shot through Ryan like a bolt of lightning. "Son of a—" The door behind Foster opened, preventing Ryan from exacting more punishment.

"Foster, baby, what's taking so . . ." A perky blonde, who appeared to be all of twenty and sounded like she had been sucking on a helium balloon, stepped out of the steamy bathroom wearing the matching robe. She tightened the belt around her waist. "You're bleeding." She scowled at Ryan. "Did he do that?"

"It's fine, doll. You go back inside. I'll be right there." The woman nodded obediently and returned to the room. Foster met Ryan's gaze. "As you can see, Lara is not here."

"No kidding."

"I don't know why you'd think she was."

"She said she saw you."

"She did. I told her I wanted her back, but all she could talk about was you and your son. How happy she was, and how her every dream had finally come true . . . yada, yada, yada."

"And the kiss she mentioned?"

"Kiss? That peck on the cheek? Hell, I've gotten more passionate kisses from my grandmother. Happy now?"

"I see you are." Ryan looked over at the bathroom door. "You didn't waste any time consoling yourself."

"I'm not one to let grass grow."

"So Lara said. You're a real bastard, Grayson."

"That may be, but I'm not the one who doesn't know where my fiancée is." Foster walked to the door. "I'm feeling charitable, so I'm going to let you leave before I decide to press assault charges."

Shelly appeared beside Foster. "Listen to him and leave already," she said. "I think you've done quite enough."

"If I see Lara, I'll tell her you're looking for her," Foster sniped.

Feeling a lot ticked and a bit foolish, Ryan left the room.

Shelly eyed Ryan, shaking her head. "I told you not to go in there, but you wouldn't listen."

"I'm sick of listening to you, Shelly!" Ryan fired. "Leave me alone!"

"Why are you snapping at me? I didn't tell you to run over here like some caveman and punch this Foster guy, and I didn't make you get with Lara. You were in love with her from practically the first minute. I just encouraged you, and it didn't take much doing."

Ryan nodded. "You're right, and I thank you, Shelly. But I don't need your encouragement anymore."

"Ryan?"

"No more, Shell. No more suggestions, and no more thoughts. I know you mean well, I do, but I don't need to hear anymore from you. I need to hear from Lara. She had me convinced we were over, because she loves Justin so much. I have to find her and fix this. I'm going to have the life I deserve with the woman I love, and I don't want or need a cheering section in you to make that happen."

Nothing Ryan tried could get Justin to talk. Lara had all but disappeared, and although he'd finally got a hold of Celeste, the little information he practically had to squeeze out of her was what he already knew. Lara still loved him, but left him for Justin's sake. Penny's questions when he dropped Justin at school the next morning didn't help matters. He had his own questions, and could think of only one person who could provide answers.

Ryan broke land speed records getting to the Lomax house. He pounded on the door. "Sue, open up!"

The door flew open with Carl on the other side. "Ryan, have you gone mad?"

"Yes, I have." He brushed past the older man and stepped into the living room. The Victorian furniture always made him think of the dollhouse his sisters played with as children. Perfect for Sue's life. The woman lived in a land of make-believe. A world where everything had to be her way. "Where is Sue? I saw her car outside, so I know she's here."

"She's upstairs getting dressed for the day."

"Fine, I'll wait." Ryan paced. "Let her know I'm here."

Carl folded his arms. "I'm sure you've already done that."

Sue bounded into the room. "What's going on down here? I heard you shouting all the way upstairs."

Ryan stormed over to her, his finger inches from her face. "What the hell did you say to Justin?"

She backed away from the accusatory pointer. "What did I say to him? I say a lot to him."

"About Lara and me."

"I didn't say anything to Justin about you and your woman. I figure he'll come to his senses all by himself."

"His senses?"

Sue stuck out her chin. "I'm not impressed with her, and I've made no secret of that. Why are you here?"

"Because Justin, if I may use your words, has come to his senses. Lara broke the engagement last night because he begged us not to marry."

The beginnings of a smile curled Sue's lips. "Oh, sorry."

Ryan's face grew hot. He stepped closer to Sue. Never had he experienced such an intense desire to hit a woman. It frightened him. "What did you say to Justin?"

Carl stepped between them. "Take it easy, Ryan."

"Something happened here and I want to know what!"

"I didn't say anything to Justin about you marrying that woman," Sue declared. "I'm not unhappy the engagement is broken, but I didn't tell him to break it."

"Maybe you did," Carl said.

Sue gasped. "Carl!"

"Be quiet, Sue. Ryan, when you and Lara dropped Justin off on Sunday, Sue was on the phone with Genevieve Converse."

"Norris's mother?" Ryan looked from Carl to Sue. "I didn't even know they were friends."

"They became friendly on Thanksgiving night. Genevieve phoned after she met Lara, and dropped by later that evening. Sue found a friend in disdain."

"Go on," Ryan urged.

"I heard the phrase 'They're going to burn in hell' said quite frequently. Genevieve called again Sunday morning. Not inclined to listen to their talk again, I decided to go outside and string the lights. That's when you all arrived and Justin rushed into the house shouting Lara was going to be his new mommy. When I came in, he was sitting very quietly watching cartoons, and Sue was still in the kitchen." Carl sighed. "I suspect Justin heard Sue talking."

Ryan's gaze fixed on Sue. Now it all made sense. Justin's upset stomach when he left Norris's kitchen, the water, air-conditioning, and hell questions. It all came together. "You should be ashamed of yourself. How could you do this?"

"I didn't say anything to him!" Sue thundered.

"You didn't have to! You heard Justin and his news coming from a mile away, so you set him up. Justin raced in here to share his happy news, and instead you let him listen to your pea-brain opinions, knowing full well what he would think. What is it you said, Sue, huh? *'Ryan and that woman are going to burn in hell if they continue with this'* or maybe *'If Ryan marries that teacher they're both going to burn in hell.'* Am I close?"

"I don't want you marrying that woman!"

"I know, and you would do anything to stop it from happening, including using your own grandson. Justin is the most literal little boy in the world, and you know this. If you said it's raining cats and dogs, he'd believe Garfield and Snoopy were falling out of the sky. So, what do you do? You use his love for Lara to suit your ends. You make him believe our being together would hurt us, so he wouldn't want it anymore. Because you didn't want it!" Ryan's body shook with rage. "Justin practically froze himself to death to keep Lara and me from burning in the hell you condemned us to." Ryan pointed a quaking finger. "You are a sick woman, and you will stay the hell away from my son!"

"No!" Sue caught his arm as he turned to leave. "Shelly wouldn't want this."

He jerked his arm away. "You'd be surprised at what Shelly wants."

"She wouldn't want you to keep Justin from me. She wouldn't want you sleeping with some other woman in her house, and God knows she wouldn't want you two married and raising her child."

Ryan grunted. "Why didn't I see this before? Here I am thinking your biggest problem with Lara is she's black, but your biggest problem is that she's not Shelly. From the moment Justin told you about Lara, you had it in for her. Lara could be as blond as me, and it wouldn't matter. It's Justin's love for Lara and hers for him that you don't like. Do you have any idea how much you've hurt him?"

"I didn't want to hurt Justin, but I wasn't given a choice. He's all I have left of my baby, and you want to take him away from me. I remember how you both were that first day, talking about Ms. Boyd. Justin couldn't stop talking about her. It was always Ms. Boyd this or Ms. Boyd that. And then he races into my house shouting that woman is going to be his mommy. Shelly is his mommy. My baby." Sue wiped away tears. "Everybody seems to want to forget that, and her. I won't forget Shelly, and I won't let you or your woman keep Justin from me."

"Nobody kept Justin from you! I asked for space, and I was asking for it long before Lara came into our lives, but you wouldn't hear it." He stepped up to her. "Hear this, Sue. I'm going to marry Lara, and she, Justin, and I are going to be a family. And you will have *nothing* to do with us. In any way!"

Carl stopped him when he reached for the door. "Ryan, I'm sorry. Sue is still struggling with Shelly's death. You have to reconsider this. She's in more pain than I thought," he said, glancing at his weeping wife. "Don't keep Justin away—"

Ryan held up his hand. "I don't give a damn about Sue's pain!" He sucked in a breath. "I need to go to my son and make his pain go away."

Ryan returned to the classroom to find the other students making arts and crafts, while Justin sat alone facing the spring picture Ryan had made for Lara all those months ago. Justin's tiny hand splayed over the image of Lara's beautiful face, and his shoulders shook with sobs.

Ryan swallowed the knot in his throat. Acknowledging Penny with a wave, he made his way to his son.

"Justin?" The boy turned around, his face streaked with tears. "Why are you crying?"

Justin dropped his head and turned away.

Ryan turned the chair around and dropped to his knees. He lifted Justin's lowered chin. "You don't want to talk, fine. I need you to listen and maybe nod. Will you do that?"

Justin nodded.

"Okay. Did you hear Uncle Norris's mother and father talking in the kitchen on Thanksgiving?"

Justin's eyes widened. His head moved slightly forward.

"Were they talking about Ms. Boyd and me?"

Fresh tears brimmed in Justin's eyes. He nodded.

Ryan rubbed his shoulder and held on to his tiny hand. "It's okay, son. Did what they say scare you?"

Justin nodded again.

"Did you hear Grandma say sorta the same thing on Sunday?"

Tears fell as he nodded.

"You still love Ms. Boyd, don't you?"

Justin threw his arms around Ryan's neck. Sobs wracked his little body. "Yes, Daddy, but I don't want you and Ms. Boyd to burn in hell."

Ryan held Justin close. "Oh, son, we won't," he promised.

"Because I told Ms. Boyd not to marry you." Justin pulled back, his eyes teary and nose runny. "I want Ms.

Boyd to be my mommy all the time, but I don't want the fire to hurt her." He used his sleeve to wipe his face. "She can't burn up."

"She won't."

"'Cause you can't marry her."

"I can marry her, Justin. It's gonna be fine."

"Uh-uh. Grandma said on the phone if you and Ms. Boyd get married you would burn up in hell. She said it. She said it a lot of times. Uncle Norris's mommy and daddy said you'd burn up, too." Justin sniffled. "They're older than us. Big people are smarter so little people have to listen to them. We're littler than Grandma and Uncle Norris's mommy and daddy."

Ryan sighed. This would be harder than he thought. "We're younger than them, but it doesn't mean they're right. Big people aren't always right."

"You said before someone does something that will make them go to hell they shouldn't do it. I don't want you and Ms. Boyd to go to hell and burn up. So, you can't marry her."

"I can and will marry her, and we're not going to burn up."

Justin shook his head violently. Tears slashed across his flushed cheeks. "You can't, Daddy," he insisted. "You can't marry her. You'll burn up. I know it. When you kissed her yesterday you made her hot. I saw her fan her face. She said you made her feel like that most of the time."

Ryan smiled. "She makes me feel like that, too, son. It's love."

"I love you and Ms. Boyd, but I don't feel hot. If you're hot now, you'll really burn up if you get married."

"Justin, Lara and I won't burn up if we get married."

"Yes, you will. You're just saying you won't. Please, don't do it, Daddy. I don't want Ms. Boyd to burn up. I don't want her to burn up."

Justin crumbled in Ryan's arms with heartbreaking sobs. Ryan held his son close, doing all he could to calm the boy who showed no signs of relaxing. How could he convince Justin his fears were groundless, when he believed them so completely?

Lara watched the scene unfolding before her tear-filled eyes. Her choice to leave Ryan was one she'd made willingly for Justin, but too many hours alone in an economy hotel had given her time to think. She could do this for Justin, but Celeste was right, she had to know, for her own sake, why she was doing it.

Arriving at the school and finding Ryan in deep conversation with Justin was the last thing she expected, but listening to the exchange put everything into perspective. She knew she loved Justin, but until today she hadn't known just how much he loved her.

Justin pulled from Ryan's embrace. "Ms. Boyd." He raced over, clinging to her legs. "I did everything I could, but it didn't work. The water and the air-conditioner didn't work. I love you, Ms. Boyd. I want you to be my mommy, but I don't want you to burn up. Please, please, don't burn up."

Lara stroked Justin's back, soothing him. She met Ryan's gaze and mouthed, "I'm sorry."

Ryan approached with the smile that had captured her from the moment she saw it. He pressed a kiss to her temple. "You never have to apologize for loving Justin." He brushed his hand against Justin's hair. "But I think we have a little problem."

"I'll try," she offered. "Justin, sweetie?" He tilted his head to meet her gaze. "I feel so special knowing how much you love me, but you don't have to worry. I can marry your daddy, be your mommy, and not burn in hell. I know you don't believe it, but it's true." She smoothed the tears from his cheeks. "Your daddy and I love you too much to lie to you."

"You're not gonna burn up?" Justin asked.

"No," Ryan and Lara answered.

"Then why did Grandma and Uncle Norris's mommy and daddy say so?"

"Justin, honey." Lara's eyes met Ryan's. He shrugged. There was no getting around this. Seating Justin in the chair, she took Ryan's hand and they kneeled before him. "Do you notice anything different between my hand and your daddy's?"

"Yep." Justin nodded. "Daddy's hand is big, and yours is little and soft."

"Yes, that's a difference, but I mean something else."

"Your hand is brown like chocolate ice cream."

"That's right. And because of that difference, some people don't think your daddy and I should get married."

"Why?"

"I really don't know," she answered, "but because we don't look the same, some people think we shouldn't be together."

"But you love Daddy, and Daddy loves you."

"Yes, and we love you, but for some people that's not okay."

Justin turned to his father. "Grandma Sue doesn't think it's okay?" New tears filled his eyes. "Is she a bad person?"

A throat cleared behind them before Ryan could answer. Lara and Ryan stood and turned to the sound. Sue and Carl approached.

"I think I should answer his question, Ryan," said Sue.

Ryan frowned. "I don't think that's . . ."

Lara took Ryan's hand and moved aside, allowing Sue passage to Justin. "I think she should, Ryan," she whispered. "Sue needs to do this."

Ryan wasn't happy, but he didn't make a fuss as Sue moved in and knelt in front of Justin.

"You asked your father if I was a bad person." Lara braced herself as the woman's gaze met hers. After a moment, Sue turned back to Justin. "I think Grandma is more of a sad person. See, I thought if you loved Ms. Boyd, you wouldn't love me. You wouldn't need me or want to see me. That you'd be gone from me like your mommy is gone from me."

"I'll always love you, Grandma. I'm not going anywhere, and I'll always want to see you. My mommy is in heaven, but Ms. Boyd is nice and she loves me and Daddy like Mommy did. She'll be a good mommy."

"That's what your grandpa said. I'm sorry I made you believe she and your daddy would burn up if they got married." She pressed her hand to his cheek. "They won't, I promise. I said that because I was scared."

"Are you still scared, Grandma?"

Sue took Justin in her arms, and turned apologetic eyes toward Ryan and Lara. "Not so much anymore, Justin. Not so much."

Later that evening, Ryan and Lara sat snuggled together on her couch while Justin watched cartoons in her bedroom. She grazed her thumb against his bruised knuckles. He grimaced. Guilt gnawed at her gut. It seemed her act had been a little too convincing. "I can't believe you hit Foster."

"That felt good, Lara. What I can't believe is you were ever contemplating marriage to that pompous jack—"

"Andrews."

"I'm going to assume you would've come to your senses even if he hadn't shown his true colors all those years ago."

"I'm sure I would have." She linked her arm with his and kissed his cheek. "Seeing Sue's true colors today really surprised me. To come to us and apologize took guts. What she did to Justin was clearly an act of desperation. She was afraid of losing her last link to Shelly."

"Whose fault is that? I told Sue time and again I wouldn't keep Justin from her, yet she pulled her stunt. I know Justin loves his grandmother, but it's going to take some time before I trust her alone with him again." Ryan drew a breath. "Now, enough talk." His finger brushed her engagement ring. "I think we should practice our wedding kiss."

"I don't think you need any practice."

"I don't, I've been married before. This practice is for you," he said with a grin, claiming her lips in a sizzling kiss.

Justin's laughter broke into their growing passion. "I need some water," he whispered in his loud way.

"I knew that was coming," Ryan mumbled against her lips.

Lara stood and extended her hand to Justin. "Come on, let's get that water."

A bright light filled the room as Lara and Justin made their way to the kitchen. Both stopped. Ryan joined them in the middle of the room, wrapping them with protective arms. The light—brilliant and so peaceful—bathed them all in a warm celestial glow.

"You finally did it, Ryan," the feminine voice said.

"Shelly?"

Hovering several inches from the floor near the back wall, a woman's form, shrouded in white, came into view. Lara blinked several times. She believed Ryan *thought* he'd seen Shelly, but she didn't believe he'd really *seen* her.

"You're my first mommy," said Justin.

Shelly smiled. "Yes, I'm your first mommy."

"Is it okay if I call Ms. Boyd 'Mommy'?"

Justin's unexpected inquiry took Lara by surprise. She'd never expected he'd want to call her "Mommy," but it pleased her that he did.

"Yes, it's fine." Shelly smiled. "She's been a mommy to you from the moment you met. She does the things good mommies do, like putting her child's happiness before her own. I can fly around happily in heaven now because your second mommy is going to take really good care of you and your daddy."

"That was your unfinished business?" Ryan asked. "Finding someone to take care of Justin and me?"

"Finding the *perfect* someone. I was so worried about you, and Justin was so quiet and shy. Then, Lara came along and brought sunshine to your lives. When you thought you lost her, you didn't care about what I needed anymore. You wanted what you wanted for you. You wanted Lara. You let go of the ghost of the past, and chose to live in the present. And that's what I wanted." Shelly turned a bright smile to Lara. "Keep making them happy, Lara. You're very good at it."

Still stunned to see a ghost levitating in her living room, Lara could only nod.

Ryan tightened his arm around Lara's waist. "Told you I saw her," he whispered in her ear. He looked to Shelly. "I guess this is really good-bye. You be happy, Shell."

Shelly extended her brand new wings to their full glorious capacity. "Finally, I am. You three will be getting an extra bit of happiness pretty soon, too. I like the name Angelica."

Lara found her voice. "Angelica?" She touched her stomach. "You mean . . ."

Shelly gave a confirming nod. "I know it's only been a few days, but with my wings come omniscient power and keen insight."

"But we used . . ." Ryan said.

"You and Lara are one in a million. I guess those odds extend to all aspects of your life. Congratulations."

The warm, sensational glow filled the room once more, and as quickly as Shelly appeared, she was gone.

"Who are we gonna name Angelica?" Justin asked. "Am I gettin' a puppy? Billy is."

Ryan's eyes matched the brightness of his beaming smile. "No, son, I think you should expect something a little bigger and a whole lot better than a puppy. Right, Mommy?"

Lara returned his smile, her hand still resting on her flat but full of life abdomen. "Right."

EPILOGUE

"I now pronounce you husband and wife. Ryan, you may kiss your bride."

Lara dabbed her misty eyes.

"You always cry at that part," Ryan said, walking into the living room with their unsettled baby girl in one arm and a bottle in the hand of the other.

"It's my favorite part of the ceremony." She stopped the DVD at the end of the kiss. "Can you believe it's been a year?"

"No, I can't." Ryan joined her on the couch. "You make time stand still. Happy Anniversary and Merry Christmas, Lara."

"Ditto." They shared a kiss that Angelica's increasing cries brought to an abrupt end. "She's hungry, huh?" Lara asked, noting the morning hour at just after six.

"Famished," he answered, giving the baby her bottle. "Here you go, Angelica. Daddy's sorry he made you wait for your breakfast." Ryan grinned at the contented little girl as only a proud father would. "Even after three months, I can't believe she's here." He gazed lovingly at the baby and pressed a kiss to her forehead as she sucked greedily. "She's so beautiful, Lara."

Angelica's brown eyes fluttered open. "Yes, she is beautiful." Lara stroked her daughter's dark curls and caressed her smooth, butterscotch cheek. "She's definitely the best birthday present you ever gave me."

"I did say I had big presents for you." He laughed.

"Big presents?" Justin raced down the stairs in his red footy pajamas. "Daddy said big presents. Can we open presents now, Mommy?" He peeked at his sister. "Angelica woke me up, and I can't wait anymore."

Lara nodded. "Sure, we can open presents."

"Yea!" Justin dashed over to the tree and started ripping away. He waved Lara over. "Come on, Mommy, you have a lot of presents."

Lara smiled, surrounded by her husband and wonderful children. Living the life she always wanted. "You're right, Justin. I certainly do have lots of presents."

The End

ABOUT THE AUTHOR

Tammy Williams caught the writing bug when a sixth-grade assignment called for the creation of an illustrated short story. From that moment, the idea of breathing life into characters took on a mind of its own.

A resident of Denmark, SC, Tammy is a member of Romance Writers of America and Lowcountry Romance Writers of America. *Choices* is her debut novel.

2008 Reprint Mass Market Titles

January

Cautious Heart
Cheris F. Hodges
ISBN-13: 978-1-58571-301-1
ISBN-10: 1-58571-301-5
$6.99

Suddenly You
Crystal Hubbard
ISBN-13: 978-1-58571-302-8
ISBN-10: 1-58571-302-3
$6.99

February

Passion
T. T. Henderson
ISBN-13: 978-1-58571-303-5
ISBN-10: 1-58571-303-1
$6.99

Whispers in the Sand
LaFlorya Gauthier
ISBN-13: 978-1-58571-304-2
ISBN-10: 1-58571-304-x
$6.99

March

Life Is Never As It Seems
J. J. Michael
ISBN-13: 978-1-58571-305-9
ISBN-10: 1-58571-305-8
$6.99

Beyond the Rapture
Beverly Clark
ISBN-13: 978-1-58571-306-6
ISBN-10: 1-58571-306-6
$6.99

April

A Heart's Awakening
Veronica Parker
ISBN-13: 978-1-58571-307-3
ISBN-10: 1-58571-307-4
$6.99

Breeze
Robin Lynette Hampton
ISBN-13: 978-1-58571-308-0
ISBN-10: 1-58571-308-2
$6.99

May

I'll Be Your Shelter
Giselle Carmichael
ISBN-13: 978-1-58571-309-7
ISBN-10: 1-58571-309-0
$6.99

Careless Whispers
Rochelle Alers
ISBN-13: 978-1-58571-310-3
ISBN-10: 1-58571-310-4
$6.99

June

Sin
Crystal Rhodes
ISBN-13: 978-1-58571-311-0
ISBN-10: 1-58571-311-2
$6.99

Dark Storm Rising
Chinelu Moore
ISBN-13: 978-1-58571-312-7
ISBN-10: 1-58571-312-0
$6.99

2008 Reprint Mass Market Titles (continued)
July

Object of His Desire
A.C. Arthur
ISBN-13: 978-1-58571-313-4
ISBN-10: 1-58571-313-9
$6.99

Angel's Paradise
Janice Angelique
ISBN-13: 978-1-58571-314-1
ISBN-10: 1-58571-314-7
$6.99

August

Unbreak My Heart
Dar Tomlinson
ISBN-13: 978-1-58571-315-8
ISBN-10: 1-58571-315-5
$6.99

All I Ask
Barbara Keaton
ISBN-13: 978-1-58571-316-5
ISBN-10: 1-58571-316-3
$6.99

September

Icie
Pamela Leigh Starr
ISBN-13: 978-1-58571-275-5
ISBN-10: 1-58571-275-2
$6.99

At Last
Lisa Riley
ISBN-13: 978-1-58571-276-2
ISBN-10: 1-58571-276-0
$6.99

October

Everlastin' Love
Gay G. Gunn
ISBN-13: 978-1-58571-277-9
ISBN-10: 1-58571-277-9
$6.99

Three Wishes
Seressia Glass
ISBN-13: 978-1-58571-278-6
ISBN-10: 1-58571-278-7
$6.99

November

Yesterday Is Gone
Beverly Clark
ISBN-13: 978-1-58571-279-3
ISBN-10: 1-58571-279-5
$6.99

Again My Love
Kayla Perrin
ISBN-13: 978-1-58571-280-9
ISBN-10: 1-58571-280-9
$6.99

December

Office Policy
A.C. Arthur
ISBN-13: 978-1-58571-281-6
ISBN-10: 1-58571-281-7
$6.99

Rendezvous With Fate
Jeanne Sumerix
ISBN-13: 978-1-58571-283-3
ISBN-10: 1-58571-283-3
$6.99

2008 New Mass Market Titles

January

Where I Want To Be
Maryam Diaab
ISBN-13: 978-1-58571-268-7
ISBN-10: 1-58571-268-X
$6.99

Never Say Never
Michele Cameron
ISBN-13: 978-1-58571-269-4
ISBN-10: 1-58571-269-8
$6.99

February

Stolen Memories
Michele Sudler
ISBN-13: 978-1-58571-270-0
ISBN-10: 1-58571-270-1
$6.99

Dawn's Harbor
Kymberly Hunt
ISBN-13: 978-1-58571-271-7
ISBN-10: 1-58571-271-X
$6.99

March

Undying Love
Renee Alexis
ISBN-13: 978-1-58571-272-4
ISBN-10: 1-58571-272-8
$6.99

Blame It On Paradise
Crystal Hubbard
ISBN-13: 978-1-58571-273-1
ISBN-10: 1-58571-273-6
$6.99

April

When A Man Loves A Woman
La Connie Taylor-Jones
ISBN-13: 978-1-58571-274-8
ISBN-10: 1-58571-274-4
$6.99

Choices
Tammy Williams
ISBN-13: 978-1-58571-300-4
ISBN-10: 1-58571-300-7
$6.99

May

Dream Runner
Gail McFarland
ISBN-13: 978-1-58571-317-2
ISBN-10: 1-58571-317-1
$6.99

Southern Fried Standards
S.R. Maddox
ISBN-13: 978-1-58571-318-9
ISBN-10: 1-58571-318-X
$6.99

June

Looking for Lily
Africa Fine
ISBN-13: 978-1-58571-319-6
ISBN-10: 1-58571-319-8
$6.99

Bliss, Inc.
Chamein Canton
ISBN-13: 978-1-58571-325-7
ISBN-10: 1-58571-325-2
$6.99

2008 New Mass Market Titles (continued)

July

Love's Secrets
Yolanda McVey
ISBN-13: 978-1-58571-321-9
ISBN-10: 1-58571-321-X
$6.99

Things Forbidden
Maryam Diaab
ISBN-13: 978-1-58571-327-1
ISBN-10: 1-58571-327-9
$6.99

August

Storm
Pamela Leigh Starr
ISBN-13: 978-1-58571-323-3
ISBN-10: 1-58571-323-6
$6.99

Passion's Furies
AlTonya Washington
ISBN-13: 978-1-58571-324-0
ISBN-10: 1-58571-324-4
$6.99

September

Three Doors Down
Michele Sudler
ISBN-13: 978-1-58571-332-5
ISBN-10: 1-58571-332-5
$6.99

Mr Fix-It
Crystal Hubbard
ISBN-13: 978-1-58571-326-4
ISBN-10: 1-58571-326-0
$6.99

October

Moments of Clarity
Michele Cameron
ISBN-13: 978-1-58571-330-1
ISBN-10: 1-58571-330-9
$6.99

Lady Preacher
K.T. Richey
ISBN-13: 978-1-58571-333-2
ISBN-10: 1-58571-333-3
$6.99

November

This Life Isn't Perfect Holla
Sandra Foy
ISBN: 978-1-58571-331-8
ISBN-10: 1-58571-331-7
$6.99

Promises Made
Bernice Layton
ISBN-13: 978-1-58571-334-9
ISBN-10: 1-58571-334-1
$6.99

December

A Voice Behind Thunder
Carrie Elizabeth Greene
ISBN-13: 978-1-58571-329-5
ISBN-10: 1-58571-329-5
$6.99

The More Things Change
Chamein Canton
ISBN-13: 978-1-58571-328-8
ISBN-10: 1-58571-328-7
$6.99

Other Genesis Press, Inc. Titles

Other Genesis Press, Inc. Titles (continued)

Other Genesis Press, Inc. Titles (continued)

Daughter of the Wind	Joan Xian	$8.95
Deadly Sacrifice	Jack Kean	$22.95
Designer Passion	Dar Tomlinson	$8.95
	Diana Richeaux	
Do Over	Celya Bowers	$9.95
Dreamtective	Liz Swados	$5.95
Ebony Angel	Deatri King-Bey	$9.95
Ebony Butterfly II	Delilah Dawson	$14.95
Echoes of Yesterday	Beverly Clark	$9.95
Eden's Garden	Elizabeth Rose	$8.95
Eve's Prescription	Edwina Martin Arnold	$8.95
Everlastin' Love	Gay G. Gunn	$8.95
Everlasting Moments	Dorothy Elizabeth Love	$8.95
Everything and More	Sinclair Lebeau	$8.95
Everything but Love	Natalie Dunbar	$8.95
Falling	Natalie Dunbar	$9.95
Fate	Pamela Leigh Starr	$8.95
Finding Isabella	A.J. Garrotto	$8.95
Forbidden Quest	Dar Tomlinson	$10.95
Forever Love	Wanda Y. Thomas	$8.95
From the Ashes	Kathleen Suzanne	$8.95
	Jeanne Sumerix	
Gentle Yearning	Rochelle Alers	$10.95
Glory of Love	Sinclair LeBeau	$10.95
Go Gentle into that Good Night	Malcom Boyd	$12.95
Goldengroove	Mary Beth Craft	$16.95
Groove, Bang, and Jive	Steve Cannon	$8.99
Hand in Glove	Andrea Jackson	$9.95

Other Genesis Press, Inc. Titles (continued)

Other Genesis Press, Inc. Titles (continued)

Last Train to Memphis	Elsa Cook	$12.95
Lasting Valor	Ken Olsen	$24.95
Let Us Prey	Hunter Lundy	$25.95
Lies Too Long	Pamela Ridley	$13.95
Life Is Never As It Seems	J.J. Michael	$12.95
Lighter Shade of Brown	Vicki Andrews	$8.95
Love Always	Mildred E. Riley	$10.95
Love Doesn't Come Easy	Charlyne Dickerson	$8.95
Love Unveiled	Gloria Greene	$10.95
Love's Deception	Charlene Berry	$10.95
Love's Destiny	M. Loui Quezada	$8.95
Mae's Promise	Melody Walcott	$8.95
Magnolia Sunset	Giselle Carmichael	$8.95
Many Shades of Gray	Dyanne Davis	$6.99
Matters of Life and Death	Lesego Malepe, Ph.D.	$15.95
Meant to Be	Jeanne Sumerix	$8.95
Midnight Clear	Leslie Esdaile	$10.95
(Anthology)	Gwynne Forster	
	Carmen Green	
	Monica Jackson	
Midnight Magic	Gwynne Forster	$8.95
Midnight Peril	Vicki Andrews	$10.95
Misconceptions	Pamela Leigh Starr	$9.95
Montgomery's Children	Richard Perry	$14.95
My Buffalo Soldier	Barbara B. K. Reeves	$8.95
Naked Soul	Gwynne Forster	$8.95
Next to Last Chance	Louisa Dixon	$24.95
No Apologies	Seressia Glass	$8.95
No Commitment Required	Seressia Glass	$8.95

Other Genesis Press, Inc. Titles (continued)

No Regrets	Mildred E. Riley	$8.95
Not His Type	Chamein Canton	$6.99
Nowhere to Run	Gay G. Gunn	$10.95
O Bed! O Breakfast!	Rob Kuehnle	$14.95
Object of His Desire	A. C. Arthur	$8.95
Office Policy	A. C. Arthur	$9.95
Once in a Blue Moon	Dorianne Cole	$9.95
One Day at a Time	Bella McFarland	$8.95
One in A Million	Barbara Keaton	$6.99
One of These Days	Michele Sudler	$9.95
Outside Chance	Louisa Dixon	$24.95
Passion	T.T. Henderson	$10.95
Passion's Blood	Cherif Fortin	$22.95
Passion's Journey	Wanda Y. Thomas	$8.95
Past Promises	Jahmel West	$8.95
Path of Fire	T.T. Henderson	$8.95
Path of Thorns	Annetta P. Lee	$9.95
Peace Be Still	Colette Haywood	$12.95
Picture Perfect	Reon Carter	$8.95
Playing for Keeps	Stephanie Salinas	$8.95
Pride & Joi	Gay G. Gunn	$15.95
Pride & Joi	Gay G. Gunn	$8.95
Promises to Keep	Alicia Wiggins	$8.95
Quiet Storm	Donna Hill	$10.95
Reckless Surrender	Rochelle Alers	$6.95
Red Polka Dot in a World of Plaid	Varian Johnson	$12.95
Reluctant Captive	Joyce Jackson	$8.95
Rendezvous with Fate	Jeanne Sumerix	$8.95

Other Genesis Press, Inc. Titles (continued)

Revelations	Cheris F. Hodges	$8.95
Rivers of the Soul	Leslie Esdaile	$8.95
Rocky Mountain Romance	Kathleen Suzanne	$8.95
Rooms of the Heart	Donna Hill	$8.95
Rough on Rats and Tough on Cats	Chris Parker	$12.95
Secret Library Vol. 1	Nina Sheridan	$18.95
Secret Library Vol. 2	Cassandra Colt	$8.95
Secret Thunder	Annetta P. Lee	$9.95
Shades of Brown	Denise Becker	$8.95
Shades of Desire	Monica White	$8.95
Shadows in the Moonlight	Jeanne Sumerix	$8.95
Sin	Crystal Rhodes	$8.95
Small Whispers	Annetta P. Lee	$6.99
So Amazing	Sinclair LeBeau	$8.95
Somebody's Someone	Sinclair LeBeau	$8.95
Someone to Love	Alicia Wiggins	$8.95
Song in the Park	Martin Brant	$15.95
Soul Eyes	Wayne L. Wilson	$12.95
Soul to Soul	Donna Hill	$8.95
Southern Comfort	J.M. Jeffries	$8.95
Still the Storm	Sharon Robinson	$8.95
Still Waters Run Deep	Leslie Esdaile	$8.95
Stolen Kisses	Dominiqua Douglas	$9.95
Stories to Excite You	Anna Forrest/Divine	$14.95
Subtle Secrets	Wanda Y. Thomas	$8.95
Suddenly You	Crystal Hubbard	$9.95
Sweet Repercussions	Kimberley White	$9.95
Sweet Sensations	Gwendolyn Bolton	$9.95

Other Genesis Press, Inc. Titles (continued)

Sweet Tomorrows	Kimberly White	$8.95
Taken by You	Dorothy Elizabeth Love	$9.95
Tattooed Tears	T. T. Henderson	$8.95
The Color Line	Lizzette Grayson Carter	$9.95
The Color of Trouble	Dyanne Davis	$8.95
The Disappearance of Allison Jones	Kayla Perrin	$5.95
The Fires Within	Beverly Clark	$9.95
The Foursome	Celya Bowers	$6.99
The Honey Dipper's Legacy	Pannell-Allen	$14.95
The Joker's Love Tune	Sidney Rickman	$15.95
The Little Pretender	Barbara Cartland	$10.95
The Love We Had	Natalie Dunbar	$8.95
The Man Who Could Fly	Bob & Milana Beamon	$18.95
The Missing Link	Charlyne Dickerson	$8.95
The Mission	Pamela Leigh Starr	$6.99
The Perfect Frame	Beverly Clark	$9.95
The Price of Love	Sinclair LeBeau	$8.95
The Smoking Life	Ilene Barth	$29.95
The Words of the Pitcher	Kei Swanson	$8.95
Three Wishes	Seressia Glass	$8.95
Ties That Bind	Kathleen Suzanne	$8.95
Tiger Woods	Libby Hughes	$5.95
Time is of the Essence	Angie Daniels	$9.95
Timeless Devotion	Bella McFarland	$9.95
Tomorrow's Promise	Leslie Esdaile	$8.95
Truly Inseparable	Wanda Y. Thomas	$8.95
Two Sides to Every Story	Dyanne Davis	$9.95
Unbreak My Heart	Dar Tomlinson	$8.95

Other Genesis Press, Inc. Titles (continued)

Uncommon Prayer	Kenneth Swanson	$9.95
Unconditional Love	Alicia Wiggins	$8.95
Unconditional	A.C. Arthur	$9.95
Until Death Do Us Part	Susan Paul	$8.95
Vows of Passion	Bella McFarland	$9.95
Wedding Gown	Dyanne Davis	$8.95
What's Under Benjamin's Bed	Sandra Schaffer	$8.95
When Dreams Float	Dorothy Elizabeth Love	$8.95
When I'm With You	LaConnie Taylor-Jones	$6.99
Whispers in the Night	Dorothy Elizabeth Love	$8.95
Whispers in the Sand	LaFlorya Gauthier	$10.95
Who's That Lady?	Andrea Jackson	$9.95
Wild Ravens	Altonya Washington	$9.95
Yesterday Is Gone	Beverly Clark	$10.95
Yesterday's Dreams, Tomorrow's Promises	Reon Laudat	$8.95
Your Precious Love	Sinclair LeBeau	$8.95

ESCAPE WITH INDIGO !!!!

Join Indigo Book Club©
It's simple, easy and secure.

Sign up and receive the new
releases
every month + Free shipping
and
20% off the cover price.

Go online to www.genesis-
press.com and click on Bookclub
or
call 1-888-INDIGO-1

Order Form

Mail to: Genesis Press, Inc.
P.O. Box 101
Columbus, MS 39703

Name _____
Address _____
City/State _____ Zip _____
Telephone _____

Ship to (if different from above)
Name _____
Address _____
City/State _____ Zip _____
Telephone _____

Credit Card Information
Credit Card # _____ ☐ Visa   ☐ Mastercard
Expiration Date (mm/yy) _____ ☐ AmEx ☐ Discover

Qty.	Author	Title	Price	Total

Use this order form, or call 1-888-INDIGO-1	Total for books _____
	Shipping and handling: $5 first two books, $1 each additional book _____
	Total S & H _____
	Total amount enclosed _____
	Mississippi residents add 7% sales tax